PLUTO RISING
A Katy Klein Mystery

✦ ✦ ✦

KAREN IRVING

Karen Irving
2000·12·09

POLESTAR
BOOK PUBLISHERS

Polestar Book Publishers acknowledges the ongoing support of The
Canada Council; the British Columbia Ministry of Small Business,
Tourism and Culture through the BC Arts Council; and the
Government of Canada through the Book Publishing Industry
Development Program (BPIDP).

Cover design by Val Speidel.
Cover image from Tony Stone Images.
Author photograph by Mitchell Beer.
Printed and bound in Canada.

CANADIAN CATALOGUING IN PUBLICATION DATA
        Irving, Karen, 1957-
        Pluto rising
        ISBN 1-896095-95-X
        I. Title.
        PS8567.R862P58 1999   C813'.54   C99-910736-4
        PR9199.3.I688P58 1999

LIBRARY OF CONGRESS CATALOGUE NUMBER: 99-64172

POLESTAR BOOK PUBLISHERS
An imprint of Raincoast Books
9050 Shaughnessy Street
Vancouver, British Columbia
Canada   V6P 6E5

00 01 02 • 5 4 3 2

I owe debts of gratitude to many people: Suzanne Holyck Hunchuck, Shirley and Gordon Irving, Clare Rogers, Dr. Marc Cezer, Dr. Robert Walker and Sheila Penney all suffered patiently through early drafts and still speak to me; Adrian Irving-Beer provided technical advice and support; Rachel Irving-Beer gave me inspiration; Michelle Benjamin and Lynn Henry believed in the project and helped birth it gently; and most of all, Mitchell Beer stood beside me every step of the way, supplying love, support, and gallons of our favourite hot brown beverage. *Thank you.*

To Phyllis and Reuben Brasloff,
patient and loving teachers
— without whom there would be no Katy.

PROLOGUE

His own screaming woke him. Panting, he lay in the dark, paralyzed by terror, his heart pounding in his throat. The threadbare sheet covering him was soaked with sweat.

It was the dream, always the same dream. He tried to focus his eyes in the thick darkness, struggling to push the horror away. The air was sweet with incense he'd burned earlier, and he breathed deeply, reassuring himself. He was home. Not there.

It was several moments before he was able to move, to thrust the damp sheet away, to sit up and feel the bare floor against his callused feet. Light from the street outside filtered down through grimy windows and, gradually, he was able to make out the familiar shapes of crosses, hung on each wall of his room.

"Holy Mary, Queen of Grace ..." he whispered, feeling along the edge of his bed for the rosary he kept near his head. He sought comfort in the familiar words, but they tumbled out of his mouth like dry leaves, falling around him.

God was punishing him, that much was clear. Prayer sometimes allowed him to forget, but tonight it did no good. Then again, perhaps that was his error: if

God was sending him the dream again and again, surely there was a message in it. A message he was meant to receive. Rather than forget it, maybe he should be trying to remember. An involuntary shudder passed through him at the thought.

You must remember the dream, he commanded himself. *You must be strong enough to suffer. God will only send you what He knows you can endure.* He closed his eyes and let the vision play itself out again. As surely as if he were still standing in that doorway, he heard the screams, saw the figure bending over the bed, in shadow. The sudden, awful silence. The figure stood, turned around, looked directly at him. And it had no face. Only eyes that glowed red, fierce and wild in the darkened room.

He opened his mouth to scream, but nothing came out. His tongue was dry, stuck to the roof of his mouth; his lips worked convulsively, trying desperately to form words. *Help me, please help me.* But even as he pleaded, he knew: there was no help for him.

1

A good astrologer should never predict a death. It's one of the cardinal rules of this business. But if I'd been the type who played by the rules, I wouldn't have seen him in the first place, right? I'd have hung up on him, told him to find someone else. That's what I should have done: passed him along. But I hadn't. That was my first mistake.

It was July when the phone call came in. The ancient electric fan thrummed and clattered from its precarious perch atop a mountain of books and unsorted papers, but its cooling properties were minimal on a day like this. The air in the tiny office was soupy with humidity, and a trail of sweat trickled casually down my spine. I grabbed for the ringing phone, spilling a generous slosh of coffee down the front of my newly-washed white T-shirt.

"Good morning, Star-Dynamics, Katy Klein

speaking." I hoped the caller hadn't heard my muttered curse. Another clean shirt, down the tubes. It was shaping up to be that kind of day.

There was silence on the other end of the line, and I was on the brink of hanging up. No, wait. Someone was breathing. Maybe a client. And the landlord would be around soon to collect the rent. I repeated my greeting, more energetically.

"Hello, how may I help you?"

"Are you the astrologer?"

The voice was male, raspy, challenging. Probably another religious nut, calling to tell me I'd burn in hell if I didn't give up the necromancer's arts. I grimaced and suppressed a sigh. If I had a dollar for each of these loonies, I'd have my own secretary. Fat chance.

"Yes, I'm the astrologer. How may I help you?"

"So how good are you, anyway?"

"Pardon?"

I bit back an impulse to ask how good *he* was. Down girl — there's a remote chance this one could be a paying customer. Be nice.

"What exactly are you looking for?" I countered. "I need to understand what you expect of me before I can commit …"

"I am asking how good you are," he interrupted. "Keep to the point. No psycho-babble. I've had it up to here with that shit. Just tell me straight out — how good are you?"

"Would you like the names of some references?" I picked up a pencil and began to scribble a random pattern of spirals on the back of an overdue phone bill.

"Listen to me carefully," the caller said, in a hoarse whisper. I covered my free ear, straining to catch his words. "I'm looking for an exceptional astrologer. The best. I don't want any bullshit, I don't want mumbo-jumbo, I don't want excuses. I need the truth, and I won't stand for one more quack trying to give me the runaround. Got that?"

His words sounded rehearsed, his voice mechanical. This was just a bit too weird, I thought, my instinct to hang up arm-wrestling with my instinct to put food on the table. Food on the table won, by a narrow margin.

"My clients have no complaints." I worked to keep my voice neutral.

"I don't give a shit about your clients or anyone else. How do I know you can tell me what I need to know?"

"You don't!" I exploded. To hell with food on the table; this just wasn't worth it. "Look, buddy — you don't know me from a hole in the ground and you have no way of knowing if I'm good at what I do, or if I'm a complete charlatan, okay? I don't know if I can give you what you need, either. I'd be lying if I said I did. All I can do is what I always do — tell you the truth about what I see in your chart. If you don't like that, I guess you're just shit out of luck, aren't you?"

There was a long silence. With my free hand, I tried to push a wayward lock of hair off my perspiring forehead. I slumped back into my chair, waiting for the caller to disconnect. I'd lost him, but damn, it was worth it. A girl can only take so much. Maybe I could borrow a few bucks from Greg to keep the slimy landlord at bay.

"Okay."

I jumped, startled that he was still there.

"Book me an appointment. What do you charge?"

I recovered quickly, naming an outrageously inflated hourly charge. If I was going to see this guy, he was damn well going to make it worth my while. I didn't relish an hour cooped up in the office with that kind of hostility; I should be getting danger pay. He accepted my terms with unexpected docility, and we set a meeting time for that afternoon. He gave me the information I asked for — date, time and place of birth — and I had the chart up on the screen of the laptop computer by the time the phone receiver was back in its cradle.

That's when it dawned on me — I'd forgotten to ask his name. I've never been very good at details.

Turning my attention to Mr. Personality's chart, I began puzzling out the mass of arcane symbols. Leo Sun in the twelfth house — desperately craves attention, even admiration, but deep down, doesn't feel he deserves it. Sun, Mercury and Pluto all hovering around a Leo Ascendant — has trouble hearing anyone else's side of the story. Bound up in his own perceptions. A Scorpio Moon in the fourth house showed a deep emotional investment in his early family environment. Was he nervous of being out in the big, bad world? That might explain his telephone manner.

Power and control issues were written all over the chart, bearing out my first, not especially favourable, impression. Furrowing my brow, I began muttering and jotting notes to myself. I'd been doing this full-time for five years now and a new chart never failed to capture my interest. It was like peeking into someone's underwear drawer, with their permission, yet. It appealed both to my need to render order from chaos and my inherent nosiness.

I worked on the chart for half an hour, then placed it in a magenta-coloured file folder to await my new client's visit that afternoon. The rest of the morning was relatively uneventful. A couple of regular clients called to book appointments and I did some phone consultations. Just a regular weekday morning in the life of a struggling astrologer.

Hanging up after the fourth call, I yawned mightily and creaked backward in my tilting chair, squirming to coax the kinks out of my middle-aged back. Glancing around, I decided a quick tidying blitz might not be out of order. The office, located above the last of the hippie-style bakeries along Bank Street, wasn't exactly luxurious, but it was comfortable enough, in a boho kind of way.

There was good light from the west and south-facing windows, though the sashes stuck in the summer humidity and rattled with winter's winds. The office walls were covered from floor to ceiling with posters and drawings of ancient astrological lore, from astrolabes and maps of the heavens, to charts indicating the herbs and minerals associated with each planet.

The furnishings themselves were minimal. A purple double futon on a polished wooden frame served as a couch, while a pine table on trestles and an ancient swivel chair made up my work space. Oversized pillows, covered in Indian cotton prints, lay scattered on the floor as auxiliary seating. Wicker baskets contained something resembling a filing system.

Reform was in the air, though. My fourteen-year-old daughter, Dawn, had recently taken it upon herself to back up my client records on our home computer. In fact, she was getting downright annoying about it, insisting that I bring a floppy disk home after work each night. Most of the time, I remembered.

A hanging lamp with rice paper shade hung from the middle of the ceiling, testament to my questionable skills as an electrician. I'd put the thing together from a kit, shorting out the entire top floor of the building when

I'd first plugged it in. How was I supposed to know the wires were meant to be attached to two different screws? I'd told my friend Greg about it, laughing, and he'd chewed me out for not calling him in to help. I shrugged; the lamp worked now, didn't it?

I swiped at the rice paper with a cloth, knocking down some of the more obvious cobwebs. I tossed the floor cushions into a pile in the corner and watered the drooping ficus plant Greg had given me when I'd moved in here. The hardwood floors could use a good mopping, but it was too damn hot for anything resembling physical labour. I satisfied myself with scooping up the worst of the dust bunnies and tossing them into the garbage. I collected several used coffee mugs and stashed them in the bathroom to wash later. One of these days, I'd get around to giving this place a thorough going-over. One of these days. Maybe when the weather cooled some.

By early afternoon I had dealt with a number of minor crises. Two couples called, debating auspicious-looking wedding dates; a two a.m. nuptial for Couple Number One was ruled out. A young college co-ed breathlessly asked me to "do everyone's fortune" at a sorority party (I declined); a new grandmother commissioned a chart for her ten-day-old granddaughter (I accepted); and a holy roller assured me I'd be doomed to eternal flames if I continued to poison pure minds with astro-filth. I told him I was willing to take my chances and hung up on him.

I was just getting down to the despised task of billing my regular clients when I heard the downstairs door open. Startled, I glanced at my watch and realized I'd forgotten all about Mr. Personality's appointment. I dug around hastily for the chart and my notes, sweeping the billing records discreetly under a file folder, while simultaneously flicking lunchtime croissant crumbs onto the floor. No, that was no good. With one foot, I pushed the crumbs further under the desk, where they'd have to rot until I got around to my twice-yearly vacuuming.

The door rattled violently as Mr. Personality announced his arrival. I jumped up, hoping he wouldn't hammer the thing off its hinges. I'd have a hell of a time explaining that one to the landlord. What was this guy's problem, anyway? No need to wreck the place, I muttered to myself. I opened the door, pasting a welcoming smile on my face.

2

He wasn't tall, perhaps a couple of inches shorter than I was. Maybe it was his wide shoulders and barrel chest that made him appear larger — he seemed to take up all the space in the narrow hallway. His hair was dark blond, thick and wild. Either he didn't own a comb, or he was working on that matted Rastafarian dreadlock look so popular with middle-class Anglo-Saxon kids these days. Except this was no kid — he looked more like someone in his thirties, but I knew from his birth data that he was in his late forties. His protruding eyes were a pale green, like unblinking gooseberries against his pallid, unwrinkled skin, which he wore like a mask over the sharp contours of his skull.

He said nothing, but peered into the office before looking at me. Despite the sweltering heat and even higher humidity, the man wore heavy black denim jeans and a wrinkled black nylon windbreaker, zipped up to his chin. He looked as though he'd slept in his clothing. If I'd met him on the street, I would have pegged him as homeless, except that he lacked the characteristic three-days' beard growth and smelled faintly of something antiseptic, rather than booze and sweat. Carbolic soap?

I took a cautious step back from the doorway. It

might have been a mistake, inviting this strange man to my office, sight unseen. There was nothing for it now, though — I'd have to ask him in.

"I'm sorry, but I don't think I got your name when we spoke this morning." I gave a wooden smile, gesturing toward the couch. "Please, won't you take a seat?"

The man entered the office stiffly, angling his body so he faced me at all times. He inched forward until he was inside the door, which he closed behind him without taking those unblinking eyes off me. Watching me intently, he stood in silence.

Didn't your mother ever teach you any manners? I thought, irritated. Aloud I said, "So. Is this your first visit to an astrologer?"

Still he said nothing. I backed into my swivel chair and sat in silence myself. Behind my new client was a poster depicting Johannes Kepler, one of the founding fathers of modern astrology. I pretended to meditate on the wise bearded visage as I waited for Mr. Personality to speak. Eventually, one of us was going to break and I was damned if it would be me. After about five minutes, during which I counted two dumptrucks, several motorcycles and at least one howling child hurtling along the street below the office windows, the man spoke.

His voice was a harsh croak, perhaps rusty with disuse.

"Yes."

Yes what? Oh right, I'd asked him whether this was his first visit.

"I see. Can you tell me what brings you here today?"

It was the same open-ended, non-threatening question I used with all my new clients. Usually it helped set them at ease, but I intuited that it would take more than a few mild questions to unwind this guy. Major tranquilizers, perhaps.

"I want you to tell me about ... you know ... myself. My life."

Where was the hostile, demanding voice that had crackled through the telephone wires that morning? This man sounded positively fearful.

"That's a pretty broad mandate, Mr ..."

"Adam. Call me Adam."

"Okay, Adam," I smiled. "Perhaps I should give you a rundown of exactly what I do. Would that be okay?"

He continued to stare, his face impassive, those pale eyes unblinking, like a lizard's. I took his silence for assent.

"When I first meet a new client, I like to look over the birthchart with them. That's basically a map of the solar system, drawn for the exact time and place you were born. The idea is that this map will form a kind of guide to your personality and future potential."

Adam neither moved nor spoke. His taciturnity was starting to get on my nerves; warning tingles jazzed their way up and down my spine. I took a slow breath and continued.

"No astrologer can ever tell you with certainty that things will turn out a particular way, but I can show you trends and inclinations. I try to work with my clients as a counselor, helping them understand their own abilities. We try to figure out areas you might want to develop further and to understand the reasons you became the person you are. I don't tell fortunes and I don't believe in fate. Does that sound like the kind of thing you're looking for?"

"Fine." He sounded like he was choking. "Just tell me what you see."

I paused. Had he understood any of what I'd said? He gave no clues.

"Okay. Why don't we start with the basics of your chart?"

Gathering my papers, I pointed to the printout on my lap. Could he even see it, from his post across the room?

"Adam, why don't you take a seat?" I offered again, gesturing at the couch across from me. He shook his head, an almost imperceptible motion; he did take a couple of tentative steps in my direction and seemed to peer at the chart. Small progress, I thought.

"Okay. You have a heavy concentration of planets in Leo, Adam. See, here's the Sun, Mercury and Pluto, all within a few degrees of one another. In fact, Leo was on the eastern horizon when you were born. That means you have Leo rising, okay?"

Adam did not reply. Sighing, I went on.

"Leos are usually very concerned with how other people see them, and they do their best when they're getting lots of admiration and praise. But look here — see, you have your Sun in the twelfth house, so it seems like you felt you weren't really appreciated when you were growing up. Maybe someone you lived with put you down, told you you weren't important. Or maybe you had to hide your true self in some way. Does that sound right?"

Adam seemed frozen in place, staring at the chart while I pointed out the details. His pale face was shiny with sweat.

"Leos can be very stubborn," I said. "Once you get an idea in your head, it can stay there a long time and you have trouble getting rid of it. It's like you have to chew things over, you know? And you hang onto everything. You might have thoughts or even relationships that hurt you, but you stick with them, maybe just because they're familiar. Especially with your high concentration of Leo planets, you'll cling to an idea right to the end, worrying it like a dog with a bone. Some people might even call you obsessed. Does that sound like you?"

Adam nodded slowly, gesturing for me to continue.

"Okay. Let's look at this Mercury-Pluto conjunction in Leo. It's right on the ascendant, so I'd say it's one of the most important factors in your life. This Mercury shows you can be very inflexible in your thinking, and when you want to get something done, you really stick to it. Pluto here shows you have a real preoccupation with power. Maybe you need to feel like you're in control, or you have to keep someone else from dominating you. In fact, the question of who is in control can feel like a real life and death issue, right?"

Adam inclined his head slightly.

"Putting these influences together, I'd say you grew up believing that knowledge is power. It seems like there were things going on around you that you couldn't understand, but you felt desperate to know about them. When kids feel that way, they can grow up with an almost insatiable desire to uncover the truth. The flip side of this is that letting other people see who you really are can make you feel exposed, and that feels dangerous. It's like giving the other person control over you, right, Adam?"

His sharp intake of breath took me by surprise, but when I glanced up at him, Adam ducked his head fearfully. I decided I'd hit the nail on the head.

"Now, if we pull the Sun into this conjunction, we get something called a stellium, where a cluster of planets creates a particularly powerful place in the chart," I said. "This shows you can go to great lengths to make sure no one ever gets close to you. Even if that means you hide yourself away from the world, that's better than feeling exposed …"

Adam let out a grunt as though I'd hit him. I softened my voice, certain now that I was on the right path, not wanting to frighten him off.

"Pluto and the Sun can both stand for the father in the chart," I said. "Maybe it seemed like your dad was so powerful he could see right through you — or maybe he had some kind of incredible control over your life, even as an adult. It looks like keeping a low profile was a real survival issue for you when you were a child — it's like you had nowhere to hide. And that feeling has followed you into adulthood. Am I right?"

Adam's already pale face was blanching by degrees and he swayed slightly where he stood. His hands clenched convulsively into tight fists.

"Nowhere to hide," he echoed, almost inaudibly. He shoved his hands into his jacket pockets and stared at the floor.

"Is that how it felt?" I tried to probe gently.

Adam recoiled at the question, then nodded abruptly, meeting my eyes for the first time. He took a step back, his eyes bulging, his body suddenly taut. My own anxiety level jumped several notches and I reminded myself to breathe.

"Am I going too fast, Adam?" I asked. "We can slow things down, if you need to. You seem upset."

Once a therapist, always a therapist, I thought, wondering how long it might take the boys from 911 to get to my office. If I could get to the telephone in time, that is.

"Tell me more," Adam demanded, his voice thick.

"Um, look, Adam," I tried to soothe him. "This stuff seems to be upsetting you. Why don't we just call it a day? Maybe you can go home and think things over, decide whether you want to continue …"

"I said, tell me more," he hissed, drawing his head back like a cobra ready to strike.

My heart pounded as I forced myself to hold my ground. Don't flinch. Don't let him see you're scared. Fear is contagious.

"Adam, stop that. I don't work like this." I hoped my voice sounded firm.

"What way?" He frowned, looking confused.

"Let's just say I prefer a little more interchange. This isn't some kind of test, where you stand there with your lip zipped, judging my accuracy. It's a process, Adam. You know — I suggest something, you respond. Like that."

An expression of puzzlement crossed Adam's face and for a moment he looked like a confused child.

"But … what do I have to do?"

My anxiety abated slightly, and I focused on trying to connect with this strange man.

"Okay. When I mentioned that you felt you had nowhere to hide, you reacted really strongly. What was happening for you there?"

The fan thrummed noisily, its desultory breeze rhythmically lifting and dropping the papers strewn across my desk.

Finally, Adam whispered, "I've never known what I needed to know. They kept everything from me. Now the visions are coming back and I don't know why. I've tried to be good, but they won't leave me alone. I don't know what's happening to me."

"What's coming back, Adam?" I tried to keep him talking. This sounded like a job for my former colleagues at the psychiatric hospital. Mentally, I started listing off referral possibilities for Adam.

"I'm not sure. That's why I came to you. I heard people like you can see … can see things. Hidden things. You have to tell me what it all means. Give me some answers."

Adam sounded like a three-year-old, trying not to cry.

"Adam, listen, okay? I work as an astrologer. I interpret people's birthcharts for them and I try to help them with what we find, but I'm not a psychic — I can't see into the future, or the past, for that matter. I'm not a psychologist, either." At least, not any more.

"If you need help figuring out stuff that you're remembering, I can give you the name of a really good doctor I know. I'm sure he can help you, okay?"

Adam stiffened slightly at the mention of a doctor and I realized I was once more treading on dangerous ground. But I couldn't do anything for this strange man. I knew my limits.

There was a long silence.

"I need the whole story. I don't know how to get at it. Please — Dr. Chisholm told me you might be able to help me."

Greg Chisholm sent me this nut? I fumed wordlessly. What in the world would possess Greg, my closest friend, an experienced psychiatrist who was well aware of the dangers, to send me a time-bomb like Adam? I cleared my throat, then feigned a prolonged coughing attack, trying to buy myself a few seconds to calm down.

"I don't think I can give you what you need, Adam,"

I said when I'd caught my breath. "I don't do magic. I can show you the stuff in your chart about trying to keep a low profile when you were a kid, but you have to fill in the details — exactly how you perceived your father, for instance. Or how you felt you were watched. Your chart can't tell me exactly what your life circumstances are, or were."

The demanding chirp of the telephone interrupted this disclaimer. I ignored it, having switched the answering machine on. But Adam responded instantaneously. He sprang backward, bumping against the futon, then leaping away from it as if burned. He glared frantically about the small office, his peculiar pale eyes feral, almost inhuman in their terror. The tightly coiled spring inside him snapped open — he knocked over a basket of files and his breath came in desperate gasps as he sought an escape route.

I jumped to my feet, then remained rooted to the spot, flummoxed by this sudden whirlwind of panic. Finally, Adam yanked the door open and was gone. The door slammed behind him and he vaulted down the stairs, two or three steps at a time.

I sank back into my chair, my heart beating a ferocious tattoo against my ribcage. Bracing my feet against the floor to steady myself, I sat forward, cupping my face in sweating hands. Deep breathing, that was the ticket. Just as my yoga instructor had taught me years ago. Gradually, my heartbeat returned to normal and I stopped shaking.

Turning back to my desk, I picked up the phone and dialled Greg's number. His secretary took the call but I decided against burdening Nina with my anger at Greg. I hung up and gathered Adam's chart, my jotted notes and a few other bits and pieces, shoving the lot into a file folder, which I crammed into my briefcase. I'd transcribe them at home when my head felt a little clearer.

On the floor near where Adam had stood I noticed a white envelope, unmarked. Picking it up, I held it at arm's length at first; if it was Adam's, I wasn't about to pursue him to return it. And he'd left no forwarding address. Still, it must have belonged to my client. I should at least make an effort. But what could it be?

Curiosity overcame my scruples and I opened the envelope. Inside, wrapped in a small white rectangle of paper, were two very crisp one hundred dollar bills. My fee. Twice my fee, actually. I began to laugh. He might have scared the living daylights out of me, but at least he paid his bills on time. How many of my more sedate clients could say that?

3

I have lived in this city for forty-five years and the summers still take my breath away. Literally. The blast furnace heat, coupled with humidity that surrounds one like a hot, damp blanket, really does leave me gasping for air. I walked slowly home along the relatively shady west side of the street. The shade cut the worst of the sun, but it was still like walking through warm soup.

Commuters drove by, heading home from their jobs in the downtown core. Those with air-conditioned cars looked smug and comfortable; the rest sweated and glared at one another over real and imagined traffic infractions and discourtesies. Adding to the mix, jaywalkers darted out from between parked cars, creating logjams of frustrated drivers and provoking honks of protest from the less sanguine among them.

The sidewalk, too, was full. Government drones hurried by in expensive custom-fit walking shoes; mothers hustled small children along to the local grocery store for last-minute supper makings; and high school kids dressed up as flower children or disco queens congregated on the corners, drinkin' java and rollin' smokes. Yeah, man. Cool. Or was it "way cool" now? I can never remember.

With its single and double-storey brick facades, and mom-and-pop businesses cramped into staid brick turn of the century buildings, Bank Street resembles the main thoroughfare of almost any small town in this part of the country. It might be prosaic, but it's part of what I love about the city — small enough that it seems everyone knows everyone else, yet large enough to have delusions of cosmopolitanism. Here, it comes as a shock to see dog poop by the side of the street. Most people in this city are clean, orderly and polite. Those who aren't stand out.

As I walked, I fumed silently at Greg, my friend and former mentor, who had referred Adam to me. What could he have been thinking? Clearly, Adam was in need of psychiatric evaluation and Greg knew I had left that part of my life behind. Besides, if they'd met in a professional capacity, Adam must have seen Greg in the Forensic Unit. Had he been one of the court-referred patients? In my years at the Royal Ottawa Hospital, I'd evaluated dozens of them. Guys who'd committed brutal, senseless crimes — the kind anyone would have to be literally crazy to commit. Which explained how they'd wound up at the Royal, telling me what the funny looking ink blot meant to them.

Was Adam one of these? And even if he wasn't, shouldn't Greg have seen the violence and fear bubbling just below Adam's too-still surface? Greg knew I worked on my own, with no back-up. What could have possessed him?

Several people glanced furtively at me before giving me a wide berth on the sidewalk; I must have been muttering to myself as I stalked home. I grinned at the realization and decided to save the full force of my fury for Greg, as soon as I caught up with the little weasel.

Meanwhile, I focused on not traumatizing innocent passersby.

Dawn was stretched out on the couch, with the portable phone propped between her shoulder and ear, when I walked into our ground-floor apartment. The place was tiny, a few renovated rooms in a subdivided Victorian mansion in the city's downtown core. I liked to think of it as shabby, yet elegant. Original leaded glass window panes, tiny rooms crowded with overstuffed furniture — and everywhere, books. Air conditioning was a luxury beyond our means, and when I'd left the hospital, I had given up my beloved Karmann Ghia, but I told myself Dawn and I were poor yet happy. Most of the time, I believed it.

Dawn had stripped down to her underwear and tied her honey-blonde hair into a loose ponytail. When she saw me, she wiggled her toes by way of a greeting. I could tell from Dawn's occasional interjections that she was talking to her best friend, Sylvie.

"Uh-huh … uh-huh … yeah … hum. That sucks. Yeah …" she murmured at long intervals. I stifled a smile; it always amused me that Dawn, so rarely at a loss for words, often had trouble inserting even monosyllabic comments into Sylvie's rapid-fire transmissions.

"Sweetie …" I tried to catch my daughter's attention. Dawn looked up and pointed to the phone receiver.

"I know, I know," I nodded, mouthing the words. I mimed lifting the receiver to my own ear. "Can you hurry it along?"

Dawn rolled her eyes, a clear signal that Sylvie was in full gear. I grimaced my disapproval, and Dawn shrugged an apology. Lord knows, Dawn might be the most wonderful, intelligent and charming young woman on the planet, but this business of hogging the phone was getting out of hand. I pointed toward the ceiling, letting Dawn know I was going upstairs to use Peter's phone.

Fifteen years ago, Peter and I had conceived Dawn. When our marriage had ended five years later, the one thing we'd agreed on was our only daughter's well-being. Peter liked to say that Dawn kept us civilized during the divorce and its aftermath; now, he lived in the apartment directly above ours. Over the years, both he and I had mellowed to the point where people wondered why we'd divorced in the first place. In fact, Peter had asked me that same question, not a week ago.

"You know why." I'd turned away, filling a watering can at the kitchen sink.

"What — the sex thing?" Peter had raised an eyebrow.

"Among others, yes. Come on, Peter, give it up." I started watering the plants on the window ledge, slopping water and potting soil over the edge of an overfilled dracaena plant. I cursed under my breath and started mopping at the mess with a paper towel.

"Katy, we're practically best friends. We live in each others' pockets and we're raising a child together. What could it hurt to have a little fun together?"

"It wouldn't feel right. We're not —"

"You mean I don't do anything for you in the bedroom department, right?"

"I don't want to fight about this. I just don't think it's a good idea, that's all."

"It's about whatsisname, isn't it?"

I had felt my face flush, and Peter had chuckled.

"Hey, never mind, kiddo. So you're still in love with the guy you dumped — what, eighteen years ago? I shouldn't feel bitter, right?"

"I'm not in love with him," I had protested. "And I didn't dump him. We dumped each other."

"Sure. Right. So what's for supper?"

Peter was at work tonight, though, and his apartment was blessedly silent. I dropped into the butter soft leather of his couch and dialled Greg's home number. His machine picked up.

"Hi, Greg Chisholm here. I can't answer the phone just now, but I'd like to return your call, so please leave your name, number …"

I waited for the beep, tapping a finger impatiently on my knee.

"It's me," I said. "I need to talk to you. Now. Yes, it's serious. No, I don't want to leave details. Let's just say your latest referral was ill-advised. You'd better call me while I'm still speaking to you. I'm at home."

I slammed the phone down and it jingled in protest.

Downstairs, Dawn was still on the receiving end of Sylvie's barrage of words. I snorted, then began searching in the kitchen for something that wouldn't require too much cooking. Six months ago, Dawn had declared that meat was murder and we'd been eating vegetarian ever since. For the most part I didn't mind, but on a hot night when cold cuts and a beer would have gone down perfectly, the range of vegetarian choices seemed pretty paltry.

I was pureeing cooked lentils in the food processor when Dawn slipped into the kitchen.

"Mom, we need an extra phone line," she announced. "I spent today getting my server up and running, but if I want anyone to use it, I need a dedicated line. Otherwise, I'll have to use our home line, and no one will ever get through. Or we just won't be able to use the phone ourselves." She smiled, wrinkling her tiny freckled nose and causing a dimple to appear at the corner of her mouth.

"Dawn, your timing could be better." I spoke slowly and deliberately. "Plus, our finances are a bit tight right now. I told you when your grandparents bought you that computer that I might not be able to afford to buy you much in the way of extra stuff for it. An extra phone line would cost money. I don't have money. I also have a headache, I'm hot and I've had a very rough day. Let's talk about this later, okay?"

Dawn seemed to recognize the effort I was putting into remaining calm and, without a word, she began to wash and tear up romaine lettuce for a salad. We worked in silence for a while and gradually the everyday tasks of putting a meal together began to ease me into a more companionable frame of mind.

We carried our plates into the living room, and just as I was settling into my customary corner of the couch, the phone rang.

"Shit. I'll bet that's Greg," I said. Considering the message I'd left, it would have felt churlish not to pick up. But the voice on the other end of the line was not Greg's.

"Oh, hi, Mama. Listen, Dawn and I are just sitting down to supper. Would it be okay if I called you back?"

"Of course, *mamaleh*, but I just wanted to know if you can come to dinner Friday," she said.

I closed my eyes and rubbed a throbbing temple. I'd forgotten all about going home for sabbath dinner; just that morning I'd agreed to go to a movie with Carmen, my lifelong friend. Never mind, Carmen would understand. She knew my mother.

"Sure, Mama."

"You don't sound happy, dear. Anything wrong? Maybe you want to come for dinner next week, instead?"

My mother rarely missed a nuance.

"No, no, really, it's fine," I lied. "Have you talked to Peter? I mean, is he coming, too?"

"Of course, he's your husband, isn't he?"

"Mama, how many times have I told you — we're divorced. Peter and I are divorced. We've been divorced for a long time. Not married. Not living together. Divorced." I tried to keep my voice steady.

"*Feh*!" My mother dismissed my protests. "A marriage is a marriage, Katy. And if you're so divorced, why is your husband sleeping in your house?"

"He's not — no, never mind." I was too tired to argue the point further. "So he's coming on Friday, then?"

"It's *shabbos*, Katy. Where else is he going to go? A nice Jewish boy like him, he needs a family, now that both his parents are gone. Besides, he could use some meat on those bones. He's been getting too skinny lately. What have you been feeding him?"

I started to argue that it was no longer my job to feed Peter, but thought better of it.

"Mama, we'll be there, okay? Around six?"

"Fine, *mamaleh*, fine. Have a good dinner."

Hanging up, I shook my head. "Remind me not to pick up the phone for a while, would you?" I asked Dawn, and we settled in to watch the nightly news while we ate.

Greg finally called, right in the middle of the Final Jeopardy Question. The answer had been right on the tip of my tongue, but the ringing phone jostled it just out of reach.

"Yes?"

"What was that message all about?" Greg demanded. "I haven't made any referrals to you." His voice, normally soothing, was edged with annoyance.

"Then who the hell was that guy I saw today? He certainly looked like your typical forensic psycho-killer candidate, and he gave me your name!"

"I haven't a clue." Greg had the nerve to sound aggrieved. "Who was he?"

"All he would tell me was 'Adam,'" I said. "He said you told him I could help him, but I'm telling you right now, I don't want this guy anywhere near me. He gave me the major willies. Looked ready to go off the deep end, talked to himself, stared at me like he thought God was talking to him through the fillings in his teeth or something ..."

"Katy, slow down, would you? I didn't send you any 'Adam', and I certainly wouldn't refer anyone to you if I didn't think he was safe."

"Then how did he get my name, and how did he know yours?"

"I'm telling you, I don't know." Greg sounded decidedly miffed. "What did he look like?"

"A bit shorter than me, dark blond hair, all matted up like he'd never combed it in his life; pale skin, weird light green eyes. Creepy in the extreme. And it was like pulling teeth to get him to even say hello, let alone sit down like any normal person."

"Wait a minute, hold on ..."

I heard Greg's briefcase click open.

"I think I might know who you mean," he said when he came back. "He's not one of mine at the moment. I saw him at the Allan, about twenty years back. Then a couple of weeks ago, he stopped in at the clinic. Wanted to make an appointment. I had to tell him I'm only seeing court referrals now, and he went away looking pretty unhappy."

"And you gave him my name? Thanks a heap!" I began, but Greg cut me off.

"Look, for the last bloody time, I didn't give him your name, okay? Do you really think I'd do that to you?"

"I guess not," I admitted. "But if you didn't, how did he find me?"

"Oh, God — wait a sec," Greg muttered. "I think I know what might have happened, Katy. Remember we'd had our lunch together that day, and you gave me your fancy new business cards?"

"Yeah …" I remembered. For the first few years of my astrology career, I'd made do with unembellished cards, which Dawn had designed for me on her computer. Finally, a few weeks ago, my decorator friend Carmen had persuaded me to visit a friend of hers, a designer. Tara had unveiled my new cards two weeks ago and I'd given a couple to Greg, who'd been impressed.

"Well, the day you gave me the cards, I came back from lunch and left them on my desk. When I was packing up later, I couldn't find them, but I didn't think much about it. You know how my desk is by the end of the day."

"Sure, it looks like a demolition site. But this doesn't make any sense," I protested. "If the guy wanted to find an astrologer, he could have looked in the phone book, couldn't he?"

"I don't know." Greg sounded tired. "I really don't know. But look — why don't we have lunch tomorrow or the next day? It's too hot to argue with you now. I'd rather do it somewhere that has air conditioning."

"Sure, that sounds good," I said, my anger rapidly

subsiding. "Greg, I'm sorry I yelled at you, but this guy scared me."

"No problem. I understand. Is twelve-thirty okay? I have a late morning meeting with Frank Curtis and some of his minions."

A lump formed in my throat, but I forced it back. Katy, it's time to get over the place, I told myself. You quit. You made the decision, and you're gone. Change the subject.

"Do you want to try out the Indian food place down the street from my office?" I asked, as though I hadn't heard Curtis' name. "I hear they have a decent buffet."

We hung up on a friendlier note. Still, while I no longer believed Greg had deliberately set me up with Adam, I was no closer to understanding how the strange man had found me. Never mind, it could wait till morning. I stacked the supper dishes and went to bed, where I lay with my eyes wide open until the first hazy light of early morning penetrated the white gauze curtains of my room. No matter how I tried, I couldn't get Adam's pale gooseberry eyes out of my head.

4

By the time I stumbled into my office the next morning, I had ten messages of varying urgency waiting on my answering machine. Rubbing the sleep from my eyes, I rewound the tape.

The wedding date I'd helped choose yesterday was no good, as the young couple's minister would be out of town; they needed some alternatives by the afternoon.

A couple of Sagittarius clients had been panicked by Madame Flora's Astro-Advice column in the *Ottawa Telegraph* — she'd predicted dire consequences as a result of Jupiter's recent ingress into their Sun sign. I wished people wouldn't read those columns. I could see the headlines now: "Pluto enters Sagittarius: One-Twelfth of the Population Croaks!" Not too likely, I chuckled to myself.

There were more hang-ups than usual on the

machine, six of them, some preceded by audible rapid breathing. I shrugged and erased the tape. Before I started returning calls, I stretched out on the sofa and drank my first coffee of the day — a rich French roast, marred only slightly by the cardboard cup in which I'd bought it.

Then I pulled my laptop over and took a moment to check out the movements of the heavens. There were no huge surprises — restrictive Saturn opposed my Libra Sun, creating obstacles and impediments. Combative Mars squared my Saturn, pitting my assertive energies against my need to stay at least marginally civilized. This explained my deep and powerful urge to deck the next person who rubbed me the wrong way, I thought. Well, bring 'em on.

I put aside the computer and began to flip through an astrological journal. What do you know — an article by Flavia. Flavia was the nearest thing I had to a penpal. We'd met over the Internet, on a usenet group dedicated to astrology, where we'd both been trashing some poor fool who insisted that the stars created our destiny. Flavia and I had hit it off instantly and maintained a regular correspondence. The article wasn't bad, a delineation of the Unabomber's chart, and I was engrossed enough to be startled by the phone.

When I picked up there was a long moment of faint breathing, then the sound of the receiver being dropped into the cradle. I had only just replaced the phone myself, when it rang again. I snatched it up.

"Adam?"

More breathing.

"Adam, this isn't funny. If you want to talk to me, do it. I'm here."

Click.

A zing of anxiety shot up my spine. Slamming the phone down, I moved uneasily around the perimeter of the office, checking the lock on the door, peering out through dust-caked windows: no sign of danger, but I could not rid myself of the idea that Adam would return.

Ruth, the first appointment of the day, arrived half an hour later, and I spent nearly two hours with her. Ruth was a bright, talented young lawyer with a solid, practical Capricorn/Virgo chart, enlivened by a dash of Aries. It was only when my watch beeped that I recalled my luncheon date with Greg. Wrapping up the session, I locked the door and followed Ruth down the stairs.

Greg was waiting for me at the dimly-lit Indian café, looking mildly professorial, with his half-moon glasses perched on the end of his long, thin nose. Years ago, he'd been my internship supervisor at the Royal Ottawa, but gradually we'd slipped into an easy collegial friendship. Greg had been distressed at my abrupt departure from the hospital, but he took my word that it was necessary, and asked no questions. I volunteered no answers.

"Hey, Katy!" Greg gestured to me. "You're not as late as usual."

"God, you're so anal," I responded, taking a seat and gulping some ice-water. "So what's up in Forensics these days? Any major affairs or betrayals I should know about?"

"Nope. Oh, except that Fowler and that intern from Addictions finally broke up. But you saw that coming two months ago. I guess I should pay up."

"It didn't exactly take a psychic. Fowler should know better by now — how many interns has she hit on? In how many years?"

Greg chuckled. "So — you going to order, or take the buffet?"

When I returned, plate piled with unpronounce-able, aromatic goodies, the conversation turned to Adam.

"Funny thing is, I didn't even meet him at the ROH," Greg said, around a mouthful of hot naan. "He was in-voluntarily hospitalized at the Allan when I was in Mon-treal doing my residency, must have been twenty years ago. Now that was one screwed up kid. The first time I saw him, he was floridly psychotic — screaming about the 'watchers' and the evil ones living in his stomach. You know the kind of thing. When we got him calmed down, it turned out he'd been hanging around with a crowd of druggies on Mount Royal. LSD and ampheta-mines don't do much for you when you're already on the edge."

I nodded, swirling spiced tea in my cup.

"So. Did he actually get diagnosed schizophrenic, or was it just the drugs talking?"

"Well, I treated him for nearly a year as an in-pa-tient, back in the days when we could hang onto some-one that long. He lost the more obvious hallucinations within a few days, but he was still pretty weird. Loads of delusions — really paranoid. By the time he was re-leased, he sounded like your average recluse. Not ex-actly nuts, but certainly happier just to be left alone. A lot of odd beliefs and rituals — like he couldn't take his eyes off you if he was talking to you."

I nodded. "That's what he was doing yesterday. Star-ing at me. Silent. It freaked me out, I can tell you."

"Uh-huh. I think his parents had money and they set him up in a little apartment on Durocher. In the stu-dent ghetto, you know. The father was obsessed with keeping Adam in line — he called me every two minutes to check on the kid."

"So how did Adam wind up doing drugs on Mount Royal? That doesn't really fit, does it?"

"I never found out the whole story. The nearest I could figure out, he started sneaking out of the family home in Westmount at night, and I guess he felt like he fit in on the Mountain. Anyway, I never heard that he received any kind of treatment after I saw him. But we had a connection. Every few years he'd drop in on me, just checking in, he said. But when I moved here, I stopped hearing from him. Then, just a couple of weeks ago, he shows up on the unit, clutching his father's obituary, looking completely weirded out. Just like the good old days."

"That's odd. If he was such an isolate, what would make him come running to you? Wouldn't he be happier just withdrawing further?"

Greg shook his head, as puzzled as I was.

"No idea. I wondered at the time, but he couldn't tell me much. Or wouldn't. It's hard to say, with him. I know when I treated him at the Allan he was pretty darn paranoid, lots of fears about being watched and so on, but underneath it all, he just seemed kind of lost. I guess I was young and green then, and maybe I didn't seem like the threatening shrink, or something. I don't know. It's not like he ever completely opened up to me, but at least he didn't just sit there staring at me. Come to think of it, that's probably how I wound up with him — all the docs who were senior to me hated that staring thing, and I guess they passed him along to the junior guy."

I laughed. "I have trouble thinking of you as the junior guy, Greg. I could swear you'd been a shrink since

Freud was in training pants. Anyway, what did you say to Adam when he showed up this time?"

"He wanted to set up a session with me, said he needed help. But you know how tight they are about patient eligibility at the hospital now. I had to tell him I could only take court referrals. I sent him along to Schneider in General Psych, got Adam to sign the release forms to get his files over here from Montreal. He wasn't happy about it, but it was the best I could do. Too bad, because I would've liked to have found out how he'd progressed over the years. Anyway, later that day I went to look for those cards of yours, and there they weren't. I have to assume now that Adam took them off my desk, but I couldn't for the life of me tell you why. And that's pretty much it."

"I think he might still be calling me and hanging up," I said. "Frankly, it makes me a bit nervous. I can't exactly call an orderly code, can I? Does Adam have any history of violence?"

"Good question. It was hard to get a complete history out of him even twenty years ago, but from what I understand, he went through a few years of elective mutism when he was a kid. Just stopped speaking, when he was about three. At first they thought he was autistic, but then someone twigged to the fact that he'd been interacting pretty well before."

I leaned across the table. "That's strange."

"Very. There was a troubled school history, and I think his parents had him in analysis while he was in grade school. Which would have cost a bundle back then, you know. I never saw him actually try to hurt anyone else, but he self-mutilated on the ward from time to time, with needles or glass or whatever. The usual — cutting his arms or legs, gouging out bits of flesh. I remember a couple of times the cuts got infected and we had to ship him out to Emerg at the Royal Vic."

There was no guarantee Adam wouldn't turn on someone else if he felt threatened enough, but I felt a bit of relief at this news. Self-mutilation may not be pretty, but it usually indicates that most of the rage the person feels has been turned inward, for whatever reason. They're less likely to lash out.

"Elective mutism, huh? That certainly sounds like my guy," I said. "I felt like I was prying words out of him, and when he talked, it sounded like he wasn't really used to the sound of his own voice. Some of what he said sounded rehearsed. Mechanical, almost — that'd match up with someone who doesn't talk much. Any idea what led to the mutism?"

"Like I said, he didn't tell us much about his past. But the first time I saw him, he was in his early twenties, and defensive as hell. What little information I got came from his parents. Nice people. Mother was French-Canadian, seemed very concerned about him, but also worn out with trying to keep him out of trouble. His father was some kind of investor or something. Not around much, and when he was, he liked to throw his weight around. But the mother was a truly sweet lady. I remember her bringing cookies and other stuff to the patients on the ward.

"Adam must have been born when they were getting on in years, because they were in their late sixties when I knew them. I think there was an older brother, but I never met him. Anyway, the parents couldn't tell me about any specific trauma. According to them, he just stopped talking one day, started wetting the bed and having night terrors. And he started that strange staring thing he does, the whole bit. But Katy, I'm remembering this from twenty years ago. I'm a little fuzzy on the specifics."

"His birth chart has a lot of stuff about an overpowering father," I thought aloud. "I wonder if that's it — he was abused as a kid? I mean, we both know that when kids have learned to talk, they don't just suddenly stop. Something must have happened. And yesterday, he was talking about things 'coming back' to him — he couldn't make sense of the memories, he said."

"It's possible, but I don't remember anything."

"Well, when I mentioned his father, he got very antsy. And he didn't deny the stuff I said about feeling overpowered. I wonder if that's it?"

Greg shrugged. "I guess we'll never know."

"Maybe there's something I'm missing in his chart." I tapped my finger against my fork. "Such a strange, scared-looking man. There's got to be more …"

"Hey, I thought you wanted him out of your life," Greg interrupted. "Come on, Katy, there's no need for you to get involved with Adam. You'll probably never see him again, and even if you do, you don't know for sure that he won't decide to disembowel you, or feed you to his pet piranhas or something."

"Oh, thank you very much," I laughed. "Yeah, you're right. I'll back off."

The rest of our lunch was filled with desultory conversation, so I walked out feeling relaxed, lulled by the dimness of the lighting, the spicy fragrance of the food and the endless feedback loop of soft sitar music. Outside, the thick, damp air engulfed us instantly. We exchanged hugs gingerly, neither wanting to press too close in the heat, and promised to call one another soon. I meandered back to work, window-shopping and hoping no one had called while I was out.

The street level entrance to my office was shaded by a huge maple tree that overwhelmed and shadowed the rear face of the building. Sometimes it irked me, not having a front entrance; but the shade was nice on a day like this. I plodded slowly up the narrow staircase, wondering for the three thousandth time when that scummy excuse for a landlord was planning to install a handrail, and perhaps even a lightbulb.

When I reached the top of the stairs, the last person I expected to see standing stiffly on the landing was Adam.

5

Adam's pale face loomed at me out of the gloom, and I nearly fell backward down the stairs.

"What do you want?" I demanded, clutching my purse to my chest as if to ward him off. My voice sounded sharper than I'd intended, and I almost felt guilty as my visitor flinched back against the door. *He* was afraid of *me*?

"I need to talk to you some more." His voice came out in a gravelly whisper. "Please?"

"Adam, I don't think this is a good idea ..." I trailed off as his gooseberry eyes bugged out even further.

"I need to," he repeated. "There is no one else. Only you."

I paused, searching for words. "Adam, I don't want you to get upset again ..."

"I'll be good," he whispered. "Please? I promise, I'll be good. I just need to talk to you again." He looked as though he might begin crying. Ignoring the tiny insistent voice in my head that kept saying, "This is a really, really bad idea, Katy," I reached slowly into my purse for my keys. My pulse beat hard against the base of my throat as I moved past Adam to unlock the office door.

"All right." My voice was tight with fear. "Come in."

He stood awkwardly, apparently waiting for permission to be seated. My mouth was dry and cold sweat dribbled down my back.

"Please, sit down." I gestured toward the couch. In contrast to his last visit, he perched cautiously on a corner of the futon. He kept his gaze trained on my face, but now and then his eyes flicked toward the door. Perhaps he was gauging his trajectory, in case a speedy exit was needed.

"Adam, I had lunch with Greg Chisholm today. He says he knows you, but he never told you to come and see me. Why did you say he referred you to me?"

Staring silence. "Talk to me, Adam. You said you would." More silence, but he swallowed audibly.

"Adam, I think you have the wrong idea about what I can do for you. You seem to be looking for certainty, for facts about the past, and I can't really give you that. I told you that yesterday, right?"

"I need the story."

"Yeah, well, what I'm saying is that I can't give you the exact story. All I can do is point out the possibilities. You have to supply the rest. I really don't think this is going to work."

"I need you to tell me the story. You know things about me."

"What do I know about you? I don't understand."

"Things. Like who hurt the child. You know that. I can feel it."

I shook my head impatiently. This was silly; we were going in circles.

"Adam, it sounds like you already know who hurt the child. Am I right?" I kept my voice neutral, trying not to set him off.

Adam's face contorted, as though he was on the

brink of tears. His words came out strangled. "You do. You know who hurt the child. You know about the father. I need you to tell me everything you know."

"Adam, I already told you. When I look at your chart, I see the *possibility* that your father was a controlling, domineering person. I see the *possibility* that he was mean to you, maybe even hurt you. Really, I can't give you any more detail than that — not unless you help me. Now, Greg told me he gave you a referral to Dr. Schneider the other day. Don't you think you could get further by talking to him? If you're having flashbacks, memories, whatever, he could help you figure out what it all means."

"He controls them, too!" Adam said hoarsely, leaning forward so suddenly that he nearly lost his precarious perch on the futon. "You're the only one he can't control. You must help me! Please! You can't know what it's like!"

I caught my breath. Who was controlling whom? He was talking in riddles now, the paranoid, stereotyped speech of someone teetering on the brink of psychosis. I didn't want to contribute to his agitation, but I needed to get him out of my office, into a more appropriate treatment setting.

"I want to help you, Adam, I do. But I don't know how to give you what you need. Why don't we just call Dr. Schneider and see if he could find time to see you this afternoon? He's good at helping people find the truth about themselves."

But Adam's frenzy had reached a fever pitch. He seemed to have forgotten his earlier promise. He jumped up from the couch, took a step toward me, staring hard. His hands were balled into tight fists at his sides, and a muscle twitched in his pale but surprisingly muscular neck. Then he jerked around toward the door and bolted, clattering down the stairs, slamming the outside door so hard the floorboards shook.

Shaking, I picked up the phone and dialled Greg's number, my breath coming in uneven gasps. It wasn't until his machine came on that I realized I was crying. I hung up. Of course he wasn't there yet. We'd just had lunch together.

For nearly half an hour, I stared blankly at Adam's chart on the computer screen in front of me. Pluto rising. Pluto, god of the underworld. Grim, inexorable in his judgments as in his actions. A loner, indecipherable. He abducted Persephone from the earth, raped her and kept her imprisoned in Hades until her mother, Demeter, allowed the crops to fail and the earth to die in her grief for her lost daughter. Eternal winter. Finally, Pluto released Persephone so she could visit her mother for part of the year, but only after the girl had eaten the magic pomegranate seeds that would force her to return to him the other six months. Keeping her under his thumb. Which makes Pluto an abductor, rapist, wife abuser and all-round not-so-nice guy.

In the heavens, Pluto is a tiny chunk of rock and ice that whirls around the Sun at a snail's pace: one circuit every 284 earth years. Like the god, the planet's symbolic psychological action is grindingly slow and relentless. When it comes into contact with the personal parts of the birthchart, it acts like a purgative, forcing poisons to the surface. Some people deal with this well; others don't. Adam was clearly one of the latter. In his chart, Pluto, Mercury, the Sun and Ascendant were mixed into a nasty stew where flavours of dark secrecy and powerful behind-the-scenes dramas could distort, even shatter a small child's world. Adam himself showed no shortage of woundedness. He was like a carrier, drawing everyone who met him into his vortex of pain. How aware was he of his impact on others? Not very, if I were to go by the rest of his chart. With Uranus and Mars rubbing shoulders in the house of friendship and sociability, it was likely Adam had a short fuse. Well, no kidding — you didn't need to be an astrologer to deduce that one.

Still, with Uranus and Mars conjunct in Cancer, a watery sign, Adam looked more likely to implode than explode, all that pain and terror spiralling inward to his very core. He would absorb every poisonous nuance in his environment and never realize that it was not actually coming from him. Then there was the Venus-Saturn conjunction — Venus longing for love and acceptance, damped down by chilly Saturn's inability to reach out. Affection would always be coupled with a sense of loss in this child's mind. A tamer conjunction than the rest, but when they were added to the mix, I could easily see Adam becoming a recluse, never comfortable with others, tormented by his own inner demons.

Finally, there was this Scorpio Moon, ruled by Pluto, sitting down there in the fourth house of early childhood and the family. The Moon represents the instinctual emotional self, as well as the mother; and it was governed by that Plutonian powerhouse on the Ascendant. Far too potent a mix for anyone, let alone a small child.

He'd stopped speaking; where had that come from? I was certain it was all linked together, but without Adam's co-operation, I had no way to find out. Weary, I exited the program and clicked off the machine. Stretching back in my creaking chair, I closed my eyes and mulled over the chart. Sometimes I found that this technique allowed images to drift into my mind, helping me make sense of a chart. It wasn't happening now, though. All I got was darkness, thick and impenetrable.

I dialled Greg's number again. His secretary put me on hold for five minutes — not bad considering how fiercely she guarded her boss's time.

"Greg? Hi, it's me again. Listen, Adam was just here. I have to tell you, this is really starting to give me the creeps."

"What did he do? Are you okay?"

"More or less. He kept insisting that I know about some secret from his past. I tried to explain that I really only see trends and make suggestions, but he wasn't having any. When I suggested we get him in to see John Schneider this afternoon, he looked like he was about to attack me, thought better of it, and bolted again."

"Katy, I'd like to tell you he's perfectly harmless, but I really don't know what he'll do if he feels cornered. I do think we need to keep him away from you."

"Nice idea, I'm all for it. But since I don't even know his last name, let alone where he lives, I really don't know how to accomplish that one."

"Oh, sorry. It's Cosgrove. Adam Cosgrove. I should have told you that. Why don't I ask around here? I'll call the Allan Memorial Institute too, and see what I can find out. I'm sure he wouldn't still be living on the same street in Montreal after twenty years, but he might have seen someone at the Institute since I was there. And I'll check with the front desk here. If he did make an appointment with John, we'll have a local address. Meanwhile, you know, you should probably call the police about this."

I sighed. "Okay, I'll give them a call. And let me know what you find out, okay?"

The police were not exactly helpful, especially since I was unable to report that Adam had actually touched me, or even uttered threats. The bored voice on the phone offered to have the neighbourhood constable check in tomorrow, if I wished. I hung up, comforted to know the boys in blue were on the job.

6

Dawn had managed to use every utensil in the minuscule kitchen, cooking up something she called Tofu Beanburger Surprise. I peered into the mixing bowl and shook in some extra salt, just to be on the safe side.

"Seriously, Mom, you've got to think about these things." Dawn pounded away at her creation with a potato masher. "I don't want you dropping dead out of the blue, like Sylvie's mother's friend did last week. No one saw it coming. And she wasn't that old, either."

"Don't worry, honey, I won't be dropping dead any time soon," I promised, crossing my fingers out of Dawn's sight. Adam is not going to do anything, I thought. He's not.

"Mom, is this an okay time to talk about that phone line? I need to know if I can tell my users the server is up and running. I called the phone company and they gave me a price, and I could pay the monthly bills out of my allowance, if you'd pay to have the line put in."

"You've been doing your homework, huh? I should have guessed yesterday." I smiled. "You had your father's look about you, the one he gets when he's hot on the trail of some story. Besides, who am I to stand in the way of socially conscious youth?"

"Yeah, but can we do it?"

"Okay," I conceded. "But you're going to pay the bills, right?"

"Sure — I can pool the allowances you guys give me," she beamed. "And thanks, Mom. This is great. It means we have a place to trade ideas, and I can post the group's newsletter on-line. We can really make a difference, you know?"

I finished packing forks, knives, plastic plates (non-disposable) and cloth napkins into the old wicker picnic basket Peter and I had received as a wedding gift. One of the city's attractions is its abundance of green space, available for people who prefer to dine *sur l'herbe*, even if they live in the downtown core. When summer heat waves settle into the region, Dawn and I like to take every opportunity to escape to the great outdoors.

We laid an Indian bedspread under one of the maples that lined the Rideau Canal, and Dawn busied herself arranging the Tofu Beanburger Surprise, some leftover cold lentil paté from the night before, a salad and a bowl of fresh sliced strawberries. We lounged on the gently sloping grass, cool against our backs, in delightful contrast to the lingering warmth of the early evening air.

The Canal wound its way through the heart of the city, from Hog's Back Falls to the Ottawa River. Formerly a transportation system, it was considered a masterstroke of modern engineering during the last century, when Upper Canada feared invasion by its southern neighbour. Now, it was a charming anachronism, much loved by tourists and boaters who meandered along its murky waters.

Joggers, cyclists and in-line skaters vied for space

along its narrow paths. The swiftest veered around the less adventurous: parents with strollers; lovers walking entwined and oblivious; dogs taking their people out for a drag; older citizens stepping out for evening constitutionals. At the height of summer, the decaying vegetation and dead, bloated carp dotting the surface smelled downright ripe, but the overall effect was still pretty.

Dawn and I lay just upstream from a bed of red and white flowers; I wondered idly if they were impatiens, but couldn't be bothered to get up and check. Overhead, a canopy of leaves blocked the last rays of the sun. If I closed my eyes and tried to ignore the hum of passing cars on the nearby road, I could almost imagine I was somewhere cool and peaceful.

We ate lazily, in no rush to return to the stifling confines of our small apartment. Houseboats, basically mobile homes mounted on aluminum floats, puttered by, passengers drowsing in canvas deck chairs and exerting themselves only to tip beer bottles to their lips.

"Do you remember, when you were little, you used to stand on the railings and wave at all the boats that went by?"

"Mom …" Dawn groaned.

I squinted up into the leaves overhead while Dawn described the wonders of her new server.

"I got the idea from Sylvie's little brother. He's such a nerd, but he says he can crack any program that's out there, and he found this one on one of the big commercial boards … but he says Rebel is nearly as good as what you can get out there, and it's freeware," Dawn rambled. "You were a hippie once, Mom — don't you love the idea of bypassing the big guys to beat them at their own game?"

My gaze drifted across the Canal and suddenly I sat up. I rubbed my eyes, blinked and stared. Without my glasses, I couldn't be certain, but I thought I recognized the figure leaning against the railing across the greeny-brown water. The same black jeans, the nylon windbreaker. And there was no mistaking the intensity of that stare. Adam stood motionless, his reflection absolutely still in the slow-moving water. He was looking right at us.

"Dawn, let's go."

My throat was tight, and Dawn looked at me curiously.

"What's the matter? I'm happy just sitting here."

"Nothing … no, it's not nothing. We have to go home. I just remembered something. Uh, I think I left a burner on."

"Mom, I was the last one using the stove. I know I turned everything off. I double-checked, just like you told me."

"I might have left the door unlocked. We have to go."

Dawn sighed theatrically, clearly humouring her capricious mother. We gathered the remains of our picnic. Despite myself, my gaze kept sneaking over to the stocky, fair-haired man who never once took his eyes off us. Anxiety buzzed up and down my spine as I hustled Dawn down the nearest side street, tugging at her elbow to keep her from dawdling.

I sprawled naked on my bed that night, covers kicked off, the inert air draping my damp skin in the darkness. Flavia. I should e-mail Flavia in the morning. She'll have some ideas. Tomorrow. When I can think in full sentences. Sleep crept up quietly, and I was gone.

FRIDAY, JULY 29
Sun opposition Moon, opposition Uranus ✦
Moon inconjunct Mars, conjunct Uranus,
conjunct Neptune ✦
Mercury square Pluto ✦
Mars square Saturn, inconjunct Uranus ✦
Jupiter square Saturn ✦

First thing next morning, clutching my coffee mug like an amulet, I bravely entered the world of modems and electronic message transferring. While I had used a computer for several years, for the most part I viewed it as a very fancy electric typewriter which did not require corrector fluid. Dawn had taught me to use e-mail, but there was something about sending messages off into the ether that worried me. Who was to say where my words disappeared to when I pressed that "send" button? Still, I wanted Flavia's input and our only means of communication was electronic.

Hi, Flavia. Got a live one here.

I punched in Adam Cosgrove's birth data, then described my interactions with him to date, not neglecting to mention last evening's performance.

So, what do you think? I'm pretty sure there's early trauma there, but I can't wrap my head around any specifics. Not that I want to provoke him any more than I already have, but I must say I'm curious. And I'm worried, too. This guy is unstable. I'm not getting any help at all from the local constabulary, but I'm looking for the key to turn Adam off. You're good at the intuitive stuff, and you're coming at it fresh. Any ideas? Let me know ASAP.

I hit the send button and switched off the computer. I drank the rest of my tepid coffee before getting into the shower as a prelude to my work day. The water was cool and needle-sharp, and it felt good against my scalp. I scrubbed my hair dry with a rough towel, then searched around for something clean and presentable to wear, bearing in mind my mother's invitation to dinner that evening.

Dawn was sleeping when I left. The sun had only just begun to gather strength and I enjoyed the relative cool as I walked to the office. The city was at its best first thing in the morning. A few of the more gung-ho worker bees headed off to their grey government hives downtown, but mostly the streets were empty of traffic. The low eastern sun flickered through masses of green leaves, and you could actually tell what colour the sky was supposed to be. In the still early morning, it was a shimmering pearly blue and the air felt clean in my lungs.

The walk took about fifteen minutes and I stopped in at Java De-Lux, the trendy corner café, for my morning tank-up. Coffee was my last bastion against Dawn's attempts to clean up my act for me. No, if I thought about it, it wasn't quite the last — once in a while I allowed myself some fries, or worse, poutine.

The phone was already ringing when I let myself into the office, and I was slightly out of breath from the stairs as I picked up. It was Greg, and he sounded perplexed.

"They're saying at the Allan that they have no records on Adam Cosgrove," he said.

"Pardon? I thought that's where you two met."

"It is … was. And they don't throw out records, no matter how brief or old. But there's no sign of him in the current files. Nothing in the archival records, either. I just picked up the message when I came in."

"I'm not getting this. You treated him for nearly a year on a locked ward, right? In-patient charts don't just vanish."

"Yup. His file was about an inch thick. Now granted, it would have been transferred to microfiche a few years after he was released, but it should still be in the system."

"It should, shouldn't it? What if he went to some other hospital after he left the Allan, and they asked for a file transfer?"

I was grasping at straws; I knew things didn't work that way.

"Only a copy would have been sent. The records department would have hung onto the originals pretty much forever. For one thing, it's illegal not to."

"I know, I know. This is just too weird. Are you sure we both didn't just imagine him? Maybe this is some kind of *folie à deux* — or *folie à trois*?

"Very funny, Katy. Look, I'm planning a trip to Montreal to see my folks this weekend anyway. I was thinking I could stop off at the Allan Monday morning and check things out. This has me curious — like you say, it's too weird. I still know some of the clerks down in Records. Maybe they'd give me a hand."

"Of course they will, Greg. They'll fall over themselves to help you — you've got some kind of magic touch."

Greg said nothing and I could imagine him blushing at the compliment. It was true, though — he was equally beloved by physicians, nurses, social workers, occupational therapists, support staff and patients. Something about the way he always looked everyone in the eye and made them feel as though they were the most important person in the world.

"Anyway, that would be great, Greg. By the way, did you get a local address for our guy?"

"No. Came up dry there, too. Apparently he didn't set anything up with John Schneider after we spoke. Big surprise. But I was thinking — he lived all his life in Montreal, and he's a social isolate, not likely to want to move unless it was for some really good reason. So he probably planned to go back there after he saw me. I'm wondering if he might be camping out at one of the city shelters."

"Good point. I'll give some of them a call this morning. Then I'm going straight to the hardware store to get a deadbolt and a chain for the office. I don't feel like taking any chances."

When we'd hung up, I hunted around my desk for my old blue plastic binder, one of the few useful remainders of my days at the ROH. It contained an only partially outdated list of the social services and mental health facilities in the region. There were a number of possibilities, from the Hostelling Association and the Union Mission for Men to the network of rooming houses spread throughout the city. None of them offered world-class accommodations, but it made sense that if Adam were just in town to see Greg, he might have decided to bunk down in one of them.

The shelter co-ordinators were all friendly and co-operative, but no one could recall having seen anyone like Adam. I described him carefully, and everyone agreed he'd stand out in a crowd, even if he weren't using his real name. But the more shelters I called, the more I began to realize how easy it is to become invisible in a city, even one as tame as Ottawa.

Especially at this time of year, Adam might have just decided to sleep in a park or an alleyway somewhere. It would certainly be warm enough; and it might fit in with his paranoid need to remain invisible. If that were the case, the only way to find him would be to prowl the city streets after dark. I suppressed a shiver at the idea.

Mid-morning I gave up trying to locate Adam, checked my machine for messages and jotted down some calls that needed attention. Then I grabbed my purse and headed out to the hardware store to buy a deadbolt. It was only as I locked the office door that I realized I had forgotten to tell Greg about Adam watching Dawn and me from across the Canal. Next time, I promised myself.

7

The hardware store was only a couple of blocks from my office, and I didn't have a long shopping list, so I decided to reward myself for the morning's spate of unproductive calls. There was a chip wagon parked on Bank Street under my office windows and I wondered idly whether they might make a decent poutine.

Poutine, for the uninitiated, is a uniquely French-Canadian delicacy consisting of french fries topped with fresh cheese curds and doused liberally with gravy. Purists eat it as is, but I have always felt a sprinkle of pepper does wonders for the piquancy of the dish. In Ottawa, the best, most disgustingly oleaginous poutine comes from cube vans that have been converted into mobile greasy spoons. These purveyors of heart disease park on street corners and lure innocent passersby into a life of shame, standing around avoiding one another's eyes, scooping poutine out of cardboard cups and trying to look inconspicuous.

I walked around the white truck that had parked under my office windows, but the operator had not yet opened the side window and the tempting aroma of potatoes frying in day-old oil was nowhere in evidence. Vengefully, I gave the truck's rear tire a swift kick and headed off toward Java De-Lux. A doughnut would have to do.

Java De-Lux was one of the factors that had convinced me to set up shop in this section of Bank Street. The café was one of those painfully trendy places that sold cappuccino, espresso, caffe latte, café mocca and, once in a while, regular coffee. Ultra-hip music, usually jazz so cerebral as to cause pain at the neuronal level, provided the background ambience.

The place was nearly empty when I arrived. I ordered a decaf latté with one percent milk and sat down directly under the air conditioning vent. The chilling blast was aimed right down the back of my cotton shirt and the effect was soothing. To top it off, for once they were playing Aretha.

"Chain-chain-chain …" I hummed, opting for a dash of cinnamon on the frothy milk topping my latte. Someone had left a trashy tabloid on the table and I absorbed myself in a first-person narrative about the CIA stealing someone's brain (evidence: the subject was clearly lacking vital parts of said organ), when a familiar voice, a deep, rich baritone tinged with the remnants of a laconic West Virginian drawl, nudged at the edges of my awareness.

"This seat taken, lady?"

"Brent? What the hell are you doing here?"

"Nice talk! Whatever happened to, 'Oh, Brent, I was just sitting here hoping you'd walk back into my life!'?"

I glared up at him, temporarily speechless.

"Hey, what's this? Your taste in reading hasn't changed much over the years, Klein!"

"Neither has your charming diplomacy, Wilkinson. If you're going to insult me, you might as well sit down and do it properly."

Brent's voice softened. "I don't want to insult you, Katy. The last time I saw you, I think we both did enough damage to last us a lifetime."

"That time you came over to deliver Peter's and my wedding present? Well, no one can accuse us of not sharing our feelings, right?"

"I think that was the first time I ever had my face slapped," he grinned. "It was definitely the last."

"You deserved it." I was unrepentant. "You were being a *putz*."

"What, for suggesting you were marrying whatshisname just to rub my nose in it? I stand by that argument to this day."

"You would. Anyway, you were the one who didn't want to commit. At least, until it was too late." I grimaced at the memory.

"Well, we had nothing in common," Brent chuckled. "The engineer and the flake. What a combination, huh?"

I laughed. "I know. Besides, you were Beatles, I was Stones. Some things you just can't reconcile."

"Well, you're looking great, Katy. You haven't changed a bit." His gaze was appreciative, and I was suddenly conscious of the pounds I'd acquired over the years. I should have blow-dried my hair that morning. Too late now.

"You are the world's pre-eminent bullshit artist, Brent," I said. "What are you doing back here? I thought you married that woman and moved to Vancouver? Isn't that where you got the big job offer?"

"Fran and I split up about five years ago."

I could not interpret his expression.

"Oh, I'm sorry," I blurted. "I didn't know you were having problems."

"Neither did anyone else. Actually, I don't think it was all that bad either, but she kept saying there was something missing."

He lowered his voice and stared into his coffee.

"I think in a way she was right — but I'd reconciled myself to it, I suppose. We never managed to have kids, and when the split finally came and I found myself living alone, I hardly even noticed she was gone. I guess that says something."

"Ouch," I said softly. "That must have hurt. You always wanted kids, didn't you?"

He nodded. "I always had this fantasy of teaching my kids calculus, you know? They were going to be the smartest, best adjusted ankle biters on the block. Funny how things work out."

"You always wanted to do things right, Brent. Remember the proposal?"

He clapped his hands to his head, groaning. "Please — don't remind me! You just sat there, looking at me like I was something you'd found on the bottom of your shoe …"

"Hey, you're the one who spilled the espresso all over my best skirt, looking for the damned ring. And that mangy girl — do you remember? You got her to sing 'Suite: Judy Blue Eyes,' but she sounded like she was about to expire of tuberculosis." I laughed, and after an awkward moment, Brent joined in.

"Typical Brent production, huh? I guess that was the beginning of the end for us. Anyway, enough of that — how's your newspaper guy?"

"Peter? He's fine. We stayed married long enough to have a little girl, realized we loved her a lot more than we loved each other, and now he lives upstairs from us. It works out okay."

"Did you ever finish your psych degree? Last I heard, you were due for your dissertation."

I checked his face quickly, but could discern no bitterness, only curiosity.

"Yeah. I finished, did my internship, started practising at the ROH, and then quit about five years ago to start a business in astrology."

"Pardon?" His eyebrows shot up.

"Don't do that. You know I've always loved astrology. Now I make a living at it, that's all."

"But you busted your butt to get that degree! Not to mention our relationship. Why the hell would you …"

"Brent, it's kind of personal. Anyway, I like what I'm doing now." I silently added a small caveat about being stalked by loonies with gooseberry eyes. "It isn't on the same scale as when people called me 'Doctor', but we're not starving. So — what are you doing back in Ottawa?" I changed the subject adroitly.

"Well, the company was getting a bit too confining, so a few years ago I took a job with the government. I've just spent a year in purgatory up North, farting around with satellite communications stuff, and when I came back to civilization, I was ready for a change. I guess this is it."

"You'd trade in West Coast weather for this? I always wondered about your judgment, Wilkinson, but even I never thought you were completely *meshuggeh*!"

He smiled, a crooked grin that made the corners of his eyes crinkle, and I felt a long-forgotten lurch in the pit of my stomach.

"Well, I guess I always knew you'd be here. That can make up for a lot of snow and ice."

After a pause, I asked, "What kind of work will you be doing here? Still engineering-type stuff?"

"More or less. Still communications engineering, but right now I'm supposed to be trying to help a group organize an information-processing lab. So I'll get to get my hands a bit dirty."

"That sounds like your idea of nirvana. Playing around with electronic thingamabobs. You've got a place here already?"

"Actually, I just got into town yesterday. They've got me at the Four Seasons downtown, but I'm taking the next few days to scout out apartments. And I did plan to call you, you know."

"Hey, I never said a word!" I blushed. "Anyway, I was going to ask if you'd like to come and have dinner with Dawn and me sometime. Dawn's my daughter. We've gone vegetarian lately, but I think we might be able to dig up something you'd find edible."

Brent laughed. "You've given up hamburgers? My God, Katy, this must be one of the signs of the apocalypse!"

"Shut up. Do you want to come, or not?"

"Sure. That would be very nice, ma'am. And frankly, I'm glad you're still speaking to me."

"As I recall, you were the one who wasn't speaking to me. Anyway, that was years ago. I can hold a grudge, but even I have limits."

"I don't recall noticing that. Maybe we just weren't together long enough. And it wasn't that I wasn't speaking to you, it's just that I was hurt that you'd marry that newspaper guy when you wouldn't marry me. I guess I never did really figure that one out."

Ignoring the barb, I suggested a time early the following week. That would give me time to sandblast the apartment and do some emergency abdominal tone-ups. Where had I put that Jane Fonda video, anyway?

Plus, Peter would be on a week-long assignment in Toronto, so there would be no chance of the former rivals meeting one another.

We parted with a friendly hug and I watched Brent lope out of the café. He'd never been able to do anything at half speed — even now, his long legs seemed to have an energy of their own, spurred on by whatever new enthusiasm had gripped his imagination.

Staring blindly at the tabloid still laid out on the table, I tried to make sense of the jumble of emotions I felt. My last conversation with Brent had taken place eighteen years ago, but it felt as raw and open as if the wound had never healed. I'd been busy earning my doctorate, while Brent had already graduated and was headed for a job in Vancouver with some communications engineering firm. It was a great professional coup for him and he couldn't understand why I hadn't been able to see things his way.

Nice of you to check with me first, I'd said. Well, I thought this would be good for both of us, he had countered. And anyway, you can always transfer to UBC — it's probably better than the University of Ottawa. Yeah, right, and I'm just supposed to dump my life and follow you wherever your precious job takes you.

We were both *eingeshpart* — stubborn as mules, neither wanting to lose out to the other. Yet it did feel good to talk to him again, with his quick smile and warm enfolding hugs. Don't put any stock in that, I reprimanded myself. One heartbreak involving Brent is enough for any lifetime.

But on the way back to my office I caught myself humming "Suite: Judy Blue Eyes." You just don't learn, do you, Klein?

8

At three o'clock I called Peter at his office to make sure he still planned to pick me up on his way to *shabbos* dinner with my parents. His secretary put me through.

"Hi, it's me. How's it going?"

"I'm busting it to get ready for the flight tonight, but otherwise okay. What's up?"

"I just wanted to touch base about dinner. Are you still okay to go to my parents?"

"Wouldn't miss it. I'll have to head out early to catch my plane, but Rosie told me she's making roast chicken. I don't pass her cooking up lightly, you know. So — when will you be ready for your chauffeur?"

"Probably not till about quarter to six, if that's okay with you. Could you pick Dawn up at home first? She should be ready for a break from Sylvie by then."

"Not a problem. Listen, I can't really talk now, but I'll see you later, okay?"

"Sure. See you then."

Around five-forty, Peter called on his cellphone to let me know he'd be swinging by the office any minute. Knowing how he hated to be kept waiting, I hurriedly gathered the day's accumulation of notes and files, shoved them into my bag, flipped the fan off, the answering machine on and locked the door behind me. Downstairs, I sat under the broad-branching maple tree that guarded the back door, taking a moment to run a comb through my unruly hair and apply some lipstick.

Peter appeared right on time, his run-down and rusted out car chugging along valiantly. However, he seemed to have forgotten something important: Dawn. I climbed into the car, which had long ago been named the Flaming Deathtrap, in honour of its state of general decrepitude. I closed the door carefully, mindful of the time I'd been less gentle and the car had been doorless for a week.

"I thought you were going to pick up our daughter. Dawn, remember? My parents' granddaughter?"

"Katy, get off my case. I went by home, like you said, but she wasn't there. I looked for her at your place, thought she might have fallen asleep or something, but there was no sign of her. Finally, I checked on the fridge and there was a note on the eraser-board — she said she'd gone to a movie with Sylvie."

I scowled. My parents only had one grandchild, and they doted on Dawn. Why couldn't she just come to the damned supper? She was not usually this inconsiderate. Maybe it was that hormone thing — everyone I knew kept predicting that Dawn would eventually succumb and turn into a True Teenager, cranky and capricious. Or maybe Dawn just felt like she had to assert her independence, and missing *shabbos* dinner would be a hard one for her parents to ignore. Well, fine. Her loss.

"I guess she's getting to the point where she wants to be a bit more independent," I said grudgingly.

"True enough. Still, I hope she thought to phone

Rosie and Bernard and let them know. I think if she's old enough to go off to movies on her own, she's old enough to at least do the polite thing."

We drove in silence for a while, the windows down to allow the tepid early evening air to swirl past our heads. Peter drove west from the city's core, along the Queensway. This expressway had been designed and built in the early sixties, a gesture to the city's spreading suburbs. Unfortunately, the highway of the future had been obsolete before it was even completed, so it was almost always overcongested. That evening, the Flaming Deathtrap tootled along at a rousing forty kilometres an hour, in a one-hundred zone.

"How's work?" Peter asked, making conversation.

"Not bad." I looked out the window, watching a green Toyota dodge from lane to lane in a vain attempt to get ahead of the rush-hour traffic. Then something occurred to me. "Listen, I'm working with a guy that I think might have been abused or something as a kid. His father was some kind of lord high mucky-muck in finance, back in the forties. In Montreal. Is there any way you could find anything out for me?"

Peter thought for a moment, his eyes squinting into the sun.

"Yeah, maybe. I think we have microfiche archives for the paper going back that far. What was his name?"

"Cosgrove. The son was Adam, but I'm not sure about the father."

"Well, I can check it out next time I'm on-line. Shouldn't be a problem to do a name search."

"Thanks, it'd be a help. So who's supposed to be coming to dinner tonight?"

My mother's dinners were legendary. Although in many Jewish households the Friday night meal is a time to gather the immediate family, Rosie and Bernard Klein had always stretched the definition, inviting a mélange of friends, distant relatives passing through town, Dad's colleagues from his days as a diplomat — anyone who needed a place to go on a Friday night was welcome.

I had grown up eating *shabbos* dinners with brick-layers from Poland, high-ranking officials from External Affairs, former bootleggers, a Canadian envoy to the United Nations, underwear manufacturers, army officers and, on one memorable occasion, two members of Parliament from opposite sides of the floor.

Peter pulled the F.D. into the long driveway, and the car wheezed in protest as he applied the emergency brake.

"Sounds like she's finally on her last legs," he commented. This was not exactly news: the Flaming Death-trap had been terminal for a number of years. Peter always swore that when the end finally came, he'd pull the plug, not let the car linger, semi-comatose and pathetic. But each time there was another crisis with her electrical system, or her exhaust or water pump or whatever, he'd sigh, curse the damned car and cough up for repairs.

He rummaged around in the back seat for the bottle of kosher wine he'd brought along.

"Peter, how long have you known my parents? You know they don't keep strictly kosher. You could have brought regular wine."

"Doesn't matter," he replied. "I like to do the right thing."

My mother opened the door before we were even half way up the sidewalk.

"Katy! Peter!" she beamed, gathering us to her in turn and kissing us. "Dawn is still in the car?"

Peter and I exchanged glances.

"She didn't call and tell you?" I asked. "She decided to stay behind and watch a movie with Sylvie. But I thought at least she'd give you a call and tell you herself. I'm sorry, Mama." But not as sorry as Dawn would be, I added silently.

Rosie's face fell momentarily at the news that Dawn would not be joining us. Then, brightening, she led the way to the living room, an arm around each of us, making introductions and kvelling about her brilliant daughter and son-in-law.

"Jean, Linda, George — this is Dr. Katy Klein, my daughter. And of course, Peter Fischer, her husband. He's a writer, you know. Famous. You might see his name sometimes, in the *Ottawa Telegraph*. They let him write the most important stories."

I tried to shush my mother, to no avail. In the living room this sabbath eve sat a man with a face that seemed to tell of at least sixty years, but whose athletic biceps and trim waist spoke of fewer. His wife matched her husband's body better than his face: she had the perpetual smile of someone who has had one too many facelifts, but beneath a heavy layer of artfully applied makeup, her eyes looked pleasant enough.

She held herself diffidently, probably because she was not accustomed to the size of her obviously revamped breasts, which pushed up alarmingly out of a sundress that might have been demure on someone less generously endowed.

Another man, perhaps a year or two younger than the other one, but certainly much older than the trophy wife, sat in the wing chair nearest the living room door.

"Katy, Peter, this is Dr. George Shapiro." My mother barely offered the guest a second glance. "Katy, Dr.

Shapiro is an old friend of your father, visiting us from Montreal."

"*Gut shabbos.*" He extended a thin, dry hand. I smiled politely and murmured a response.

Shapiro — the name was familiar. Wasn't he one of Montreal's elder statesmen of neuropsychiatry? I was sure I'd read something on post-traumatic encephalopathy with his name on the top, in my previous life as a psychologist. Though Shapiro was dressed in golf slacks and a casual shirt, I had no trouble visualizing him in a white lab coat. He had the piercing, critical gaze of one accustomed to wielding authority.

"And this is Jean Marois, and his wife Linda," Rosie continued. "Mr. Marois worked with your father all those years ago, when he first started at External Affairs. Remember when Dad was taking all those trips to the embassies?"

I did. From the time I was about eight years old, my father had spent more time on the road than at home, doing site inspections and overseeing the installation of ventilation systems in Canada's embassies abroad. I'd resented his time away from home, and had made no bones about it; that was one of the reasons he'd taken a desk job while I was in my teens.

I greeted Mr. and Mrs. Marois and found a seat, sinking into a deep wing chair. Within moments I felt as though I'd regressed back to about six years of age, content to sit politely and listen to the grown-ups converse. My gaze wandered around the room, touching on the familiar decorations — the mahogany pie-crust table with its cluster of silver-framed sepia photographs of Dad's family; the lone bronzed baby shoe gracing the mantelpiece; the Lalique crystal vase, filled just now with baby's breath.

"Bernard, you remember that embassy in Mexico City?" Marois asked my father. "The one where you had to re-do all the vents? I was visiting Mexico just a few months ago, and do you know, the system you designed still worked perfectly. Sometimes the old principles hold water the best, *non*?"

His voice was rich and mellow, pleasantly accented with just a hint of French. Well-educated, I thought, and socially adept.

My father smiled gently. "I remember. It must have been … 1962?"

It was clearly an effort for him to speak. His voice sounded a bit weaker than it had on my last visit a couple of weeks earlier. When he'd had his stroke a year ago, everyone predicted a steady decline, but he'd fooled them all. He'd been up and around within a week, and his gait had improved to a mild limp; only his slow, halting speech gave any clue that he'd been ill. Tonight, I could see the fatigue in his face — his eyes were shadowed, the lines around his mouth more prominent. One eyelid drooped, but that was the only sign of anything more than weariness.

"So, Jean, what have you been doing with yourself lately?" Shapiro asked, without looking at the older man. "Last I heard, you were working with External Affairs?"

Shapiro inserted himself awkwardly into the conversation, in a tone that seemed almost deferential. Funny, he didn't seem the type to defer to anyone.

"I'm still with the public service, yes." Marois dismissed Shapiro with the tiniest of smiles.

Marois looked to me like a born diplomat. Though the weather made it foolhardy to wear a suit, he was nattily dressed in taupe slacks with a military crease and a brilliant white cotton shirt, into which he had tucked a tasteful silk cravat. His shoes, the kind with little tassels on them, were buffed to a gleaming shine; he did not look the sort to wear sneakers much.

Shapiro turned his gimlet eye on me. "And you, Dr. Klein? Are you a physician?"

The question I dreaded. I took a deep breath.

"No, I'm not. I have a doctoral degree in psychology." I hoped my lack of medical credentials would give Shapiro a bone to chew on — some doctors could go on for hours about whether a Ph.D. entitled its holder to be called "Doctor" or not. Such a discussion could divert him permanently from the question of what I did for a living these days.

However, Shapiro was not one to be put off so easily.

"I see. And where do you practice?"

"Actually, I gave up working in psychology several years ago."

"How … interesting," Shapiro said. "What do you do with your time now?"

"I have a private practice in astrology." I tried to sound as though this was the most ordinary career choice in the world.

There was dead silence in the room. I wondered whether I should simply have announced that I was a not-very-high-class hooker, or perhaps a purveyor of child pornography. It might have elicited a more positive response. I shot a ferocious glare at my mother, the instigator of my current discomfort, but Rosie just smiled beatifically back, impervious to the sudden temperature change in the room.

"My goodness, that is fascinating," Mrs. Marois began, in a timorous voice. "Do you …"

But she got no further.

"That's preposterous!" Shapiro interjected. "Astrology is all superstitious nonsense! Charlatanism! How can you justify taking in ordinary dupes, letting them believe in fairy-tales? You've squandered your education on utter bilge, young woman. Your parents must …"

He checked himself abruptly, remembering where he was. His thin face was nearly purple, bursting with indignation.

"If I truly thought astrology was superstitious nonsense, I wouldn't have chosen to practice it, now would I?" I tried to keep my voice level, but a tiny quiver betrayed my anger. Still, it wouldn't do to shed blood on a Friday evening, I thought. Especially on my mother's immaculate beige carpets. Hard to clean. But I hoped someone was keeping track of my self-control, marking it down in my big Permanent Record in the sky.

Jean Marois stepped into the breach.

"Actually, George, I have recently read an excellent article on this very subject. It would appear that, contrary to logical belief, the movement of the planets does seem to have some effect on human affairs. There have been studies bearing this out, you see. Astrology would seem to be perhaps more complicated than one might think."

"Thank you," I whispered under my breath. Aloud, I said, "It's refreshing to hear a more progressive viewpoint, Mr. Marois."

"Ah, my dear. There are many things in science itself that cannot be logically defended, correct? How can something be both a wave and a particle simultaneously? We just do not know these things. It would be arrogant to pretend otherwise."

Shapiro was beet-red by now, but appeared to decide that it was not worth taking on Marois, particularly not just before the sabbath meal. He sank back into his seat, looking glum. I flashed a quick grin of thanks at Marois, who acknowledged me with a wink and a nod of his elegant grey head.

9

My mother stood, ready to light the sabbath candles.
It was a little early, since the summer sun had not quite
sunk below the horizon, but to Rosie, serving food pip-
ing hot took precedence over technicalities. The group's
attention turned to the dining table. Rosie struck a
match and lit the two candles in their ornate silver can-
delabra. She motioned over the flames with her hands,
then covered her face while whispering the blessing.
Finally she beamed toward the watching group.

"*Gut shabbos*, everybody," she proclaimed.

This was my cue. I struggled out of my very soft and
comfortable seat and went to the kitchen to help serve,
a task I'd had since I was old enough to hold a salad
bowl in my arms.

"Holy cow, Mama, you were expecting maybe an
army?" I teased my mother, surveying the kitchen
counters, piled high with food.

Rosie snorted. "You never know who might be hungry. I make a little extra, just to be safe."

She ladled pale yellow chicken soup into bowls
which already contained a *knaidle*, a large matzoh
dumpling that had been simmered in the fragrant broth
to absorb its flavour and puff up nice and tender.

If it had been only the family gathered for dinner, on any other night of the week, we might have eaten the boiled chicken whose flesh had contributed its savory juices to the soup. It would have made a nice chicken salad later, maybe. But for tonight's guests, Rosie had extravagantly roasted a fresh plump capon, which reposed on a large and elegant antique platter.

Nor was that the end of it. In the fine Jewish tradition of wasting nothing, Rosie had had the butcher save the bird's neck skin, which she had stuffed with *schmaltz*, onions and matzoh meal. Then she'd sewn it up with string and roasted it to a beautiful golden brown in the pan under the capon. This delicacy, known as *helzel*, would be served in small, delicate slices. I could have eaten one all by myself.

Rosie had not stopped there. She had slaved over a hot stove all day, making *chremslach*, tiny nuggets of mashed potato and onion, fried dark and crispy in still more *schmaltz*; and there were thin, tender-crisp stalks of asparagus, stuffed green peppers full of rice and vegetables, and a salad of romaine lettuce and the reddest of ripe tomatoes, glistening under Rosie's special vinaigrette dressing.

But the real centrepiece was always the *challah*, a light, tender bread made moist with eggs, twisted and braided into an ornate shiny crown. It sat regally on its own silver tray, covered by an embroidered cloth that had been handed down through generations of Kleins.

I began to take bowls of steaming soup to the table. Between trips, I hissed into my mother's ear, "I really wish you'd stop telling everyone I'm still a psychologist. You know I don't practice any more. It just gave Shapiro an excuse to give me a hard time, which I don't need."

"I don't see what's the problem, *mamaleh*," Rosie smiled. "You are a psychologist, even if you do mess around with that star stuff."

"You're not getting the point on purpose, Ma. I can tell."

Rosie shook her head, as though she didn't understand. "You should be proud of all the hard work you put into that degree, even if you don't hang your diploma on the wall." She was serene in her pride over her daughter's accomplishments.

"Ma, I might as well talk to the soup tureen. How come I can never win an argument with you?"

"It's *shabbos*. You shouldn't argue with your old mother," Rosie shot back. "It's bad luck."

I sighed. I was never certain whether or not my mother made up these obscure edicts, but I was sure I wasn't going to make a dent in Rosie's logic.

The meal, as always, was delicious. Rosie bobbed up and down, bringing food, clearing plates, bringing still more food. She was really working it, and I knew better than to interfere. The planning, preparation, decoration and serving of food were serious business to Rosie. It was a point of pride that her table never be empty, and that each guest leave the meal surfeited and groaning.

The conversation, too, remained innocuous after its inauspicious beginning in the living room. Linda Marois, seated next to me, struck up a conversation about astrology, asking some fairly intelligent questions. I relaxed in a stuffed stupor; the fine wine, wonderful food and subdued conversation were doing their work, and I felt the tension of the past week begin to lift.

"It must be just fascinating, your job, I mean," Linda said. "Do you get a lot of people who just want to test you, to find out if astrology really works?"

"Actually, most of the people I see are pretty well informed," I said. "Although I do get some real doozies now and then. Right now, I've got this guy coming to me for information about his childhood, and I'm having a hell of a time convincing him I can't be as specific as he wants."

Jean Marois pricked up his ears from across the table. "But what can he be looking for? Would someone not already know all there is to know about his own childhood? Why would he need you to tell him?"

"I don't honestly know," I said. "This guy is quite the character. Strange-looking, and a real loner. I think he may have some sort of trauma that he's repressed, and now he's having flashbacks he can't understand. Unfortunately, he's kind of latched onto me."

"Why you, though? Why not a psychiatrist? Someone who could really help him?" Shapiro looked at me sharply and I shrugged.

"Beats me. Maybe I do have a few insights, but I'm not really sure how wise it is to tell someone in his state what I know. For instance, I don't think I should say anything about his father abusing him. I'm worried I might just tip him over the edge, you know?"

"You can really tell that from the arrangement of stars in a person's chart?" Even Marois sounded sceptical.

"Planets, actually, not stars. No, it's not as cut and dried as that. I'm just giving you the abbreviated version. I'm putting together the hints my client has dropped, and what the chart seems to show. It's not magic, you know."

I chatted happily with the Marois', shutting out Dr. Shapiro's evident sullenness. Still, when he thought no one was looking, the doctor gave me several hard, questioning glances. Taking a page from my mother's book, I feigned obliviousness.

After dinner, tea was served in the living room. As I left the table, I offered my father my arm and he leaned on me heavily. As we shuffled toward his customary chair, he squeezed my hand and whispered, "I love you, sweetie."

I responded by kissing his cheek. The flesh felt strangely flaccid, not the taut whiskered skin I remembered from before the stroke. Well, they'd said there would be a loss of muscle tone.

Shapiro seated himself next to me on the sofa, and during a momentary lull in the conversation, he tapped my arm.

"It seems to me I might know one of your former colleagues." He was obviously making an effort to be sociable. "A Dr. Curtis? Yes, I believe his name was Frank Curtis. We met at the Canadian Psychiatric Association conference this week. He's head of Forensics at the Royal, isn't he?"

I froze, tea halfway to my lips. I set the cup back into its saucer as well as I could, but it clattered and some of it spilled. I opened my mouth to answer Shapiro, who watched me with curiosity. No words came, and I tried again, but succeeded only in expelling an inchoate noise from my throat. I was sweating, though the room suddenly felt frigid. I got up and bolted from the living room, tripping over the edge of the carpet on my way out.

"Was it something I said?" Shapiro looked confused.

"I'll help her," Peter volunteered, and excused himself, overruling Rosie's objections.

He found me in the bedroom I'd used as a child. I

sat on the bed, staring at my old debating team trophy from high school. Funny how the wood looks so much darker now, I thought. I'd swear the wood has darkened. It was much lighter before. I'm sure of it. Don't you think so, Peter?

I am in the medications room, bottles of haloperidol and chlorpromazine, clonazepam and perphenazine spilling to the floor. I back against the shelves, as far as I can. He is angry, pushing me back, further and further. I can't exactly hear the words, he's whispering, he doesn't want the nurses to know he's there. His face is nearly purple, eyes blazing. I can't speak, he's gripping my neck, and I cringe backward even further.

Peter put an arm round my shoulders.

"You're shaking. Are you cold?" he asked gently, and without waiting for an answer, he opened a dresser drawer and hauled out a blanket. Wrapping it around me clumsily, he sat on the narrow bed with me, waiting it out.

"Mama … Dad … they don't know, do they?" I asked in a frozen voice.

"Not unless you told them something. I wouldn't, you know that, Katy. I just told them you have a stomach bug or something. I said I'd make sure you were okay."

I blinked, but Peter's face still blurred in front of me, obscured by the damn tears that just would not stop.

That purple, fiercely whispering face loomed up again. *He's going to hurt me; I can feel it, but it feels like a numbness, not a terror. When I found out, I should have gone to Greg. Now he's going to hurt me, and I can't stop him. I'm in the meds room with Curtis, and I can't stop him. I shouldn't have told him what I knew. The administration. I should have gone to them. They could have handled it.*

He grabs me by the shoulders, hits me on the ear with a closed fist. It doesn't hurt, but there is a funny ringing sound. I fall to the floor, pushing at him, trying to wriggle out from under. He grabs my hair and pounds my head against the shiny, polished floor. The lights in here are very bright, I think.

He has his hands around my throat, tightening them, and I gag, push ineffectually at him, choking. Then he changes his mind, starts fumbling with his belt, pushing my skirt up, ripping fabric. I paid a lot of money for that skirt. I hope I'll be able to fix it. I wonder if blood stains come out of wool. I wish my ears would stop ringing. Where is the night nurse?

Rows and rows of bottles stand at floor level, full of little pills, hundreds of them, and if I could only count all of them, one, two, three, maybe he'll go away, maybe I won't notice what he's doing, fifty-six, fifty-seven, maybe he'll just leave me alone.

Interesting that they make the pills all those different colours. They say it's so nurses can make sure they're not giving the wrong pill to the wrong patient. Interesting.

He finishes, and I am lying on the floor, one cheek pressed into the cold linoleum covering bare concrete. I think I might be crying. I can't hear much, through the ringing in my ear. I don't want to make any noise. He might hurt me again. He zips his pants up, and spits on me. The warm spittle trickles down my cheek. I should lie here a while, give him time to leave the unit, get out of the building.

I knew I shouldn't have confronted him. He always did have a temper. It's my own damn fault. I should have gone to Greg. He would have known what to do.

Peter held me, rocked me back and forth in his arms, crooning gently as I shook and wept.

"It's all over, Katy. All gone. You didn't know he'd do it," he said, over and over. "It wasn't your fault. You couldn't have known he'd do that. You thought you could stop him on your own. It wasn't your fault, Katy. You're here with me, now. He can't hurt you. You're safe."

The right words, but somehow they didn't get through. Peter had said them when it first happened, and they hadn't worked then, either. I'd made the horrifying discovery myself, and in my arrogance I'd thought I could handle it on my own.

"He's still hurting me, Peter." I gulped back a sob. "He cost me my career five years ago, and he's taking away my self-respect now. I let him drive me out, and I never reported him. Not for what he did to me, or for what he did to his patients. He drugged them, Peter, and he raped them. And I still haven't said a word. Not a single fucking word."

"How could you? How could you say anything against the Director? Come on, Katy, we've been through this before. You know the odds — he had charm, money and credentials. You were just a junior psychologist. And he might not stop at rape next time."

"I know." I sagged against his damp shoulder and reached for a handful of tissues from a box on the bedside table. "And there's Dawn to consider. I know. And you know what, Peter? Sometimes I can even convince myself that I did the right thing, walking away from the place."

"Sure you did," he soothed. "What else could you do?"

"I don't know. I could have let you have your way. I could have let you write an exposé or drop an anonymous tip or something. I was just too scared, Peter. It's funny — I must have taken a hundred showers that week, and none of them made me feel clean. Isn't that weird? I did that for a long time. And then, I just let it drop. And I haven't really respected myself since."

"I respect you, honey. You know that. And it probably wouldn't have solved anything, letting me get involved. Who would I have told? The hospital board? Curtis had them all wrapped around his little finger — he would have just accused you of false accusations or something, and it would have been your word against his. He was a dangerous man, Katy. You did the right thing. And you survived because of it, and you protected Dawn. That's worth something, isn't it?"

I tried to smile. "I guess. I just wish I was as strong as everyone seems to think I am."

10

I sat on the edge of the bed for nearly forty-five minutes before the shakes died down. Peter held me, wrapped in an old comforter, and handed me tissue after tissue, until I was able to go to the bathroom and wash my face. Peter is good that way.

He followed me into the bathroom, apologizing that he'd have to be leaving soon.

"Do you think you'll be okay?" He rubbed my shoulders. "I feel bad just leaving you like this."

"Really, I'm fine. Shapiro took me by surprise, that's all. And it's been a stressful couple of days, with that Adam character lurking around. The thing about Curtis just knocked the wind out of me. You should go, you'll miss your flight. I'll take a taxi home. Don't worry."

Bernard peered anxiously, and Rosie stood at the ready with a bottle of Pepto-Bismol when I returned to the living room. Shapiro had left already, but Jean and Linda Marois were still there. Linda flashed a quick sympathetic smile. No one said a word about my emergency catapult from the living room.

"Everything all right, sweetheart?" my father asked.

"I'm fine now, Dad. Really, it was nothing — just a bit of a stomach bug." That was what Peter had told everyone, wasn't it? If you're going to lie, at least make an effort to be consistent. That's my motto.

"I'm so sorry I caused a scene," I apologized to the group, mustering a smile to demonstrate that my distress was past. Nothing quite like someone bolting from the room, clutching her mouth to keep the screams in, to liven up any party.

Peter left a few minutes later, and as he kissed my cheek at the door, he promised to get back to me with the archival check on Adam's father. Closing the door behind him, I wished, not for the first time, that I could get excited about my ex-husband. He's such a good guy. Sometimes we just look at one another and giggle at the improbability of our relationship. He always said we should have been siblings, not husband and wife. Except that would make Dawn … no, never mind. Some avenues are best left unexplored.

Jean and Bernard sat reminiscing about the good old days, when they'd been students together at McGill University. I blinked — if they'd gone to school together, that must make Jean at least my father's age. Dad was seventy-three, but Marois looked a decade younger. Maybe it was the trophy wife on his arm that seemed to peel away the years? Funny, too, because in the early forties, McGill had been such a bastion of English-speaking values and sensibilities in Montreal. Jean, elegant and well-spoken as he was, was most definitely not your traditional old school tie anglophone.

What had things been like for a young French man, attending a place where his language, his heritage and culture were either ignored or actively disparaged? And my father, too, had been one of the first Jews allowed to attend the engineering program — so despite their very different backgrounds, the two men had something in common. My mother and Linda Marois listened to their husbands indulgently, exchanging slight smiles as the two men dredged up stories they had obviously told at least a hundred times. This professor or that who'd married a student, or the time they'd blown up the football goalposts or snuck into the girls' dorm after hours.

"Now, Major Payne, he was my science prof." Dad's words were slow and stiff. "He never seemed to notice that we laughed at his name, did he, Jean?"

"I thought you two met when Dad was at External Affairs," I remarked.

"Oh, no," her mother put in. "I first met Jean when your father brought me back to Canada. We had gone to that little place up in the Laurentians. Your father, so sweet he was, he wanted to give me a little honeymoon. And there we met Jean, who knew Bernard from when they were students, isn't that right?"

Bernard smiled at Rosie, more than fifty years' worth of love in his eyes. Rosie had been only fifteen years old when she was deported to Auschwitz, along with her own mother and a baby sister she would never see again. When she was released from the death camp, two and a half years had gone by and she had become old.

I have never heard her speak a word of Polish in my life. Having renounced the language of the neighbours who had abandoned her and her family to the Nazis, she spoke English with a slight Yiddish accent. No family, no relatives, no friends and no home remained to Rosie after Hitler was defeated. In a Europe that had been tipped upside down and viciously shaken, she could find no bearings. She was sent initially to a Displaced Persons camp near Vienna, where members of the newly-formed Joint Distribution Committee fed her ravaged body, tried to ease at least her physical pain.

Bernard, just shy of his nineteenth birthday at the time, youngest son of an old Montreal family, had travelled all the way from Canada to join in the relief work. When he first met Rosie, he said, her ankles and calves were the size of a normal person's thigh, the result of severe malnutrition, cold and dampness.

My parents came back to Canada in 1948, already married, and I was born three years later. They poured their hearts into caring for me, their only daughter, and the act of nurturing a new life helped in part to heal them of the old. That's what Dad always said, anyway.

"Right, Rosie," Bernard said. "But we didn't see Jean again until we moved here. He recommended me for the post at External — and then I don't see him for years, until last week. Such a beautiful surprise, to hear from an old friend."

Jean Marois was all modesty. "You deserved that job, Bernard. You were made for it. And now we have come full circle, *non*? Two old friends, reminiscing over our youth. Whoever would have thought?"

I sank into the down-filled cushions of the couch and stopped paying attention to the conversation. I might even have dozed a little. It had been a long day. By the time Rosie nudged me awake, the coffee table had been spread with photos of Bernard's halcyon days as a student at McGill, plus a few I hadn't seen before: my father and a bunch of unidentified people, horsing around, dancing, swimming, in front of an old-fashioned lodge in the country, complete with wraparound verandah.

In one, I spotted my parents, very young and absorbed in one another; in another, Jean stood with his arm draped around the shoulder of a shy-looking young woman wearing a frilly apron, who gazed like a frightened rabbit into the camera lens. Rosie gathered the photos up and replaced them in the shoebox she kept at the back of a cupboard upstairs.

"Such memories," she sighed.

Jean nodded. "We lived charmed lives back then," he agreed. "But now, *mes vieux*, Linda and I must be on our way. Thank you for a wonderful evening."

Jean and Linda would not allow me to call a taxi, insisting on dropping me off at home. I hugged my parents, assuring them again that my "stomach bug" was now completely under control. Rosie looked suspicious, but said nothing.

Rosie and Bernard stood in the doorway, waving and smiling as Jean, Linda and I pulled away in the black BMW. It was a beautiful machine, really. Given time, I might be able to get used to the plush interior, smooth drive, and best of all, the air-conditioning. The ride home was quiet, everyone absorbed in their own thoughts. From time to time, Linda and Jean exchanged murmured words in the front seat, but I was too tired and drained to contribute much in the way of sparkling repartée.

As a rule, I do not go off the deep end every time Frank Curtis' name comes up in conversation, and I wondered what had touched off this evening's violent response. That's the problem in training as a psychologist — you can never just freak out about something, you have to analyze it to death, figure out all the unconscious material that might have contributed to your behaviour. It can be a real pain.

Knock it off, Katy. You had a long day, it's been a hard week and Shapiro caught you off guard by casually naming the man who'd raped you to preserve his own power in the hospital's chain of command. That's all there is to it — end of story. It had nothing to do with the curl of fear you felt when those staring gooseberry eyes fixed you in their gaze, or the jolting terror that thudded up and down your spine when you spied Adam watching you and Dawn. Nothing at all.

I hardly noticed that we were driving down my street, until Jean eased the car to a silent halt in front of my apartment building.

"Once again, Katy, it has been a real pleasure to meet you." He extended his hand backward over the seat to clasp mine in farewell. I shook it, and said good night to them both. The car slid away into the night and I checked my mailbox before digging out the keys. Junk mail mostly, one hand-addressed envelope that I put aside as I fumbled for the light inside the apartment. Where the hell was Dawn? It must be well past eleven, and her curfew was ten-thirty. There was no sign of her in the apartment, and I felt a minuscule inkling of panic at the base of my spine as I checked Dawn's empty room. Where was she? I bounded up the stairs two at a time to Peter's place, but his apartment, too, was dark and still. Even so, I checked each room thoroughly, fighting back my fear.

"That kid … I swear, I'll ground her for a week … no, a month … what the hell is Sylvie's number? If she's over there, she's going to get such a blast …" I muttered as I searched room after empty room, not allowing myself to imagine that Dawn might not be at her best friend's house.

The phone rang several times before anyone picked up. Sylvie answered, her voice thick with sleep.

"Sylvie? This is Dawn's mother." I enunciated clearly, despite my chattering teeth.

"Mrs. Klein?"

"Is Dawn there with you? I need to speak to her. Now."

"Dawn?"

No, Rudolph the fucking red-nosed reindeer, I thought furiously, trying desperately to remain calm. I took a deep breath.

"Sylvie, I need to speak to Dawn. Now. Please."

"Uh … she's not here. I haven't seen her all day."

"What do you mean?" I shrieked. "She said she was going to the movies with you! Why isn't she there? Where is she?"

Sylvie sounded a little more awake now, but no less confused.

"Really, Mrs. Klein, I haven't seen her since this morning. She came over to get something from my brother for her computer, and then she left. Honest, if I'd seen her, I'd tell you. Is something the matter?"

I hung up, my teeth chattering wildly now, independent of my control. Maybe she's really here somewhere and I just missed her, I thought. Remember the time when she was a little girl and she hid in the closet, and I thought she'd been kidnapped, and I looked everywhere and finally called the police, and the officer found her sound asleep in the laundry basket, covered with clothing, and she wasn't hurt at all, not dead, just hiding, and everything was okay, she was fine, I didn't need to panic at all. I don't need to panic. Don't panic.

Peter had said Dawn left a note on the fridge. Here it was:

Dear Katy and Peter: I have gone to see Mission Impossible *with Sylvie.*

Sorry about missing supper. Love, Prairie Dog.

This could not be right. For one thing, hadn't Dawn

spent the entire summer informing me in no uncertain terms that she had no intention of ever subjecting herself to that particular movie? And Dawn detested being called Prairie Dog. When she was in kindergarten, some little stand-up comic had decided her name was "Prairie Dawn," like the goody-two-shoes character on Sesame Street. Inevitably, someone on the playground heard and nicknamed her "Prairie Dog," and Dawn had come home in tears for several days because of the taunting, until we'd asked the teacher to intervene. Why would she revive the despised nickname now?

Was she trying to say that the note was not really from her? That she had not wanted to write it? It hit me with dull certainty that Dawn had not wanted to write anything at all, and that she had left this message to convey precisely that. So if she hadn't wanted to write it, why had she done it? She must have been under some kind of pressure —

Adam, I thought. Adam made her write the note.

The realization made me gag. My throat constricted, my mouth suddenly dry, and I gripped the edge of the kitchen table, afraid of falling. Adam had done something. Call the police. Call someone.

I did call the police, and they laughed at me. A teenaged girl, missing for a couple of hours on a Friday night, did not strike them as the crime of the century. Was I sure Dawn wasn't just out smoking dope somewhere, or trying to get into a bar with a fake I.D.? Maybe she was … uh … with her boyfriend? This last idea was suggested with a slight snicker. I tried to explain that Adam, a dangerous lunatic, had been staring at us across the Canal as we ate the other night, but the officer wasn't buying. Call us back tomorrow if she doesn't show up, the man said. Don't worry, lady, she'll be fine.

They all are. They come home when they get hungry. Or when they need money.

I slammed down the phone, then picked it up again, my fingers tripping over themselves as I dialled Greg's home number. It was like one of those terrible dreams where you're trying to call someone, but you can never make the number come out right. I must have tried ten times, persisting despite cold, unco-operative fingers, and finally the phone started ringing at Greg's end.

He picked up on the first ring.

"Greg — I think something has happened to Dawn. I can't find her anywhere, and I'm afraid Adam …"

I couldn't finish. My throat swelled, cutting off my words. Greg didn't waste time on niceties.

"I'll be there in ten minutes. Don't go anywhere."

I waited, huddled on the couch, hugging my knees, whispering Dawn's name over and over again. Never a religious person, I now begged someone to listen to me. Make Dawn safe. Please make her okay. Please.

Greg's car screeched to a stop on the quiet street, and he ran in and hugged me hard. Then we looked at the note together.

"What happened?" he asked.

I told him about the *shabbos* dinner, and how Dawn never missed them, and how she'd left the strange note and not even called her grandparents, and how Sylvie hadn't seen her all day. I told him about the unhelpful police officer. I left out the part about this being my second major bout of hysteria in one evening; I didn't think it was relevant.

We were debating whether to go out and scour the alleyways and streets of the neighbourhood, or check out the bars and nightclubs in the Market area, when the phone rang. My heart thundering in my ears, I answered.

"Mommy?" quivered Dawn, her voice strangely high and childlike. "Please come..."

I heard a rustle as the phone was passed to someone else.

Adam, his voice a low, emotionless rasp.

"Is this the astrologer? I've got your daughter."

11

"Adam? Where are you? What have you done with Dawn? Please, don't hurt her."

Funny, my voice sounded calm. Maybe I was, and I just didn't know it.

"You wouldn't tell me the truth before." Adam's voice was flat. "Now you will."

"Please, don't hurt her," I repeated. "Where are you? Please tell me where you are."

"You have to tell me everything. The whole story."

"Adam, I'll tell you everything I know, but you have to let me speak to Dawn. She's a good girl, she doesn't know anything about this. Whatever you think about me, she isn't to blame."

"I'm in a safe place. I will tell you how to come here, but if you bring anyone else, I will hurt your daughter." He sounded like one of those computerized telephone operators who tell you that the number you have reached is no longer in service.

"Adam, hold on a sec. Greg is here with me now. You remember Greg — Dr. Chisholm, right? He knows you, you trust him. Can I bring him with me?"

Even after five years away from the business, I slipped easily back into psychologist mode. Keep your voice calm, soothing, mention the subject's name frequently so he knows you're talking to him, keep your sentences short and to the point.

There was a long pause.

"Dr. Chisholm? He's with you?"

"That's right. He has his car, so we could come and pick you up. Then we can talk, and I'll tell you what I know. Maybe Greg could help, how's that?"

Another long pause.

"All right. I will wait here with the girl. I will wait for half an hour only. Go out the Rockcliffe Parkway to the sewage treatment plant. Go to the parking lot on the right. Turn off your lights and wait there. I will come to you. If you call the police, I will hurt her."

"Adam, please let me speak to Dawn. I need to make sure she's all right."

Smooth, clinical, not panicked at all. Yeah, right.

There was the muffled sound of the phone being passed, and then Dawn's voice, young and scared, not her usual confident self, but still Dawn.

"Mom? Are you there?"

"Right here, honey. Has he done anything to you? Are you okay?"

"I'm fine. We walked a long way. But I'm fine, don't worry. Mom, he says you know things …"

The phone was snatched away.

"I will wait for half an hour."

The connection was cut.

Greg and I dashed from the apartment, crashing into one another as we both tried to get through the front door. It might have been comical, another time. We leaped into his car, he gunned the engine and we squealed away from the curb, just like they do in the cop shows.

"Where are we going?" Greg asked.

"Out the Rockcliffe Parkway. I think they're near the Green's Creek treatment plant. He wants us to meet him in the parking lot. I think I know where it is."

Now that my worst nightmare had come true, I felt bizarrely composed. My heart pounded in my throat, but the urge to scream and wave my arms had passed. I was coping.

The Parkway follows the cliffs above the Ottawa River for several kilometres, from Sussex Drive all the way out to the eastern boundaries of the city. It cuts a circle around Rockcliffe Park, an enclave where Ottawa's version of the rich and famous reside. Then it meanders out past the meadow where the RCMP keep the horses they use in their Musical Ride. The road passes the Rockcliffe Airport, and after that there is little to see but scrubby woods and the pathways used by bikers and joggers.

We drove until I spotted the sewage treatment plant on our right, its huge orange flare belching upward at intervals, releasing the pent-up gases that were the end result of the treatment process. We almost missed the parking lot, and had to turn around and drive back a few hundred metres. Greg pulled the Audi into the lot, killed the lights and pocketed the key.

Without the air-conditioning on, it soon became unbearably stuffy in the car, so we opened the doors and sat back to back, legs out on the pavement. The moon had risen, full and enormous. It cast a dim silver glow over the parking lot, which was surrounded with thick brush leading back to even thicker scrub forest. Neither Greg nor I spoke, because neither of us could think of anything to say.

We just sat there in the warm heavy darkness, illuminated periodically by the sudden flash of fire from the treatment plant. Once Greg turned, reached over and squeezed my shoulder encouragingly. I did not acknowledge him, but just stared into the woods, silently willing Adam to emerge with my daughter. She's going to be fine. She's going to be fine. He won't hurt her. He can't. Don't let him.

The night was tranquil, except for the frogs and crickets, who kept up a constant chirping back and forth, telegraphing messages to one another through the muggy summer air. The trees hung motionless, no hint of a breeze stirring their leaves. The only moving things were the plump, low-slung groundhogs that grazed placidly on the grassy embankment. And beyond them, just still, dark forest.

Someone tapped my arm from behind and I leaped up, knocking my head on the doorframe. I stopped my scream by stuffing half a fist into my mouth. In a cold sweat, I turned to greet Adam.

His huge pale eyes gleamed in the darkness, like some nocturnal animal's. He held Dawn in front of him, gripping her bare arm with one white hand. In the other hand, he held a long and nasty-looking hunting knife, its edge glinting orange intermittently. The blade was inches from Dawn's throat. I caught my daughter's eye, trying to reassure her silently. She looked terrified, but I could see no outward sign of injury.

I began to climb out of the car, but at a gesture from Adam, I obediently sat back down. A car's headlights approached from the west along the Parkway, and I held my breath lest Adam think we had brought the police to ambush him. But the car slowed for the curve past the parking lot, then continued along the road. I expelled my breath.

"Adam, we need to talk. Why don't you and Dawn

sit back there? That way, you won't be so visible." Greg sounded as though he was perfectly accustomed to meeting crazed men holding young girls at knife-point in darkened parking lots.

Without a word, Adam opened the back door, thrust Dawn in before him and climbed into the car himself. Dawn scrambled gratefully to the far edge of the back seat. Even in the dark, I could see the streaks of dirt and tears on her cheeks. Adam left his own door open, and laid the knife across his lap, a visible reminder that he was in charge now.

Greg and I turned around, trying to make eye contact with Adam. In hostage situations, eye contact is very important.

"Adam," Greg said, "can you tell us exactly what it is you want?"

Another gas flare burped upward, filling the car with yellow-orange light that vanished almost as quickly as it had appeared.

"She knows what I want." Adam pointed to me. "You know I keep seeing the child get hurt. And you know who it is. I could tell, that first time I met you. I could see it in your aura. You knew, and you tried to keep it from me. You must tell me."

"Adam, I can only see part of the picture." I felt my way, trying to calm him, give him what he wanted. "I can give you more if you tell me what you can see, what you hear."

He stared hard at me, his strange eyes pale and iridescent in the moon's light. I kept my own gaze level, but not so direct that he'd think I was trying to challenge him. I wanted him to trust me enough to talk; I would make no mistakes, say nothing careless to throw him off-balance. More off-balance, that is.

"Please, Adam," I urged. "Just try to tell me what you see. I want to help you."

He looked away from me, addressing himself to the dark forest. Greg and I strained to hear him.

"Screaming, crying, she never stops. Until the end, and then … then, there's nothing. I see it, I see it all the time. I can't make it stop. And you know how it all happened. I could tell the first time I met you."

He looked at me, half accusing, half hopeful.

"Do you know who the child is?" Greg asked. "Can you see her face?"

"No. Not her face. I can hear her. I know someone is hurting her. I can't …"

Adam's face contorted, his eyes filling with tears, his mouth working desperately to find the right words.

"You can't help her?" Greg prodded.

Wordlessly, Adam nodded, tears spilling down his pale cheeks.

"Adam, I want you to think about this carefully." Greg's voice was hypnotically slow and gentle. "You're watching this terrible thing, and you can hear but you can't see what's going on. I want you to tell me where you are in relation to the child."

"She's … she's in her bed. And I can see someone … not too far away. In front of me. And then she cries, and then she stops."

"Are you big or little?"

There was a long pause.

"Little. Too little. The other one, the big one, he's bigger than me …"

"You can see him? You know he's a man?"

"Only his back. His hair. Shiny. The moon … it's coming in the window, shining on his hair. *Good night moon. Bye-bye, room.*"

"Adam, try to stay with me, okay? Do you know who the man is? Is he anyone you know?"

"I … I can't see. That noise, the screaming, it stops and he stands up, and she's just lying there, and he starts to turn toward me … No! No! I can't see you! I can't see his face!"

Adam pounded his fists savagely against his forehead, screaming hoarsely, as Greg, Dawn and I watched in mute sympathy.

"Adam," I asked, "who was the child? Do you know?"

He looked up at me, as though surprised that I could speak.

"I think … she might be … my sister."

Greg looked puzzled. "I didn't know you had a sister, Adam. I don't remember hearing about her when you and I were seeing one another."

Adam said nothing.

"Do you have any other memories of her?" I asked. "Earlier, maybe? She might have played with you …"

He shook his head violently.

"I don't know, I don't know," he moaned, over and over.

Suddenly, he looked up, his eyes wide with terror.

"He's going to find out I talked to you. I talked … I talked … they know when I talk. They always find out. They can hear everything I say, everything I think!"

In his realization that he had broken some rigid inner code, some unspoken rule that had sentenced him to silence for years, Adam rocked back and forth against the back seat of the car, his pale green eyes luminous in the moonlight, throwing off orange glints every few moments as the gas flare erupted nearby.

"Adam. Adam, listen to me." Greg was trying to reach the part of him that might still be able to connect with reality. "You were not responsible. No one is going to find you. No one is going to punish you. We want to help you. Do you understand me?"

Adam rocked harder, shaking his head and moaning.

"They know I'm here now. How could I be so foolish … I should have thought … they can hear me telling you, and they show no mercy to traitors, traitors, and the one who speaks must die, die instantly, no mercy given … Jesus, please help me! Jesus, I have made my penitence, Holy Mary, Mother of God, grant me your mercy …"

He grabbed my bare arm, his jagged untrimmed fingernails nearly puncturing the skin. I fought the instinct to pull away, and instead placed my free hand on top of Adam's, trying to soothe him. Adam sobbed, begging someone, anyone, to protect him from the demons that inhabited his tortured mind.

Dawn's face shone with tears, too. She reached out to touch Adam's arm. As her fingers brushed the nylon of his windbreaker, he looked up and froze with fear. Another car had entered the parking lot, its lights casting harsh shadows across our faces.

Adam made a choking sound, and scrambled out of the car, dropping his hunting knife with a clatter on the tarmac. He crashed through the bush, disappearing into the forest within seconds. Gingerly, not wanting to touch it, but not wanting to just leave it there, I picked up the knife, stashing it in the glove compartment.

The other car toured the perimeter of the lot, then stopped several metres from Greg's Audi. A young man in uniform approached us, carrying a flashlight. Finally — the police.

"Everything okay here, folks?" the cop asked. He sounded polite, but authoritative. He'd probably thought we were a couple of horny teens from Rockcliffe, making out in Daddy's expensive car. "This isn't a good place to park at night — you never know who might be hanging around. Had a couple of rapes out here last year."

He turned to leave.

"Hey! Wait a second!" I called after him, and he whirled around, startled.

"Yes, ma'am?" There was an edge of impatience in his voice, but I didn't care.

"Something …" I groped for words. "Something just happened here. Something the police should know about."

I swear his ears perked up. "What kind of thing?"

"A kidnapping. I want to report a kidnapping."

The officer peered into the car again, a puzzled expression on his smooth, tanned face. "Who was kidnapped? Maybe you'd better start at the beginning, ma'am."

I got out of the car and leaned against the hood. "It was my daughter. We got her back," I explained hastily, as he gave me a disbelieving look. "There was this guy, Adam, you see, and he thinks I know things about his past, but of course I don't, but he wanted to force me to talk to him, so he kidnapped my daughter at knife-point and brought her all the way out here. That's what we're doing here, getting her back."

"Getting her back," the cop repeated, with a slight shake of his head.

"Yes! I mean, if some loony had your daughter out in the woods in the middle of the night, wouldn't you come to get her back?"

"Sure. Sure, I would. Ma'am, could you tell me your name, please?" He patted his jacket, searching for a pen. I handed him one. He dug in his hip pocket for a pad of paper and laboriously spelled my name.

"K-l-e-i-n."

"Yes. Look, should we be coming in to the police station to fill out a report, or press charges or something?"

"Not necessary. I'll take care of it for you. Now, could you describe this Adam person?"

I gave as complete a description as I could, and he made copious notes. When he was done, he pocketed my pen and thanked me.

"Fine, no problem," I said automatically. "But what about Adam? He's back there in those woods somewhere, and he's pretty distraught. Don't you think you should go and find him? I mean, he could hurt himself. He needs help, and soon."

"I'm going to radio headquarters right now," the cop said, flashing me a big, reassuring smile that somehow did nothing to calm my brittle nerves. "We'll have tracking dogs out here within ten minutes. Don't worry, ma'am, we'll find this guy. Now, why don't you go on home? We'll be in touch if we need you for anything else, okay?"

"Sure." I climbed back into the car, and rested my head for a moment against the cushioned seat.

"Mom, what are they going to do to Adam?" Dawn's voice sounded very far away.

"I don't know, honey. I assume they'll take him to the hospital, get him committed for observation for a couple of days. Poor guy, he's not in any shape to take care of himself right now."

Greg drove slowly out of the lot, and the last I saw

of the cop, he was sitting in the front seat of his car, radio transmitter in his hand. Halfway home, I reached
backward to grip Dawn's hand. Dawn returned my tight
grasp, and her hand trembled convulsively. Neither of
us stopped shaking until we reached our apartment
building.

We must have looked like hurricane victims:
stunned, pale, grateful to be alive, wondering what hit
us. In the apartment, Dawn and I huddled together on
the couch, chilled despite the warm, unmoving air in
the room.

12

Dawn's face was grey with fatigue and emotional overload. Haltingly, stopping frequently to sip the hot sweet tea Greg had made for all of us, Dawn told her story.

She had been working on her computer server, but found something she couldn't quite understand. There had been a notation in the log file of someone logging off, but no trace of that person ever having logged on. Dawn was good with computers, but this one had stumped her. She decided to take the problem to Billy, Sylvie's nerdy younger brother, who always helped her out because he had a secret crush on her.

"And he's only eleven, Mom, isn't that gross? As if." Dawn rolled her eyes. She had spent some time at her friend's house that morning, and arrived home just before noon. As she'd pushed open the heavy oak doors of the apartment building, an arm had snaked around her throat, pushing the edge of a knife up under her chin. She had tried to scream, but a hand had clapped over her mouth.

Adam led her to the apartment door, and she had no choice but to let him in. Dawn had tried to ask him what he wanted, but he'd refused to answer. He told her to make up some excuse to explain her absence, and that is when she'd written the cryptic message on the fridge magnet board.

"I knew you'd understand it, Mom," she explained. "You know me well enough to figure it out."

I wondered why Peter hadn't twigged to the strange note, too; but that question could wait until he got home.

Adam had insisted that Dawn fill two empty pop bottles with water, and they had started walking. He'd stayed right behind her, giving her terse directions, and she had complied, knowing he had a mean-looking knife concealed under his windbreaker.

"How in hell did he survive, out in the noonday sun in that black jacket?" I asked. "It must have been like a steambath in there."

Dawn shrugged. "He didn't complain. In fact, I never saw him sweat the whole time we were together. He's a strange guy, Mom."

"I suspect physical comfort wasn't his first priority," Greg said. "Go on, Dawn — what happened then?"

"We walked for ages — maybe a couple of hours, I don't know. Every now and then, he'd tell me to stop and take a drink. He never took any himself, but he said he didn't want me getting sick," Dawn said. "He gave me some soda crackers, too, but I didn't want them. I was still afraid he was going to hurt me." Her eyes filled with tears.

"All I could think about was you and Dad," she said in a low voice, "and how you'd both feel, knowing I'd died alone and scared."

I pulled her even closer, and Dawn's breathing slowly returned to normal.

She and Adam had continued their trek, following

Sussex until it met the Parkway, then using the bicycle path that led past the sewage treatment plant. When they'd finally reached the parking lot where Greg and I had met them, it was late afternoon. Adam had marched her into the forest, where they sat down to wait.

The mosquitoes were out in full force, swarming them continuously. Dawn had been fearful that any quick motion to prevent them biting her would alarm her captor, so she had endured the stinging and itching as best she could.

Finally, as darkness settled and the frogs and crickets took up their evening serenade, Adam had begun to call me. He called at precise fifteen-minute intervals, allowing the phone to ring only three times before hanging up. When Dawn wondered aloud why he was doing this, he said only that he didn't want to let anyone find him, and he had to keep it short.

This made no sense to her, so she dropped the subject.

"But how did he call, Dawn?" Greg asked. "I didn't see any phone booths out there."

"He had one of those little fold-up cell phones in his jacket pocket," Dawn explained.

Greg and I exchanged glances.

"That's bizarre!" I said. "Paranoid people don't use cell phones — they're usually too afraid of having their calls monitored. If you're afraid you're being watched, why invest in a technology that makes it easy for your persecutors to track you down? It doesn't make sense."

Dawn shrugged. "He didn't say."

Adam had spent much of their interminable wait in silence, but as night drew on, he tersely informed Dawn that it wasn't his intention to hurt her. He only wanted information, he said, and he was sure her mother would co-operate now.

"He sounded really satisfied," Dawn said. "It was the closest he came to smiling the whole time."

"Well, it worked. I would have told him the sun rose in the west and his father, the Shah of Iran, had murdered the entire royal family and was now living in a grass hut at the North Pole, if that's what he'd wanted to hear. All I wanted was to get you out of there, honey."

By three in the morning, Dawn lay curled next to me, the day's events and her earlier terror giving way to natural exhaustion. Greg and I talked, our voices hushed.

"Is he schizotypal, do you think?" I asked.

"Not much doubt," Greg said. "He meets most of the criteria, from the magical thinking right down to the social anxiety. He might have delusions, but I wouldn't say he was frankly schizophrenic. No word salad, no pressured speech, no hallucinations that we know of. I'd say definitely schizotypal."

Schizotypal personality disorder is one of the diagnoses given to the wacky loners, the guys (for they are mostly men) who sit around talking to the walls because they can tolerate human company even less than they can tolerate themselves. What separates the schizotypal from the merely unsociable is the strange behaviour patterns and beliefs, the odd, stereotyped speech. Schizotypals may not have arguments with the martians living in their stomachs, but they are in the murky borderlands that separate the odd from the diagnosably disordered.

"Where do you think he got it?" I wondered. "I mean, he clearly witnessed, or thought he witnessed, something terrible when he was a child. That would tie in with the elective mutism you were telling me about. Would that be enough to warp his development so completely?"

"I doubt it. That initial trauma must have been followed up with a childhood full of mental or physical torture, I'd think," Greg said. "Watching a child being hurt, even being a victim of abuse himself — those wouldn't explain the business about being watched."

"Yeah, he talked about some mysterious entity who could read his thoughts. I couldn't figure that out."

"I don't get the thing about his sister, either. Without the files I can't be certain, but it seems to me there was an older brother somewhere. No sisters, and no sibs close to his own age."

"Haven't a clue. But the way he described it was pretty vivid, wasn't it? Is it possible he was at a friend's house and witnessed something? Maybe for a sleepover …"

"We'll probably never know," Greg said. "Not unless he decides to pay a return visit."

"Oh, thanks, Greg. Now there's a comforting thought," I shuddered. "Although if we could get him to consent to a voluntary hospitalization, you did seem to be able to reach him."

Greg was on another track.

"You know, the thing about the cell phone bugs me. I've never yet met a paranoid person who trusted one of those things. My paranoid patients are always going on about the deadly brain waves, and the spies listening in on them, and so on."

"Maybe he thought the benefit was worth the risk," I said. "Besides, with no pay phones for miles around, what other choice did he have? I mean, if he wanted to reach me that badly, he'd have to take a few chances, I guess. It must have been a trade-off."

"True. He might be able to broadcast his thoughts, but it's not usually as reliable as good old Ma Bell," Greg chuckled. Then he sobered. "Anyway, Adam doesn't strike me as a hardened criminal type. He took Dawn because he figured that was the only way to get you to talk to him. In his warped world, getting information out of you was more important than the fact that he was committing a crime."

"You know, the funny thing is that his chart does have a lot of indications that his family life was violent and painful. But to just hand that nugget of insight over to someone who seems to be coming unglued — well, it struck me as unwise. Maybe I should have just given him the works, let him do with it what he would."

"Nah. I think you did the right thing. You couldn't have known he'd take Dawn."

I recoiled as if I'd been slapped. "You couldn't have known …" There was that horrid phrase again.

"Greg, one of the reasons I got into astrology in the first place is that in a world where I can't know, I can at least get a few clues. I want a competitive edge on the fates. I don't want to not know."

Greg chuckled. "That's my girl."

It was four in the morning, and although Greg valiantly offered to spend the night doing guard duty on my lumpy sofa, I shooed him away home. He still planned to drive to Montreal to see his parents in the morning, and I didn't want him attempting the two-hour drive along a busy highway without at least a few hours' sleep. He left his beeper number, though, insisting that I page him immediately if anything untoward should happen.

I shook Dawn gently until she groaned in semi-waking protest; then I hoisted her up under her armpits and guided her, stumbling and still snoring slightly, to my bedroom. I was not about to let Dawn out of my sight for the next little while. While I valued my sleep, I valued my daughter a whole lot more.

With Dawn stretched across the bed, there wasn't much room for my large frame, but after a few pokes and prods she moaned again and rolled away. I lay balanced on my side, watching Dawn breathe. In this position, I finally drifted into an uneasy sleep myself, punctuated by Dawn's occasional twitches and cries as she relived her kidnapping on the big-screen television of her dreams.

13

I woke with Dawn's head nudging its way persist-ently into the crook of my arm. She'd been that way as a baby — a determined little nurser, even in her sleep.

My right hand began to tingle, the circulation cut off, and reluctantly, I eased my way out of my sleeping daughter's embrace. Dawn stirred briefly, then snored once, loudly. I left her sleeping, her long hair fanned out against the white pillow.

In the kitchen, early rays of sun filtered in through the high small windows, and I went through the motions of preparing my Saturday morning pot of coffee. Just as if it were any other Saturday, and I had not almost lost my child the night before. Funny how things just continue, the small motions and rituals of life ticking right on by, even when things have been inalterably changed. The kitchen looked the same as it had the morning before, and I was surprised at its untidy familiarity.

On weekends, I took the time to grind my coffee by hand. I spooned the polished black kernels into the electric grinder, pulverizing them into an aromatic powder, which I tapped into an unbleached coffee filter while I waited for the kettle to boil. Then I poured the freshly boiled spring water over the black powder, watching it bubble as it slowly drained into the waiting pot. I heated a small pan of milk just until it began to foam up slightly. Then, holding the coffee carafe in one hand and the pan of milk in the other, I swirled the scalding black and cream liquids together into the huge chartreuse mug Dawn had bought for my birthday.

Just as if it were any other Saturday, I carried my coffee over to the computer my parents had insisted on buying for Dawn, and started catching up on my weekly inputting of case notes. I transferred the contents of a floppy disk onto the hard drive, and then checked each file, adding comments or questions. Then, as Dawn had commanded, I checked my electronic mail box for messages. Sometimes I thought I might actually be getting used to living in the age of electronic information; I even had my own Internet service provider, though I couldn't have said what this actually did. Still, it sounded important. ISP.

The first e-mail was from Flavia, my electronic penpal. I had almost forgotten writing her — it seemed like about a month ago.

Flavia wrote:

Hi, Katy!

This guy Adam sounds like a handful ... not my idea of a dream date. All that Pluto activity sounds most obsessive and mysterious; mind if I free-associate a bit here?

Father: heavy, domineering, maybe a policeman type, or a detective. Keeps his kids in line, suspicious of them, or maybe even threatening. He exerts a strong grip on Adam, inhabits a very important place in his psyche. Won't let go, even after death. Adam may over-identify with father's 'dark side' — either take on father's guilt, or become even more scary and powerful than Dad, just to survive. Adam can bury the taboo aspects of the father, unable to acknowledge or integrate them without feeling overwhelmed. Any of this ringing a bell so far?

Sun-Pluto types often have trouble coping with the powerful people they meet. Their own egos can feel too vulnerable, too open to attack. With a father like the one I'm describing, who can blame them? Perhaps a fear of usurping or challenging the father's authority and position. Or a fear that Dad would rather see him dead than asserting himself, telling the truth to the world. Your guy might also have a secret 'superman' complex, wanting to defy his father in secret — because if he did it openly, Dad would kill him, right? At least, that's the fear. Loads of guilt here, too — a kind of inverse megalomania, where somehow ADAM becomes responsible for all the bad things in the world. Where only HE has the power to put things right, to outwit the bad guys and save the damsel in distress. Only, the damsel might very well be himself.

He has an incredible need to KNOW — both himself and his own deepest psychological recesses, and everything around him. Like you said, to him, knowledge is power, and the key to his survival.

That's why he's latched onto you — he thinks there are secrets out there that can threaten his very existence. And you, of course, are the Mystical Goddess Who Knows All and Sees All.

If you want to know where his secrets really lie,

look to the father, and possibly to the siblings. One thing I've come across is a link between Mercury/Pluto conjunctions and the death or injury of a sibling. You know, Merc as third house ruler, third house including brothers and sisters? Attach Pluto to that, and you've got the death of sibs, and the death of the words to talk about it. Like, say, there was a child stillborn or dead before Adam was even born, but somehow he picks up on the nuances and undercurrents in the family. Pluto types are great at undercurrents, though they don't always interpret them right. Maybe he's decided his words or actions were responsible for the loss? You mentioned a reluctance to speak, and that ties in with this theme, too. There might be a feeling that his words are ugly or deformed, or that his own existence might be threatened if he speaks. Maybe he feels more in control when he's not talking? Don't forget that silence can be a very powerful communication.

Sorry I'm running off at the keyboard a bit, but hey, I'm having a Mercury transit to my Sun, and that always makes me a little chatty. Hope this is all useful to you, and let me know how it turns out, okay? Oh, by the way, have you thought about looking at the transits and progressions?

Cosmic greetings and much love, Flavia.

I printed out the letter, then set the machine back to Dawn's server. She wasn't having much luck attracting new users, but she liked to keep the machine open to receive callers anyway. I took Flavia's letter into the living room and curled up on the couch to re-read it. The words rang true to me, but I still couldn't form a picture of Adam's tormented life. Dead or injured siblings, powerful and threatening father — it all made a kind of sense, but it wasn't enough.

For example, what had happened to the child whose screaming image had been seared into Adam's consciousness? Had that child been a vision of himself, suffering some kind of abuse? The face of the aggressor had been hidden — because he dared not see it? Or had his vision really been obscured, the abuser turned away from him? Had it been his father, the powerful dark figure who overshadowed his childhood?

If Adam was thinking of killing his father, as Flavia seemed to suggest, it looked like he was out of luck — hadn't Greg said both parents were old when Adam had been born? Adam himself was forty-seven now, so his parents could be in their eighties or nineties. How much could they threaten him, at that age? Oh, right. Greg had said Adam showed up at the hospital clutching his dad's obituary. Okay, check patricide off the list.

Flavia was right, though — Adam's father seemed to have a life of his own, in his son's mind. Maybe he'd come to me looking for a way to kill Dad off symbolically. Like an exorcism, perhaps. I sighed and took a sip of the cooling coffee. Try as I might, I just couldn't seem to insert myself into Adam's shoes.

When I'd practised as a psychologist, one of the tricks I'd used to reach difficult clients was something I privately called "entering their reality" — letting myself slip into the imaginary worlds they'd created for themselves. I would allow myself to feel what they felt, dream what they dreamed, crave what they craved. It wasn't easy, and sometimes it left me feeling just as slimy as some of the killers and rapists and child molesters I assessed. But it was effective; I could reach my clients, understand what made them tick. The hardest part was always removing myself, coming back to being just Katy Klein.

But with Adam, I couldn't do it. I couldn't get past the barricade of fear. When I tried to view the world through his eyes, I kept smashing into an impenetrable wall of terror and paranoia that surrounded him like a bristling shield. I always wound up on the outside, staring into his pale bulging eyes that gazed out at a hostile, monstrous world, in a state of … what? Shock? Horror? Rage? I just couldn't tell.

Dawn padded into the living room, carrying a bowl of muesli topped with sliced peaches and fresh yoghurt.

"So. Did I dream yesterday, or what?" She sounded hopeful.

"I wish. Listen, with Dad away, I'm not really thrilled with the idea of letting you spend time here alone, while I'm at work. Would you be willing to go stay with Zayde and Sabte for a while?"

Dawn hesitated, visions of days spent being fed and cossetted by her grandmother competing with her wish to remain at the side of her trusty computer.

"I'm not sure. Can we talk about it later on? I mean, you'll be around all weekend, and maybe the police will catch Adam, right? Didn't Greg say he could have him hospitalized or something?"

I swirled the remains of my coffee in the bottom of the mug.

"Mom? They're going to catch him, aren't they?"

"Um, sweetie, I'm not sure. We'll call today and see."

Tears formed in the corners of her eyes. "He really scared me, Mom. I don't like knowing he's still out there. Aren't the police supposed to catch people like that? It would be for his own good, wouldn't it?"

"Sure it would. So listen, here's what we're going to do until we know he's some place safe, okay? We're going to stick together like glue for the next couple of days, and then when I go back to the office Monday morning, you are going to stay with your grandparents until your dad gets home. At the first hint of any kind of trouble, we are going to call the cops and get this Adam person fitted for a lovely white jacket with really long arms." I smiled and threw an arm around Dawn's shoulder. "Think of it as an exercise in mother-daughter togetherness. Bonding."

Besides, I thought, there's always the handgun I bought after the episode with Frank Curtis. I kept the gun, unloaded of course, in my bedside table. It was one of those futile gestures, closing the stable door long after the horse's exodus, but it had helped me get a little sleep in the months after I'd left the hospital.

"Mom, I don't need a babysitter," Dawn snorted, tossing her hair back. "You don't need to go overboard about this."

I smiled. Sure, Dawn needed to make a show of thinking her mother was a Grade-A Number One Moron; that was just part of being a teenager. But she hadn't rejected my plan, and she'd probably go along with it.

"Hey, you want to help your aging mother out? Why don't you go get me another cup of coffee?" I asked, grinning at Dawn's exasperated expression. "Come on, we're practising for when I'm old and you have to wipe the drool off my chin."

Dawn's retort was interrupted by the telephone.

"Ms. Klein?" The voice was male, official sounding. I answered cautiously.

"Yes?"

"Ms. Klein, this is Detective Benjamin calling. Ottawa-Carleton Regional Police. Do you have a moment?"

I was silent for a few seconds. This didn't sound like

the cop I'd met last night. "What can I do for you? Is there something wrong?"

"I'm calling about a Mr. Adam Cosgrove. I believe you're acquainted with him?" The detective sounded businesslike, probably accustomed to confused people wondering what on earth the police could possibly want with them.

"Adam? Yes, I know him slightly. Did you find him?"

"I beg your pardon?"

"Did you find him?" I repeated the question more loudly, in case this guy was hard of hearing.

"Yes, yes we did," Benjamin said slowly. "Ms. Klein, I think you should come to the police station as soon as possible. Mr. Cosgrove was found this morning by one of our officers. He's dead."

14

I scowled, blinked and held the phone receiver away from my ear. I looked at it stupidly, unable to credit, or even fully understand, what I was hearing.

"I don't understand." My voice was thick and muffled. "How can he be — what you said? Dead? What happened to him?" This dopey, disconnected feeling was happening far too often for my liking. Maybe I ought to check out the planets transiting my chart — surely they would reveal something about a constant feeling of stupefaction.

"Ms. Klein, I'd appreciate it if you could meet me here as soon as you can." The detective sounded patient, as if he were talking to a three-year-old. "Say in about half an hour?"

"Half an hour, sure," I said. "Sure. What was your name again?"

"Detective Benjamin. Steve Benjamin. Major Crimes Division. You can just ask for me at the front desk, okay?"

I nodded silently, and seeming to grasp my addled state, Benjamin asked more gently, "Would you rather I have a cruiser drop by to pick you up? That might be easier for you."

A cruiser? A cop car at my door? Just what the neighbours needed, I thought — the sight of me being led away in a cop car would give them something to chew over for months afterward.

"No, thanks. I'll be there." Slowly, like a boxer who had sustained one too many direct hits to the jaw, I placed the receiver back in its cradle.

"What is it, Mom? Did you say someone was dead? Is everything okay? What's going on?"

Dawn was all over me, demanding answers.

"I'm not sure. It was the police. They're saying Adam is dead. They want me to come to the station."

This news silenced Dawn, but only for a moment.

"He's dead? How can that be? And what do they want you for? Do they think you had something to do with it? Do they think you killed him? Are they going to arrest you?"

"Dawn, stop it. Calm down, okay? I don't know what they want, but we'll find out soon enough. I have to be there in half an hour, so if you want to tag along, you're going to have to hurry up and get dressed."

"Mom, he's dead. You don't need to keep me in your sight, you know. He can't hurt me now."

"You're right. So why don't you stay home? I'll tell you all about it when I get back."

"Never mind," Dawn said. "I'm coming."

It was a short walk from our Centretown apartment to the police station, and Dawn and I arrived only a couple of minutes late. When we asked at the desk, a tall, bulky man with too much wavy reddish hair combed across a wrinkled forehead appeared almost immediately to greet us. His suit hung from wide shoulders, making no attempt at all to conform to his frame; and it looked like he'd bought his purple and green tie

at Big Bud's Discount Superstore. At least he wasn't
wearing a pinkie ring, I thought irrelevantly.

"Ms. Klein, good of you to come." He pumped my
hand as though welcoming me to Steve Benjamin's Used
Car Lot. He ignored Dawn. "Let's go to my office. We
can deal with the formalities later."

Formalities? Dawn and I exchanged glances, and
followed the detective obediently through a maze of
identical cubicles. Benjamin's "office" consisted of a
desk and swivel chair, two shabby burnt-orange plastic
chairs and a filing cabinet, all surrounded by green fab-
ric-covered sound baffles. The baffles did nothing to cut
the noise, but did succeed in adding an extraordinary
touch of ugliness to the general decor. The carpeting
was a matching avocado green, stained with who knew
what.

There were other officers in their own cubicles, but
it was pretty quiet around Benjamin's desk. He waved
us toward the auxiliary seating, and we sat in unison,
hands folded in our laps, like truants expecting the
worst from a visit to the principal. Benjamin looked
solemn, but the laugh lines around his eyes indicated
that his expression was not always this funereal. This
gave me some encouragement.

"I'm not really sure what we can do for you, Detective," I said. "My daughter and I were only very mini-
mally acquainted with Mr. Cosgrove. I don't see what
his death has to do with us."

Damn. Too defensive. I hoped he wouldn't take this
as an admission of guilt. Not that I had anything to admit. That is, I wasn't really guilty of anything, was I?

"Sure, I understand." Benjamin sounded as though
he dealt with people like me all the time. "But we have
reason to believe that you were the last person to speak

to Mr. Cosgrove while he was alive, so naturally we have to ask you a few questions, if that's all right with you. Did he have any relatives that you're aware of?"

I shook my head. "I don't know much about him. I heard his parents were quite old when he was born, but I don't know if they're still alive. No, that's not true," I contradicted myself. "His father is dead, now that I think of it. I don't know about the mother. And I understand he might have had an older brother, but I wouldn't know where he is, or how to reach him."

Here Dawn piped up.

"Actually, Mom, he told me he had no brothers or sisters. Just a father, he said."

Benjamin looked at Dawn as though she were a stone that had suddenly been gifted with speech. Furrows developed between his bushy eyebrows.

"Are you trying to tell me your daughter has met the deceased, too?" he asked me. "In what capacity?"

"Hey!" Dawn burst out. "You could ask me that, you know. She's my mother, not my spokesperson."

Benjamin ignored her, just kept waiting for me to answer.

"I guess you didn't get the report, then?"

Benjamin looked blank. "What report would that be?"

"Well, you know, about the kidnapping! I told the cop last night all about it, so I thought it would at least be in your records system by now."

The furrows between his eyes reappeared. "Wait a second. What kidnapping? What cop?"

I decided this might be as good a time as any to tell Benjamin the whole story, or as much of it as he would be likely to believe. So I told him about being an astrologer, and about Adam coming to me to find out the truth about some strange visions he'd been having, and about my inability to give him what he'd wanted. I told him about Adam's meeting with Greg, and the stolen business cards, and Greg's earlier work with Adam in Montreal. I told him about Adam's strange reaction at our second encounter, and how he looked about ready to jump at me, but then stopped himself and ran away instead.

I told him how Adam had taken Dawn and threatened her with harm if I didn't tell him what he wanted to know. I told him Greg and I had handled it, and Adam had dashed off into the bush afterward.

"And then you spoke with a police officer. A police officer in a uniform?" Benjamin spoke slowly, as if he thought I was slightly retarded.

"Yes! I'm trying to tell you, I gave a full report to this guy, and he said he'd take care of everything."

Benjamin said nothing, just wrote in his notebook. Finally, he glanced up at me.

"Now, I don't suppose you know the name of this alleged officer?" he asked.

"Alleged? You don't believe me, do you?"

"I have no reason not to believe you. But I also haven't heard about any reported kidnappings. That's not a common occurrence in Ottawa, you know — I'm pretty certain I would know if one had come in."

"Look, I'm telling you what happened. It's not my fault if your staff don't tell you what's going on. I trusted you guys to look for Adam, to keep him out of danger, and now look — he's dead, and you're accusing me of lying? What's that?"

"Ms. Klein, please. No one's accusing anyone of anything. I'm just trying to find out exactly what happened here. Now, did the … officer tell you his name, or did he not?"

"No. He didn't. I don't know his name, he didn't tell me. But the last I saw, he was on the radio to headquarters, calling in some dogs or something to look for Adam. We were worried about Adam, you know, all alone out there in the bush. I was afraid he might hurt himself. Turns out I was right to be worried."

"And did this 'officer' show you his badge?"

Badge? I stopped in my tracks. "No …" I said slowly. "He didn't. But it was kind of an emergency. Maybe he forgot?"

Again, Benjamin scribbled something in his book. This was really starting to get on my nerves. Detective Benjamin seemed to doubt everything I said, and I didn't like feeling like a little kid who'd been caught in a lie. Especially when I was telling the truth.

So I didn't bother to mention the missing files at the Allan Memorial Institute; and I skipped over Adam's belief that his father (alive or dead) was able to read his thoughts; and I forgot all about the knife I'd gummed up with my own fingerprints. Nor did I mention that Greg was planning to do some amateur detective work in the archives at the Allan, nor that my ex-husband had been recruited to do some digging about Adam's father. It just didn't seem relevant.

Benjamin had scribbled everything I said in pencil on a small notepad he'd pulled from somewhere deep in his tweed jacket. He looked to me like the kind of man who'd seen and done it all; even the news that I read the stars for a living didn't seem to faze him. By the end of my narrative, I felt a bit better. At least I'd told my story, and whether or not he believed me, Benjamin had accepted it without much comment.

"I'd like to ask you some questions now, if that's okay," I said. "To start with, can you tell us how Adam

… that is, Mr. Cosgrove, died?"

"We aren't sure. He was found in the Canal early this morning, just under the Pretoria Bridge."

"Oh." I blanched. Although I knew Adam was dead, the image of him floating in the Canal hit me with unexpected vividness. I could see him clearly, his matted dirty blond hair spread out around his head, undulating softly in the fetid water. My stomach churned. I reached for Dawn's hand, and swallowed hard.

"Well, if you found him in the Canal, doesn't that mean he must have drowned?" Dawn asked, trying her best to sound adult.

A flicker of a smile crossed Benjamin's heavy face. "Not necessarily, little lady. Anyway, we'll have to wait for the autopsy before we can really say anything."

Dawn's spine straightened. She gave Benjamin a hard stare of outrage and opened her mouth to protest this form of address, but I jumped in and headed her off at the pass.

"One thing I don't understand. How did you know to contact me? I mean, I'm not a lifelong friend or a relative or anything. He'd only really known me a few days."

"Actually, that was easy." Benjamin grinned, pleased that I had asked such an obvious question. "He had one of those little fold-up cell phones in his jacket pocket. Your number was the last one recorded to that account. Took me one phone call to trace it. Oh, and he had your business card in his pocket, too. A bit wet, but still legible."

Dawn, still smarting from being called "little lady", said coldly, "Well, wouldn't the Canal water have damaged the phone?"

Benjamin smiled again, apparently unaware of the effect of his ill-chosen words. "The phone was a rental.

We just called the rental place and checked out the serial number. The calls are logged to a computer, just like when you call long-distance, you know?"

I nodded. In a way, Adam had been right. The "others" had known his every move. After the fact, at any rate.

"Well, that's about all I have to ask you for now, Ms. Klein." Benjamin tucked his notes into a brand new clean file folder, which had already been labelled "Cosgrove", with a bunch of numbers after the name. "The only other thing I have to ask you is to identify the body."

I flinched. He might as well have slugged me in the stomach; I was getting that familiar dazed feeling again.

"I didn't know that was part of the deal. And what about my daughter? She's nearly fifteen, but …" I certainly didn't want Dawn to see her abductor lying lifeless in some drawer or something.

Benjamin nodded reassuringly. "She doesn't have to go. I only need you. And don't worry, it's not like on TV. You don't have to be in the same room with the body. It'll only take a few seconds."

I looked at Dawn, who had grown paler. "You can wait for me in the lobby, honey. I won't be long."

Dawn acquiesced with only a token protest. She'd hit her tolerance level for emotional trauma in a twenty-four hour period.

I accompanied Detective Benjamin along a series of corridors, down some stairs, and through another maze of buildings to a room with a small discreet sign over the door: "Morgue". He guided me into a small antechamber, where we stood in front of a wide plate-glass window, darkened by a heavy curtain that hung on the other side.

"Are you ready?" he asked, barely waiting for my answering nod. "Okay, Jim," he said into an intercom on the wall.

The curtain opened, seemingly by magic, revealing a stainless-steel gurney covered with a very clean-looking white sheet. On top of the sheet, a man lay absolutely still, his greyish-white face registering mute surprise at his present circumstances. It looked to me as though he were play-acting. Any minute now, he'd jump up and start hammering on the plate glass, demanding that I tell him the truth, release him from his nightmare. But no matter how hard I peered at him, I could detect no signs of life in Adam's still body.

His hair was not only matted, but now was randomly decorated with twigs and leaves and other Canal detritus. His black jeans and windbreaker were grubby and sad, still clinging damply to his dead flesh in the harsh overhead lights.

All the fear, all the desperation, all the energy had drained from him. His eyes were even paler than they had been while he was living, but they still seemed to bulge from their sockets in silent shock.

"That's him," I whispered. I turned my head away, not wanting to stare any longer. Adam needed his privacy now.

"You need to say his name," prompted Detective Benjamin.

"That's Adam Cosgrove," I muttered.

The curtain was closed again. I signed a paper declaring that to the best of my knowledge the person I had seen on that gurney was Adam Cosgrove, of parts unknown.

"Well, you've been a big help, Ms. Klein," Benjamin said. "Thanks."

I scurried to keep up with him; if I lost him, I might wander in this underground maze forever.

"So — that's it?"

"Yep. That's it."

"Aren't you going to tell me not to leave town, or something?"

Benjamin slowed down and gave me a look. "Why? Is there something you're not telling me?"

I shook my head. "No, of course not. I just thought …"

"This isn't *Dragnet*, Ms. Klein. If I need to speak to you again, I'll call you. Meanwhile, thank you for your help, and good-bye."

We had reached the lobby, where Dawn stood fiddling with the leaves on a stunted geranium plant. Without another word, Dawn and I left, walking home in the late morning haze.

"How was it?" Dawn asked.

"Don't ask. I never wanted out of anywhere so badly in my life." I shivered, despite the glare of the sun. Tears filled my eyes and threatened to spill over onto my cheeks; I wiped at them angrily. Sure, I was relieved that Dawn and I would now be safe, that Adam's compulsion to understand and exorcise his demons would no longer collide with our lives.

"It's sad, isn't it?" Dawn asked, squeezing my hand.

I nodded. "You know, I kept thinking back there — his whole life, all that suffering, and it came down to this: floating in the Canal like a piece of garbage. Lying on some gurney with only strangers to tend to him. No kaddish, no last rites, no mourners, no candles. Nothing."

"We couldn't do anything for him."

"I know. But he asked — no, he screamed for our help, and all we could do was look on. We watched him suffer, we said he was nuts, but we didn't help him. In the end, we turned away from him."

"I know. I thought that yesterday, when we were sitting in the woods together. All he wanted was to make sense of things."

I said nothing. Someone should mourn for Adam, shed at least one tear for his constricted, tortured life. It might as well be me.

15

SUNDAY, JULY 31
Sun inconjunct Jupiter, opposition Uranus ✦
Moon square Pluto ✦
Mercury square Pluto ✦
Mars square Saturn ✦
Jupiter square Saturn ✦

On Sunday morning the weather broke.

All the sultry, dense air congealed into one enormous black cloud, a wind whirled up out of nowhere, and the skies opened to release a torrent. The rain pelted down in streams, battering windows, flattening flowerbeds and creating rivers down the middle of downtown streets. Lightning forked skyward, splitting the darkness so you could glimpse the pure white energy behind it.

Nine times out of ten, these summer storms are simply the result of too much steamy air collecting in the basin of the Ottawa Valley. They drop their rain, which then evaporates into more steam, and the storm disappears without having much effect on the sweltering heat and humidity. A flash in the pan.

But this was one of those truly wonderful, weather-breaking downpours in which an actual cold front sweeps across the valley, smashes roundly into the warm front that has taken up residence there; and the two battle to the death. The hot wet air sneaks off the battlefield in disgrace, muttering imprecations over its shoulder, and the cold front, triumphant, paints the sky a snappy shade of blue. The temperature drops precipitously and all the grouchy tempers in the city improve exponentially.

I went shopping at the farmer's market and picked up a ridiculous amount of fresh produce for two people, merely because it was all dirt cheap. Humming to myself, I strode homeward. A cool breeze riffled through my hair and my shorts felt almost too light for the weather.

At home, I had finished unpacking my vegetable treasures, cramming the small refrigerator with broccoli, spinach, bundles of lettuce and parsley, cherry tomatoes, cucumbers, peaches, the first of the tart shiny local apples and even a jug of maple syrup left over from the spring run.

I was at the kitchen table going through the week's accumulation of bills, when I came across the plain hand-addressed envelope I had put aside Friday night in my panic to find Dawn.

There was no stamp and no return address. Someone had scrawled, "K. Klein, Astrologer" across the front in thick, black ink. It didn't look like a mass mailing from some out-of-work political party soliciting funds, or a worthy but obscure organization representing a disease I hoped I wouldn't get. This alone made it more interesting than ninety per cent of my mail. Intrigued, I slid a knife along the crease.

Three small black and white photographs fell out. The first was a head and shoulders shot of a small blonde girl, her hair a froth of curls around a chubby face. She wore a white cotton blouse, starched and embroidered with stylized ducks on the peter pan collar. Her expression was shy, her large eyes cast down, but a small smile played at the corners of her cupid-bow mouth. Cute, timid, maybe about two and a half or three years old.

At first glance, the second photo looked like a replica of the first, but when I compared them, I noted that the second child had slightly darker hair and the mouth was not quite the same. Judging by the cowboy motif on the identically pressed shirt, Child Number Two was a boy. The pictures might have been taken in the early fifties or so, I thought.

They looked like the studio shots parents get made of their kids, displaying them in all their finery, improbably clean and neat. Both children wore expressions that were hard to read: camera-shy, perhaps, or just plain shy. Not unhappy, exactly, but not bubbling over with childish enthusiasm, either.

The third shot had been taken outdoors. An older woman held both children on her knee. The kids might have been a few months, even a year older. Their faces weren't quite so round, not so babyish. A scarf covered the woman's hair, and a large cross hung from a chain round her neck. She held her head back from the children, as though trying to get a good look at them. She smiled, but held them away from her body.

In this shot, the kids wore light-coloured woollen coats, identical tartan pants, and knit caps. They held hands, looking down and smiling those mini-Mona Lisa smiles. Next to them sat a man, older still than the woman, his face shadowed by a snap-brimmed fedora. Though his eyes were hidden, it was clear he was scowling. He wore a three-piece suit and tie, and held a pipe in one hand. A watch chain hung from his vest pocket.

A number of other adults stood behind the couple and kids, though I couldn't tell whether they belonged with the family group. There was a tall young man wearing a light sport jacket and sweater, with a dark ascot tucked into the v-neck. He wore sunglasses and a crewcut, and looked down at the older woman, expressionless. Maybe he was the father, and she the grandmother, I thought. Or did he even belong in the picture? He could have been a passing stranger, caught forever by the camera. It was impossible to say.

Another man seemed to walk away from the group, his hands thrust into the pockets of an overcoat. His lips were pursed, as though he were whistling. And a plump, dark-haired young woman wearing a scarf over her head clutched a handbag to her stomach and gazed off into the distance. She was slightly out of focus.

Dawn bounced into the kitchen. "I need to talk to Billy the Nerd again. My stupid server program isn't making any sense … Hey, what are these?"

She picked up a photo and turned it over.

"Beats me." I shrugged.

"Huh. Where did they come from?"

"Your guess is as good as mine. They came in Friday's mail."

"Weird. I wonder who these kids are? They don't look very happy."

At that moment, the phone rang. Dawn picked it up, and the flash of her smile was brilliant.

"Dad! No, we were just sitting here. I know, I'm sorry

I didn't let you know, but … but … Dad, you haven't even heard … Yeah, fine. Here she is."

She handed me the phone, all her animation gone. Peter, a stickler for propriety, must have reprimanded her for missing Friday's supper.

"Hey, Peter, how's it going?"

"Not bad. You okay now?"

"Okay? Yeah, why would I … Oh," I stopped myself, remembering that last time Peter had seen me, I'd been a weeping, pathetic puddle of mush at my parents' place. That all seemed very long ago.

"Sure, I'm fine," I said. "Listen, about Dawn not coming to my parents' place …"

Peter interrupted. "I already had a word with her about that. Told her it was damned rude to let them down without calling or anything."

"Mmm. Right." Maybe Friday night's adventure could wait till Peter was back in town. No point worrying him while he's away.

"So listen," Peter continued. "I just wanted to tell you I found a bunch of stuff about the Cosgrove family, dating back to the forties and fifties. Seems they were really in the big time back then."

"Big time? How do you mean?"

"I mean Julian, that is, Mr. Cosgrove Senior, was a real hot-shot financier, rated up in the major leagues back in his day. Into a lot of different businesses in Montreal and the States too, from the *shmatte* trade right on up to banking. You know that old saying that money makes money? He cottoned onto that one in a big way."

"So, where is he now?"

"Pushing up daisies. He died only a few months ago. Alzheimer's, plus some kind of heart thing. He was pretty old — ninety-six, I think. The article was in the financial pages, though, and they were more concerned with his assets at death. Something in the range of fifty million."

"Wow." I sucked in my cheeks, trying to imagine what life would be like with that kind of money to worry about. I should be so lucky.

"What about Mrs. Cosgrove? Is she still around?"

"Nope. Seems he was 'predeceased by his beloved wife, Micheline', but it doesn't give a date of death for her. But I'll tell you, if that's what he thought love was, he had a screw or two loose."

"How so?"

"I mean, I found three separate stories chronicling his run-ins with the law, each time for beating his 'beloved Micheline' to a bloody pulp. Once in 1949, once in 1953 and once in 1960. They were small items, in the City News section, but they were definitely about Cosgrove."

"Which means he was probably beating her up on a regular basis in between times, just not getting reported for it. Did he actually go to jail for any of this?"

"Nope, not even for a day. Each time, the Crown witness, a.k.a. his wife, would refuse to testify. And this was the fifties, when no one thought much about wife battering, as long as you didn't kill the poor woman. They'd assume she was either lying or exaggerating. Besides, you can imagine the kind of legal power someone like Cosgrove could purchase. So he'd get off and she'd be called crazy."

I shuddered. "I know. It was that way when I was volunteering at the shelter, and that's not all that long ago, either. Hubby flies off the handle, bashes the wife around, and she leaves, swearing she'll never go back.

Until he shows up, tail between his legs, claims this time for sure he'll go straight, this time he'll show how much he really loves her. Or else he threatens her: you drop the charges, and maybe I won't hurt you so bad next time. Or I won't hurt the kids. Or your dog, or your cat, or your mother."

Peter snorted. "We're way too cynical, you know that?"

"Yeah, but you know it's the truth, don't you? And if the woman stays in the marriage, her shrink will say she's masochistically entangled, or weak-willed, or just not very bright. It's a no-win. Oh, except for the husband, who still has his human punching bag to practise on. So — what about the kids? Any mention of them in the articles you found?" I changed the subject abruptly.

"Actually, it's funny. In the obituary for Julian, it mentions his 'only son, Adam.' But I remember you saying there were two kids, one older and one younger, so I went looking for other references. There's only one, in the social pages back in the late forties. It doesn't mention the kid by name, but there was some fancy dress ball in Montreal, and the guests included 'Mr. and Mrs. J. Cosgrove, and their son.'"

"That kind of bears out the idea of a much older brother, doesn't it?" I asked. "Adam was either a baby or not yet born then, and I'm sure his parents wouldn't have brought an infant to a formal party in those days, right?"

"Um-hmm. But your boy Adam is due to hit the jackpot, I'd say. Most of his money is held in trust, but it looks like his dad set aside about a million 'for his use and enjoyment', administered by Daddy's financial advisor. Whom I happen to know, by the way."

"There's a small catch, Peter."

"What's that?"

"Adam is dead. I identified his body yesterday morning."

"Pardon?" Peter spluttered. "I thought I just heard you say he's dead — how can this be? What the hell happened?"

"I don't know. Apparently they fished his body out of the Canal, but the cop I spoke to wouldn't say anything about the actual cause of death." This would be a good time to let Peter in on the rest of the story, I told myself, but somehow the words just wouldn't come.

Peter expelled a long breath. "So … how come you got to identify him?"

"Just lucky, I guess. They found my name on him," I hedged. "Anyway, I saw him, and it was definitely Adam. Unmistakable. So now what happens to all that money?"

"No idea. I'm no lawyer, but I'd guess it might go to Adam's estate, whatever that might be. From your description, he doesn't sound like the type to have made out a will."

"Probably not. Well, it's not our concern, anyhow. I was just wondering." I was lying. In reality, I was speculating frantically: could the prospect of a tidy sum of money have provoked person or persons unknown to push Adam into the Canal? And should I tell the police about this new development?

"Well, th-th-th-that's all, folks!" Peter said. "I've forwarded everything to your e-mail address. If I see anything more, I'll let you know."

When I hung up, Dawn was still engrossed in the baby pictures. Without looking up, she said, "You didn't tell him about Friday. What is this, some kind of state secret?"

She did not sound happy.

"No, not at all." My words sounded more tart than I'd intended. "I just don't think there's any sense in worrying your father when he's out of town. There'll be plenty of time when he gets home."

"Fine." She looked away from me.

"Dawn, look, I'm going to tell him, but you know how Dad worries about you. If I told him now, he'd be on the next flight home and he'd screw up this big assignment that means a lot to his career. If I wait, no one gets hurt, and it helps him get through a week that's going to be tough enough as it is."

"Yeah, well you sure left me hanging in the breeze, didn't you?" Dawn turned back to face me, tears forming in her eyes and spilling over. "He gave me royal shit about missing dinner Friday night, and it wasn't even my fault! You could have at least told him that!"

"You heard what I said, Dawn. I did try, and believe me, he'll hear the whole story the minute his plane sets down, okay?" I stroked her hair. "I'm sorry, sweetheart. I didn't mean to make things bad between you and Dad. Look, I'm thinking of stir-frying some broccoli and tofu for supper. Do you want to make one of your marinades?"

Grumpy at first, but with more enthusiasm as she measured out tamari sauce and grated a stump of fresh ginger to a pungent paste, Dawn worked beside me. By the time we were ready to eat, she was on speaking terms with me again.

16

First thing Monday morning, I called Detective Benjamin from my office. It seemed the thing to do; I had to let him know about Adam's recent financial windfall, even if Adam was no longer in any condition to spend the money. I'd already withheld a few tidbits of information from the police. This was an opportunity to right the balance, at least a little.

"Okay, Ms. Klein, I'm making a note of that." I could just picture him with his stubby pencil at the ready.

"Good." Then, ever so casually, I asked, "So — any idea what Adam died of yet?"

"We're still waiting for the complete report. The body was found early on the morning of July 30, and you claim to have seen the victim late the previous night, so that does narrow down the timing, but it can be hard to establish a cause of death in a case like this."

"Well, isn't it possible he just fell into the Canal and drowned? Wouldn't that be the simplest explanation?"

"Actually, no. If he had drowned, his body would have spent some time under water before the gases forming in the decomposing tissues forced him to the surface. He would have been under water at least a day or two, even in the heat we've been having," Benjamin explained. He was enjoying this. "And his body wasn't bloated or decomposed when we found it, the way it would have been if he'd drowned."

"Yuck. I'm sorry I asked." If the sight of Adam lying dead on that gurney had nauseated me, the idea of him dangling underwater until his body bloated up and bobbed to the surface like a grotesque black-clad cork appealed even less.

"It's not pretty," Benjamin agreed.

"But wait a second," I said, more to myself than the detective. "If he died some other way, wouldn't there be marks? Bullet holes, or knife wounds, or even rope burns or something? Wouldn't you know?"

Benjamin heaved a sigh. "I've told you as much as I can, Ms. Klein. Look, you'll be the first on my list to call when we get any more news, okay?"

"Yeah, right. Don't humour me, okay?"

"You've been a big help to us, Ms. Klein. I'll be in touch," he said, as if I hadn't spoken. Joe Cop, handling the troublesome witness.

"Sure." I made a rude face into the receiver. "Let me know if I can be any help."

"Oh, we will, believe me."

What the hell was that supposed to mean? I wondered, as I hung up. A chill coursed up my spine. Did he suspect I had something to do with Adam's death? Well, I hadn't, so they could just go find someone else to pick on. It wasn't my fault the guy died. It wasn't.

But what if … I stretched back in my chair and studied the watermarks on the ceiling.

You're just feeling guilty, that's all. Yes, you, Katy. You feel guilty because you think you could have given him more, done more, you could have calmed him down, and then you and Greg could have driven him to the hospital and he'd be fine now, instead of lying in some giant refrigerator with a tag on his toe.

There. I'd thought it. I did feel guilty, and ashamed that I'd allowed my fear to get the better of my compassion. I didn't like it that I'd let Adam run off not once, not twice, but three times, without offering him some alternative, some relief. I'd let someone kill him, when I could have helped.

Funny — now I was assuming someone had killed Adam. Well, it was pretty obvious he hadn't just decided to go for a leisurely midnight swim in the fetid waters of the Canal. No, he had not been ready to die. Expecting someone to kill him, perhaps, but not ready to go. Suicide didn't make sense, psychologically speaking. He'd needed some kind of closure — a sense that his riddle had been solved, that he'd done what he set out to do. As of just after midnight Friday night, he had not achieved that. His internal dragons had still been breathing fire in his face; he hadn't faced them down yet.

So what had happened? Had he been rolled by some kid wanting spare change for his next high? Had he got himself into a fight with some of the other homeless people who roam Ottawa's streets on hot summer nights, looking for the best places to sleep or shoot up in privacy? Or had he finally met the mysterious "him", the one who could read his thoughts, track his every move? Katy, there's such a thing as getting too far into a client's reality.

With a jolt, I sat upright in my chair. It hit me: I still thought of Adam as my client. He was my responsibility, a part of my life, and he would be until I found my own closure with him. Was it my compulsive need to control the world by knowing everything I possibly could? Or was it simply that I wanted to know there was nothing more I could have done?

I mulled over these questions as I took care of the mundane tasks of running a business — billing clients, writing cheques for rent and electricity — until the phone rang. I let the answering machine pick it up.

"Hello, this is Star-Dynamics, Katy Klein speaking. I'm with a client at present, but your call is important to me. Please leave your name and number ..." My disembodied voice droned on, and the machine emitted a series of beeps.

"Katy, are you there? It's Greg. I'm in Montreal —"

I lunged for the phone. Feedback screeched in our ears.

"Hang on, I'm going to turn this stupid thing off," I yelled. "There, that's better. What's up?"

"I just thought you might like to know what I've been finding," Greg said, with no preamble. "It's weird. I'm calling from the Allan, and it's just as if Adam Cosgrove never existed here."

"*Nu?*" I asked, which is Yiddish for "so get on with the story, already!"

"I've been through all the electronic records and there's no trace of him. Nothing at all. So I went down to the archives and there's a slot where his file should be, but there's a place-marker there. That means the file was taken out and not returned, but there's nothing to indicate who might have taken it, or why."

"Greg, I have to tell you …"

"No, no, let me finish. This is so bizarre, Katy. To take a file out of here, you have to sign it out with the clerk at the front desk. According to the date on Adam's place-marker, the file was removed in May of this year, but there's no record of anyone leaving the archives with it during that time period."

"So — where is it? Did someone surreptitiously smuggle the thing out under their lab coat or something?"

"The clerk and I had a long talk, and he thinks Adam's file probably got put back in the wrong place. That's not supposed to happen, they're very strict about it. So he's assigned one of the junior clerks here to try and locate it for me."

"You've got the touch, Greg — how come you can always get people to do what you want?"

He laughed uncomfortably. "Anyway, what did you want to tell me?"

"Oh, right. Well — Adam is dead." I hadn't meant for the words to come out sounding so flat, but there they were, hanging between me and Greg, stuck somewhere on the line between Montreal and Ottawa. There was a long silence.

"Are you there?" I asked. "Greg, I'm sorry, I —"

"It's okay. I'm here. What happened?"

"I got a call from the police Saturday morning. They'd fished him out of the Canal in the early morning and they wanted me to identify him."

"Why you?"

I laughed, more of a snort. "Good question. Why me? Well, then again, why not? Apparently, they can trace calls made from those little cell phones everyone uses now. Oh, and he had my business card on him. Like Adam said, nothing he did was a secret. Maybe he wasn't as out to lunch as we thought." I was rambling, but Greg cut me off.

"Oh. So how did he die?"

"They don't know yet, but the detective in charge of the case is kind of keeping me informed. I think he almost believes I might have done it. I mean, I was the last person to see him alive. And you and Dawn, of course."

"Oh."

"Greg, look. It came as a shock to me, too. We can talk more about this when you get home, okay? And don't worry, I don't think I'm the prime suspect or any-thing — it's just that he died suddenly and alone, and they always ask a lot of questions when something like that happens. I don't think it's even a murder investiga-tion yet. At least, that's what Steve Benjamin, the de-tective in charge, told me."

"Okay."

Greg took a deep breath, then exhaled slowly. It took a great deal to ruffle him, and I knew that when he started doing his yogic breathing exercises, he was feel-ing close to the edge. Welcome to the club.

"Okay," he tried again. "Look, I'm leaving Montreal in about half an hour or so. Why don't we meet for lunch?"

"You buying?" I teased. "Nah, forget it, it's my turn. But I can only afford hot dogs, okay?"

Cautioning Greg to drive carefully, I said good-bye. He seemed to be suffering from the same kind of mind-lag that had afflicted me the past several days; not a good state to drive in.

I went back to work, writing up a chart for a baby born less than two weeks ago. I loved these charts. They reminded me of the feeling of starting a new school year, with brand new pencils, unblemished notebooks, erasers that have not yet become grimy with a year's worth of frustration and error. A new baby gave everyone a chance to start over. And with luck, I might be able to give the parents some tips that would protect this new, fragile life from the kind of damaged, crippled childhood Adam must have led.

At half past noon, I realized Greg had not yet appeared for our promised lunch. He was the most compulsively on-time person I knew, and his absence worried me. Still, I kept working, figuring he'd been delayed in Montreal, or that traffic on Highway 417 had been unusually nasty. By one-thirty, though, I was getting concerned; when the phone rang at one forty-five, I pounced on it.

"Katy?"

Greg sounded tired, thready, distant. Something like ice surged through my body, and I nearly dropped the phone.

"Greg? What's wrong?" It shouldn't be this difficult to sound calm.

"I'm in the hospital. In Hawkesbury. There was an accident …"

"Oh my God, what happened?" I cried. "Are you hurt? Dammit, I knew I shouldn't have told you about Adam! I distracted you, and now look! Greg, I'm so sorry!"

"No, no, don't worry. I'm okay — I've just got a dislocated shoulder. And my head hurts, but they don't think it's too serious. The car isn't totalled, but it's not going on any trips anytime soon."

I sniffed back tears. "How did it happen?"

"You won't believe it, Katy. Someone tried to run me off the road."

"You're right, I don't believe it. Greg, that only happens in James Bond movies, and you know I hate them. This is Ottawa: the nation's capital. Houses of Parliament. Tulip festival. Changing of the guard. Peace, order and good government. People don't run one another off the road here."

"Well, it happened to me." He sounded weary.

"Okay. Sorry. It's just — no, never mind. Listen, I'll be right there. Don't go anywhere, okay?"

"I wasn't planning any trips," he said. "But it's not necessary for you to come all this way. They told me they're going to keep me overnight for observation, and let me out of here in the morning. I'll be fine, really."

"Hey, I promised you lunch. Katy Klein promises you a hot dog, you gonna get a friggin' hot dog." I sounded like a cross between Sonny Corleone and Yosemite Sam, and Greg gave a weak laugh.

"See you soon, then," he said.

I called Dawn at home and told her to wait for me on the front porch. Then I called the nearby car rental agency and reserved a sub-compact, the cheapest on the lot, for pick-up in half an hour. I closed the office, picked up the car, picked up Dawn, and the Klein Rescue Mission hit the road.

17

We were on the Queensway heading east by two-fifteen. If we hadn't been on our way to assist someone who'd just been in a car crash, it would have been a great day for a road trip. The sun was brilliant in a deep blue crystalline sky, the air felt fresh and clean against our cheeks and the local "classics" station was playing Otis Redding.

"So, what happened to Greg, Mom? Is he badly hurt?"

"I'm not really sure. He said someone tried to run him off the road, but he sounded pretty dozy, so he might have been imagining it. I mean, how likely is that?"

Dawn was silent for a moment. "Not likely at all. But Greg isn't the kind of person to imagine stuff like that. How come you don't believe him?"

"It's not that I don't believe him, it's just — I don't know. I mean, who would want to hurt Greg? And why?"

"The same person who wanted to hurt Adam, maybe?"

"You watch way too much television, kid. You sound like that guy from *The X-Files*."

"Fine, don't listen to me." Now I'd hurt her feelings. "But I bet I'm right. You'll see."

Hawkesbury is a smallish town along old Highway 17, the roadway that hugs the shore of the Ottawa River all the way to its junction with the St. Lawrence. Thirty or forty years ago, someone had got fed up with taking the scenic route, meandering along a two-lane country highway, passing picturesque towns and hamlets on the way to Montreal. That is when Highway 417 was conceived, the eastern extension of the Queensway.

The 417 roars rather than rambles, and there's not much scenery, unless you count endless fields alternating with second-growth forests. But it's fast, with four lanes separated by about twenty metres of grass median. This is a good thing, because many of the people who drive the stretch between Ottawa and Montreal seem to have obtained their driver's licenses as prizes in their morning boxes of cereal.

Dawn and I were averaging about 110 kilometres an hour and we were being passed by nearly every other car on the road. Some drivers actually flipped me a contemptuous finger as they zipped by.

"You'd think we were getting in their way on purpose," Dawn remarked.

"I've got my foot on the floor," I said. "I don't think this thing goes any faster than this."

"Next time, we take the Batmobile."

I stuck to the right lane, playing it safe. This vehicle couldn't even begin to approach the Flaming Deathtrap in terms of body rust or mechanical caprice, but it lacked F.D.'s get up and go. Even at this speed, the little car vibrated and shuddered alarmingly. Periodically, I slowed down, just to give the poor beast a rest.

The turn-off for Hawkesbury came up faster than I expected. The hospital wasn't hard to find, given the many blue "H" signs with little arrows on them that directed me right to the door. It was a small building, two stories, probably not more than ten or fifteen beds. This was a good sign. When accident victims are taken to small local facilities like this, they are only held and treated if their wounds are minor enough for the hospital to handle. If they require more sophisticated treatment or equipment, they are shipped off to regional treatment centres, like the ones in Ottawa or Montreal. I explained all this to Dawn as I parked the car.

"So he's probably okay?" She looked hopeful.

"That'd be my guess. Come on, let's go see."

Greg was sitting up on the edge of his bed in the tiny emergency ward. Another good sign. His left arm was in a sling, and his head was bandaged alongside his ear, but there were no signs of more serious injury. "I'm afraid to hug you," I said. "Where doesn't it hurt?"

"Nowhere. But go ahead — I could use a hug." He tried to smile, but didn't quite make it. "I've got a hell of a headache, but otherwise I think I'm all right. Anyway, where's that hotdog you promised me, Klein?"

"I lied," I said. "You're going to have to take a raincheck. When are you allowed out of here?"

"They just did a skull x-ray, and apparently I'm no worse off now than I was before the accident. They said I could leave when you guys got here, as long as I get my head checked when I get back home."

"What about your car? How much damage?"

Greg loved his Audi, one of the first purchases he made after his wife of twenty years ran off with her personal trainer.

"They're saying she'll need a panel on the left-hand side replaced, and some dents and gouges ironed out, but it doesn't look like there's as much damage as I thought," Greg said. "I had the car towed back to Ottawa, to Marcel's place. He just called."

"Who's Marcel?" Dawn asked.

"Greg's mechanic," I said. "He knows that car inside out and backwards. Which I would too, if it was paying for my kid's university tuition."

"Marcel doesn't overcharge," Greg protested. "He's a specialist. He knows everything there is to know about that car."

"Yeah, right. I should be a specialist like Marcel. So when can we check you out of this hotel? I think some fresh air will do you good. You can start saving up to get your car out of hock when we get back."

"Har-de-har. I'm all set to go. I just want to thank the head nurse."

Greg got up, and I assessed his gait carefully as he crossed the room to the nursing station. Slow, but no wobbles, no visible listing. Despite the negative x-ray, I didn't want to take any chances with possible brain damage. Post-traumatic encephalopathy could be a killer, literally.

Greg thanked the plump woman who sat behind the desk and she positively glowed with pleasure as she replied to his flawless French. He also thanked two nursing assistants who stood giggling by the door, and a cleaning lady who had apparently had the honour of emptying his wastebasket during his brief stay. I was used to Greg's effect on all those who cross his path, but Dawn was deeply impressed.

"How come he knows all these people already?" she whispered. Greg was engaged in another bout of handshaking, this time with the two ambulance attendants who had brought him in.

"Take notes, kid. Greg is sweet to everyone, and he

goes by the motto that one should choose one's enemies sparingly and one's friends broadly."

"Not like you, huh?" Dawn poked me gently.

"Hey! I'm not that bad!" I protested. Dawn rolled her eyes expressively, but said nothing. The queen of tact, my daughter.

We settled Greg into the car as comfortably as possible, placing Dawn's jacket behind his head for cushioning.

"Okay, buddy, spill the beans," I said, as soon as the car reached the main highway. Dawn, in the back seat, leaned forward to hear.

"Well, it was the strangest thing I've ever seen," he said. "You know how you tend to see the same cars over and over again when you're all going the same direction on the highway? That's normal, right?"

Dawn and I nodded in unison.

"Well, there was this one guy, a real hot-shot type, in a beat up old bazou with not much in the way of a muffler, and I kept noticing him behind me. I didn't think much of it, but I noticed he kept cutting people off, diving in and out of lanes, tailgating, that sort of thing. I figured he was just having a bad testosterone day."

"Sure. I hate that. I've always believed driver's licences should be mandatory — I hate it when they let morons like that out with the rest of us."

"Right. So this guy keeps coming up behind me really close, tailgating and then backing off. I thought he was playing some elaborate game of chicken. Also, I was thinking more about the missing files at the Allan than about the local yokels you meet on this road. Then, as we were going around a curve, he came up behind me really tight, and I actually felt the nose of his car hitting the left rear bumper of mine. I have to say I panicked a bit, and I sped up. So did he."

My eyes widened. "Christ," I muttered.

"By now, I'm starting to get extremely nervous, and I'm wondering how much damage he's done, so I look back for just a second. He's this young guy, crew cut, wearing reflective aviator glasses, but the look on his face is … well, grim. His lips clamped shut, just fierce. The thought goes through my head, 'He's doing this on purpose!' but I still really can't believe it, you know?"

"Oh, yeah." I nodded emphatically. "I've been having that feeling for a few days now. It's starting to feel normal to me. If things keep up like this, I'll wind up in a permanent dissociative state, just completely numbed out."

Greg chuckled. "Exactly. So anyway, just as I glanced back, this guy gunned it, and I felt this hard crunch and a kind of grinding noise, as his car hit mine along the left side. And then I just completely lost control of the wheel. The car spun once, twice, and then I was off the road altogether. I wound up in the ditch with a very bad headache and my arm pinned against the door. The last I saw, the guy who did it was tearing off toward Ottawa. I think I lost consciousness for a while after that."

"Did you get a make and a licence number?" Dawn asked.

"The police asked me that when they got me here. No, I only know the car was old, one of those huge gas hogs from the seventies. Rusted out in places, I remember noticing that when I passed him earlier on. I think it was light blue."

"Well, what about the guy? Did he look at all familiar?" Dawn was still fixated on her conspiracy theory, apparently.

"I'm not sure," Greg said. "At one point he flashed me this smile, and I thought, 'hey, I've seen this before' — but that was right before he hit me that last time, and I haven't been able to place him."

"See Mom, I told you!" Dawn sounded excited. "There's no reason for a stranger to try a stunt like that — it has to be connected to Adam! I bet it was the same guy who killed him!"

"Dawn, he said he wasn't sure. And there's still no evidence about how Adam died. There's no point getting carried away about all this."

"Dawn could be right," Greg put in. "I just wish I could remember …" His voice was thready, and I looked sideways at him. His eyes were closed, his face white.

"Hey, I'm sorry. We're pushing you, and what you need is rest," I said. "Why don't you put the seat back and try to get some sleep? You've had a hell of a day."

We drove a while in silence, punctuated by light snoring sounds from Greg. Finally, Dawn spoke.

"Mom? Even if it was the same person who killed Adam, why would anyone do that to Greg?"

I shook my head. "Honey, I wish I knew. Maybe it was one of his patients? I can't really believe that, because most of his patients love Greg, but maybe one of them went off the deep end. It's a risk you run, in his business. Or maybe it's that road rage thing you hear about these days — some guy just decided to vent his anger on the nearest expensive, shiny car."

Dawn scowled. "That doesn't make much sense. Greg's super-polite — we just saw that. He wouldn't piss anyone off. And how would a patient know where to find him?"

I shrugged. "Well, a couple of days ago I'd have blamed Adam. But we both know where he is. And I don't believe in ghosts. Your guess is as good as mine, Dawn."

"Well, I told you my guess, and you don't believe me," Dawn retorted.

I sighed. "Let's talk about this when we get home, okay? I don't want to wake Greg up with our arguing."

Dawn sat back in her seat and closed her own eyes.

We drove in silence until we reached the outskirts of the city. I turned on the radio, trying to get some local news and weather.

"It's six o'clock in the capital," the deejay said, and I gulped, sitting up very straight.

Monday afternoon, soon to become Monday evening. Had I not invited Brent, former love of my life who still sent a certain thrill up my spine, for supper this evening? Shit. Double shit. I'd wanted to clean up the apartment, wear something nice, make something tasty yet vegetarian, preferably not tofu-based, for supper.

There is very little point in inviting former loves of one's life to dinner if one cannot fully impress upon them that one's own life has gone on in a dramatically positive direction since they left. Ignobly, I wanted to do a little posturing about the happiness and fulfillment I now enjoyed, amply demonstrating that losing Brent had not, in fact, meant losing all that was worthwhile in my life.

And now I had a bare fifteen minutes to rush home, install Greg in my bed to rest, shove the newspapers and magazines that littered the floor of the apartment into an already overstuffed cupboard, and maybe order a pizza. Vegetarian, of course, in deference to Dawn. This was not how I'd planned it, and I was not pleased.

On the other hand, when we'd been lovers, Brent

had invariably been late for our assignations. He was one of those people who believed in the physics of Star Trek — "Beam me up, Scotty!" It had always irritated me that Brent's idea of being on time was to leave his house at the exact time when he was supposed to be arriving on my doorstep. I'd expressed this concern to him often, to no avail. He'd claimed I was trying to control him, we'd fight, and he'd be twice as late the next time, just to make a point.

How ironic, I thought, that one of Brent's most irritating habits might actually buy me some time to prepare a bit more adequately for his visit. I entered the late-day Queensway traffic jam, and was forced to slow the car to a crawl. This did not improve my mood.

We pulled up in front of my apartment building at exactly six twenty-eight. I slammed the car door as I got out, waking Greg and startling Dawn, who'd been dozing in the back seat. Too bad. Just as I had feared, there was Brent, lounging nonchalantly on the front verandah, watching our arrival through half-closed brown eyes that always seemed so sleepy, yet never missed a single detail. Was that a look of smug superiority I detected on his face?

He still wore that bloody Stetson, his idea of formal wear, but at least he'd lost the snakeskin boots. I supposed I ought to feel grateful for small mercies.

18

It was all I could do to remain a gracious if some what frazzled hostess. I yelled a welcome to Brent, while I assisted Greg from the car and informed Dawn that we were home and would she please go ahead and open the front door so I could attend to our wounded friend. Dawn grumbled a bit at being wakened so unceremoniously, and wandered up the steps rubbing her stiff neck.

Brent came down the stairs, glancing from me to Greg, who leaned on my arm for support.

"If this is a bad time, I can always take a raincheck," Brent said.

"No, no, Greg is just a friend who got in an accident," I explained, concentrating all my remaining positive energy into a high-wattage smile. "How have you been, Brent? I'm glad you could come. Sorry we're late."

"I'm feeling a lot better now that I'm here." Brent wrapped his long arms around me. I fought an almost overwhelming urge to hug back and disengaged myself politely, staring pointedly at Brent's hat.

"So — where'd you park the hoss?"

Touching the brim of the Stetson, he grinned at me. "Still don't like it, huh?"

"No, no, on you it looks good." Which was true. "Listen, I'm really sorry. I'd planned to make you a wonderful meal, but Greg's accident really threw things off today. I thought we might just order a pizza, or some Chinese food. Or there's a Vietnamese place down the street that does pretty good take-out."

"I didn't come for the food. I came to see you."

"Cut it out, you're embarrassing me." I could feel myself blushing. Smiling awkwardly, I led the way into the apartment.

Inside, Dawn had scooped the newspapers and empty coffee cups and computer manuals off the living room floor. I silently blessed her, wondering where she'd managed to stash the stuff. Never mind, we'd cope with that little detail later. I'd have to remember to ask, though, or risk opening a cupboard and having a pile of junk crash down on my head.

"Brent, this is my daughter, Dawn." I draped an arm around my daughter's shoulder.

He smiled one of his heart-melting smiles, the one that could make you think you were the most wonderful thing that had ever crossed his path.

"Just as beautiful as her mother." He took her hand in his firm grip. Dawn coloured up a bit, but looked pleased.

"And this is my friend Greg," I added as Greg stumbled out of the bedroom, looking dazed and tired. "He's going to rest here for a while. Will you eat with us, Greg? I think we're going to order out."

The men shook hands and eyed one another the way men do when they think women don't see — who is this guy anyway, and what's he doing here? Like dogs circling one another in the park, unsure whether to roll over or go for the throat. The mutual once-over complete, they relaxed a little, Brent staking out a corner of the sofa and Greg excusing himself to lie down a bit before dinner.

By the time I got back from phoning in an order for pizza, Dawn was perched on the arm of a chair, chatting enthusiastically with Brent, who seemed to know everything there was to know about computers, servers and the much-vaunted Internet. I tried my best to keep up.

"What's the difference between upload and download?" I asked. "I've never really understood that. How do you decide what's up and what's down? It doesn't make any sense to me."

"Mom …" groaned Dawn.

Brent was kinder, but eventually I decided that the humiliation of being an electronic ignoramus outweighed my responsibility to contribute to the conversation. I shut up and let them carry on. The pizza arrived, and no one but me noticed. Not that I was miffed or anything — it was nice to see them getting along so well.

I set the table, deciding to depart from our usual custom of eating our dinners on our laps while watching the nightly news on television. When I returned to the living room, Dawn and Brent had disappeared to the tiny alcove that served as a study. They hunched in the bluish glow of the computer screen.

I cleared my throat.

"Excuse me, dahlings, but dinnah is served in the main dining room," I intoned.

"Mom! Can't it wait a sec? I'm just showing Brent my server," Dawn protested. "Look, see, here's the users list. It's not huge, but it's growing. And when I get more features, more people will want to join in."

"Great!" Brent said. "But we'd better get a move on. Your mom's gonna kill me if I keep you from being on time. She's got this thing about promptness."

I ignored the barb, and we trooped out to the kitchen. Greg ate with us, and the pizza was actually pretty good: lots of cheese, not too much green pepper, and the crust was thick yet not soggy. Brent produced a bottle of red wine, which added a festive touch along with the candles I lit. As we pushed away from the table, I realized I'd mellowed considerably.

Afterward, we sprawled in the living room. I put on a J.J. Cale album, and Greg repeated the story of his highway adventure to Brent.

"So you don't know anyone who might have a grudge against you?" he asked. "You're a shrink — I mean, a psychiatrist, right? What about any of your patients?"

Greg shook his head, then winced at the pain. "Can't think of anyone. And the guy looked kind of vaguely familiar, but if he'd been a patient, I'd have remembered. I'm in the dark on this one. But the police took my statement, so I guess it's all in hand."

"You're sure the guy wasn't just a real bad driver?" Brent pressed him. "I recall some pretty terrible driving along that stretch of road. You Canadians take out all your aggression when you get behind the wheel."

"I don't think so. I saw his face and he looked absolutely focused. Determined. He wanted to hit me, I could see that. I can't think why, though. Unless he thought I was someone else."

"I wondered about that too," I put in. "I mean, at the hospital, all your patients think you're next up for sainthood. And now that Adam ..." I stopped myself, and Greg gave me a warning look.

Brent narrowed his eyes, looking at each of us in turn.

"Who's Adam?" he asked.

"Just this guy. We've had some trouble with him recently. It's a long story, I'll tell you all about it some other time. And anyway, he died over the weekend. So it couldn't have been him."

Brent's eyebrows shot up so quickly that I couldn't suppress a giggle.

"No, we didn't ice him, Brent. He … that is, we don't know yet exactly how he died. The cops are still waiting for the results of the autopsy."

"Hey, I wasn't trying to accuse anyone," Brent said. "Sounds like you guys have been busy. But I'm not offended that you won't tell me about it. Not at all."

I laughed. "It's not a state secret. I will tell you, I promise. But it's just a bit — odd. I haven't completely processed it myself."

"Katy, I'm really sorry, but I think I need to lie down again," Greg interjected.

"Why don't you take Peter's bed upstairs? He's on assignment in Toronto, so I'm sure he wouldn't mind. Then you'd be able to get a good night's sleep and we can check on you now and then," I offered. "Dawn, can you take the key and open up Dad's apartment for Greg?"

They headed upstairs, and Brent smiled at me.

"You've got a wonderful girl, Katy. I'm glad things worked out for you, even if we couldn't quite get it together. Though it's never too late," he added in a low murmur.

I ignored the innuendo. "Thanks. I'm glad you got a chance to meet Dawn. We're pretty proud of her. And she seemed to like you, too. I'm a bit of a loser in the computer field."

Brent stretched his arm along the back of the couch, brushing my shoulder, which tingled alarmingly at the gentle touch. I moved away slightly, not trusting myself to respond.

Dishes. Yes, that's it, the dinner dishes needed stacking. I jumped up and busied myself with a household task I loathed and usually ignored as long as I could. Brent stood too, and followed me into the kitchen. He ran one finger down my spine, which promptly transformed into a very sweet and warm liquid. He wrapped his arms around me and nuzzled my hair with his chin.

"You're a brave man, Brent. Not too many guys get away with that, you know."

"You feeling a little skittish?" he teased. "You're like a jumpy horse — every time I get close, you dance away."

"It's just —" I began, but I was interrupted by a slamming door that announced Dawn's return. I squirmed out of Brent's embrace, though I could still feel the imprint of his arms around my waist. I severely reprimanded the part of myself that was urging me to pull him back. Forget it, Katy. It's over — you can't go back in time.

But it had felt so damn good. Hey, cut that out. You're a middle-aged single parent with a good crop of grey hairs, more than your fair share of stretch marks, and a reasonably decent life, and you have no business getting yourself involved with a man you know to be inconsistent, difficult to pin down and not particularly interested in contributing to your personal growth and autonomy. Plus, you know you can't spend ten minutes with him without arguing. You need this? Yeah, like a hole in the head.

While I argued with myself, Brent turned to Dawn.

"We were thinking it might be nice to have some ice cream for dessert," he smiled, pulling his wallet from his pocket.

He didn't need to say more; Dawn eagerly volunteered to run to the corner store for a carton of double chocolate almond marshmallow fudge deluxe, and grabbed the bill from his hand before I could object.

"Ah, *ma cherie*, at last we are alone," Brent purred as the door shut behind Dawn.

"Knock it off, Brent. Maurice Chevalier you ain't. And we've been through this already, remember? Didn't we swear off one another a number of years ago?"

He looked hurt, but said nothing, aiming his sad-puppy eyes at me. I tried again, the voice of mature responsibility.

"Come on, Brent, don't be like that. I just don't think it would be wise to get involved again. It's all water under the bridge. And neither of us was good at being close, even at the best of times. You must remember that, at least."

"You're not leaving any room for the possibility that we've changed," he countered. "What about all those fancy ideas you used to have, that people grow and mature? We're not in our twenties any more, Katy. I know I'm different now, in a lot of important ways."

"Point. But even if we've both become completely mature and self-actualized human beings in the last eighteen years, which I seriously doubt, I'm still not ready to just throw myself into your arms. There's this little thing called reconnecting. Getting to know one another. You know?"

"Okay, let's do it your way." He ruffled my hair. "I just need to know that you're willing to let me get my foot in the door."

"An unfortunate metaphor, but I'll overlook it. Can we talk about something else before Dawn comes back with the ice cream?"

Brent was unusually obliging. We talked about my work, my decision to leave the hospital, which I attributed to a disagreement with the unit's director. We talked about Brent's marriage to old what's her name, and his disappointment at never having had children, and his work as a computer nerd, for which it appeared he was now getting paid handsomely by the federal government.

We finished the ice cream, polished off a bottle of wine and I made some decaf. Dawn wandered off to work at her computer, and still Brent and I sat talking. It felt good, seriously good, and it was past midnight when I reluctantly shoved him out the door. It seemed the mature thing to do.

He was back five minutes later, having forgotten that stupid cowboy hat. This time, he pulled me to him, or I pulled him to me, it didn't matter. We hugged. I think that has to have been the longest hug in recorded history. We might have stood in the darkened vestibule for forty-five minutes, saying nothing, not moving, just pressing up close to one another and listening to each other's breathing. Neither wanted to be the first to pull away, and so it did not end.

Gradually, when our legs began to give out, we just sat down right where we were, and continued hugging, making gentle crooning noises. Brent whispered something in my ear, and it seems to me we kind of wafted into the bedroom, where we lay side by side, still pressed tightly together, unmoving, unspeaking.

There was so much to say, and it was all being said in that hug. I don't exactly remember where our clothing went, but I do remember looking at the row of geranium pots on my window ledge and watching the moon set. And in the morning he was still there, and I woke feeling his ribcage rise and fall under my cheek, and that felt right.

19

TUESDAY, AUGUST 2
Sun inconjunct Jupiter ✦
Moon square Venus, square Mars,
conjunct Saturn ✦
Mercury square Pluto ✦
Mars opposition Jupiter ✦
Jupiter square Saturn ✦

It did feel right, waking up with Brent, but I was none too certain how my daughter might take it. I rummaged under the bed for my nightgown and made straight for the kitchen, cautioning Brent to stay where he was until the coast was clear. He looked amused at my concern, but obediently lay back on the pillows, pulling the sheet up under his chin.

Dawn, always an early riser, was whirling something brownish and thick, with darker specks in it, in the blender. She barely glanced in my direction as I staggered toward the coffee machine.

"So, was your back giving you a lot of trouble last night?" she asked, all concern.

"Um, no, not really, why?"

"Oh, nothing. It's just that I woke up a couple of times. All that moaning and groaning, I thought for sure your back must have gone out again. '*Aaah, Oooowww*' — I almost came in to see if you needed help, or something."

I looked sideways at her. No trace of a smile, but then her long hair was falling forward, shielding her eyes from view.

I stood uncertainly at the counter, wondering how to broach this particular subject. Having Brent stay the night had seemed like a good idea at three a.m., and waking up with him had been delicious, but explaining his presence to Dawn might be trickier than I'd first thought. I had never brought a man home for the night before, and I felt unaccountably self-conscious. And had we really made that much noise? I stood frozen for a second, trying to think of something to say.

Then I saw her shoulders shaking. The little *pisherkeh* was laughing at me! I swatted her on the tush with the lid from the coffee cannister and her giggles got louder. I started laughing too, and soon we were hanging onto one another, nearly falling down. Finally, I wiped my eyes and leaned against the counter.

"Sweetie, I wasn't sure how to talk to you about this," I started, but Dawn interrupted.

"Mom, look. You don't have to explain. You and Dad have been divorced a long time. I never really thought much about you being with anyone else; I guess it just never occurred to me. I mean, you being with Brent is fine, he's a nice guy — I was just a little surprised, that's all. But at your age, you really should watch out for your bad back," she added.

"You were surprised?" I asked. "Oh, right, I forgot you didn't know about my sordid past. Brent and I were actually together for nearly five years before your dad and I got married, so it's not like he's some kind of one night stand."

"Well geez, now I can thank God my mother's not just some kind of tramp," Dawn said, and I took another swipe at her.

"Watch your mouth, kid," I laughed. "Though I guess you come by that honestly enough."

Brent wandered into the kitchen, drawn by our giggles, looking confused. He had never been a morning person, and the concept of two people laughing their guts out before they'd even had a shower and a cup of coffee was alien to him. I didn't bother to explain.

"Coffee's on in about five minutes," I said, but he shook his head reluctantly.

"I was supposed to be at the office fifteen minutes ago. I'm real sorry, honey, but I just have to dress and run. Can I call you tonight?"

I opened my mouth to protest, but the memory of past arguments about whether Brent spent enough time with me silenced me. I smiled, and even allowed him to kiss me on the nose.

It was just as well he had to go, as I had to run up to Peter's place to check on Greg, anyway. Dawn had looked in on him last night before bed, and he'd been sleeping peacefully. This morning he was up and about, a little stiff and favouring his injured side, but basically okay. I helped him make Peter's bed, then assisted him down the stairs.

Dawn had actually managed to ingest whatever she'd been making in the blender, and had cleaned up after herself, too. She was dressed and champing at the bit to join Sylvie. They'd arranged to go downtown to look at computer programs.

"Sure, love, see you soon." I kissed her cheek and tried to quell the nagging worry that now seemed an automatic part of letting Dawn out of my sight.

"I really think we need to talk," Greg said when I returned to the living room.

"My thoughts exactly."

"Too many things have happened in the past few days," he said. "I feel like I'm drowning in information, and none of it makes sense."

I went first. I told him about being summoned by Detective Benjamin to identify Adam, and about the uncertainty over the cause of death. I got out Flavia's e-mail and showed it to Greg, too.

"The powerful and scary father part we've already pretty much confirmed," he said when he'd read it. "But this bit about siblings who get hurt is interesting. That sort of came up when we talked to Adam in the car, didn't it? I didn't believe he'd actually had any same-age sibs, but I'm not sure if my memory is working well. Damn, I wish I could lay my hands on that file at the Allan."

"I know. It's just a bit too coincidental that it went missing, isn't it?"

"Makes you wonder. And how peculiar that right after I borrowed the phone at the main desk to let you know about the missing file, I get run off the road."

"Now who's being paranoid? Do you really think there's a connection?"

Greg picked absently at the surgical tape on his temple.

"Do you think maybe someone was listening in while you made the call?" I asked.

"I really don't know. It didn't occur to me that Adam's file would interest anyone else, so I didn't lower my voice or anything. But you have to admit it makes sense, in a macabre sort of way. If someone had hidden the file on purpose, and they heard I was determined to find it, they might want to scare me off."

"Well, what could be in that file to get anyone that excited? You could have been killed, Greg. That's pretty bloody serious."

Greg rubbed his forehead in frustration.

"I don't know. I just keep thinking there are so many connections. So many puzzle pieces that look like they all belong to the same picture, but I can't figure out how, or why."

"Wait a second." I leaped to my feet. "I almost forgot these." I ran to the kitchen, where I'd stashed the envelope in a basket of peaches on top of the fridge.

"Look, Greg. These arrived in the mail Friday, but with all the excitement that night, I forgot about them until yesterday afternoon. Do you think there's any possibility they might be connected to Adam?"

Greg put on his glasses and peered at the photos. He turned them over, then squinted at them again.

"I feel like I should know these people," he said, to himself as much as me. "Wait a sec. The older woman in the group photo, the one holding the kids — I'm pretty sure that's Mrs. Cosgrove. She looks a bit younger than when I met her, but she's got that same wistful expression. It was hard to forget."

"Are you saying one of the kids on her lap might be Adam? Who's the other one? And what about all these other people?" My mind was racing.

"Hold on, hold on," Greg cautioned. "I can't say anything for sure. Let's say I'm right, and based on a twenty year old memory I really can identify Mrs. Cosgrove in a forty year old black and white photo.

There's nothing to prove this kid is Adam. He could be her grandson, or a visiting nephew, or a neighbour's child."

I was quiet for a moment.

"But what if that is Adam? Is the little girl his sister? They look like they could be twins. They're the same age, and dressed almost exactly alike. What happened to her?"

We stared at one another. It seemed clear that the photos had come from Adam, but why? Had he wanted me to understand who he'd once been? Or to let me know that his visions of someone hurting a child had been real, not his own private delusions? Why entrust me with this information? He'd felt I was keeping the details of his chart from him, and he really had no reason to trust me.

"I hate to sound like the private dick in a grade-C whodunnit, but Adam obviously put these in my mailbox before he kidnapped Dawn. Did he know he might die that night? I can't really imagine why he'd give me something so personal, especially when he thought I was holding out on him. But if he knew he was going to die, this kind of points toward suicide, doesn't it?"

"Katy, I think it's almost impossible to guess what went on in his mind. He was so fearful by the time we met him, he probably couldn't have explained what made him give you the pictures. But they sure call the no-sibling theory into question, don't they?"

"They call a lot of things into question. I think we've been making a lot of false assumptions about Adam. All we could see the other night was a guy who'd been driven nuts by his own pain. We don't know where that came from, or why he was so fanatical about finding the truth. Whatever it was, it must have been damn powerful, because talking about it ran counter to every instinct in his body. Maybe giving me the pictures was his way of passing the torch."

"Like saying he couldn't go any further? You could be right. I think our best bet now is to turn these over to the police, then hope my clerk at the Allan finds Adam's file. Maybe that'll tell us something."

Greg drained his coffee mug and stood up. He'd lost his wobble, but he was still pale.

"I'm going to call the office and let them know I'm running late," he said. "And I hope Marcel will be done with the car soon. Mind if I use your phone?"

"Sure. You know where it is. I'm just going to check something on the computer."

It was time to follow Flavia's advice: check out what the planets had to say about the night Adam died.

20

I called up Adam's chart first, then pressed a couple of buttons to display the planets as they'd appeared Friday night. I wasn't surprised to see transiting Saturn squaring Adam's Mars — here was his frustration, his feeling that no matter which way he turned, he'd be thwarted by someone or something bigger than himself. This would have pumped up his already overloaded nervous system to the bursting point. It was a slow-building transit that he would have experienced as a mounting pressure, resulting in an inevitable explosion.

On the night he died, transiting Mars had been squaring off against Adam's Uranus/Mars conjunction. He'd have felt impelled to seek freedom, no matter what the cost. Both transits showed Adam in danger's way, whether through his own recklessness and nervous energy, or through forces beyond his control. Maybe an accident involving electricity, or machinery of some kind? Whatever it was, there'd been too much energy flowing through his body.

Next, I looked at Adam's progressed chart. Once again, a Mars connection: impetuous, angry Mars squared Adam's Sun, showing a time of conflict with authority. Angry confrontations, injury and physical danger. In fact, with the progressed Sun opposing Pluto, Adam's choices had boiled down to this: dominate, or be dominated.

This did not look like the chart of a person who'd committed suicide. Rather, Adam had tried to break free of something, and it had cost him his life. Who had he been defying? He'd been a recluse, rarely speaking to anyone. What authorities could possibly have had it in for him?

Yet he'd kept insisting that "they" would not let him speak, that "they" controlled his thoughts and actions. The father? But Peter had said the father was dead. Still, he hadn't thrown himself into the Canal — he'd been dead when his body hit those greeny-brown waters. Someone else must have been present at his death, hauling his body all the way from Green's Creek into town. That certainly seemed to argue for a non-accidental death.

"Katy?"

Greg came into the room, holding the phone.

"There's a Detective Benjamin on the phone, wants to speak to you."

I grabbed the receiver. Maybe Benjamin wanted to tell me how Adam had died.

"Yes?"

"Ms. Klein, Detective Benjamin here. I was wondering if you'd mind coming down to the station this morning. I've got a few more questions to ask you."

"Well, I have a few questions for you, too." I stopped myself. No point antagonizing him unnecessarily. "That is — is there any word yet on how Adam — I mean, Mr. Cosgrove, died?"

"I really can't discuss that right now. But can I expect you here in an hour or so?"

He sounded official, cold; once again, I felt unaccountably guilty. What kind of questions could he have? Did he think I'd killed Adam?

"Oh, and I was wondering if you know where I could find Dr. Chisholm?" Benjamin added. "We called his office and they said he wouldn't be in today."

"He's right here. Look, Detective Benjamin, you don't think we — I mean, we really didn't have anything to do with Adam dying, you know." My words sounded lame, false to my own ears.

"So far, this is just an investigation of a suspicious death, not a murder," Benjamin said. "You're not being accused of anything, Ms. Klein. Now, may I speak to Dr. Chisholm?"

Wordlessly, I handed the phone to Greg.

"Yes, yes of course," Greg was saying. "Sure, if I can help you at all, I will. Right. See you then."

How could he sound so damn mellow? I followed him into the living room.

"Do you think he thinks we killed Adam?" I blurted.

Greg looked at me quizzically. "Why would he think that? It's just that we were the last people to see him alive, and the police need to cover all the bases. Let's just meet this Benjamin fellow, answer his questions, and I'm sure he'll be satisfied. Oh, and we should remember the photos. They might be important."

"Do we have to? I feel like Adam left them to me. Like they were a gift, or something."

"I think that would count as withholding evidence, Katy. I know you feel a sense of personal responsibility about Adam, but what happened wasn't your fault. Yes, he gave the pictures to you, but if they can shed some light on what happened, don't you think it's better to give them over?"

"Fine." I avoided his eyes. "But Greg—the police only see Adam as a body. He's a corpse they fished out of the Canal, nothing more. I feel like I was a witness to some of his pain, and I don't want to turn my back on him, now that he's dead. And these pictures are all that's left of his life. I don't want them rotting in some police file."

"But you're going to give them up, right?"

"Right," I said, half-meaning it.

The police station was bustling with activity. Phones jangled and officers yelled to one another over the partitions on the floor where Benjamin worked. He ushered Greg and me into his cubicle, his expression as neutral as it had been a few days ago.

"Thanks for coming. A few questions have come up about Mr. Cosgrove's death, and we're hoping you can fill us in a bit more on what happened that night."

"Anything we can do to help."

Benjamin actually cracked a smile. "To start with," he consulted his notes, "Ms. Klein stated you arrived in the parking lot near the sewage treatment plant at around midnight?"

Greg and I exchanged glances. We hadn't exactly been timing ourselves that night.

"I think so," I said. "I got home from dinner at my parent's house at around eleven-fifteen, I think. I couldn't find Dawn anywhere, so I called her best friend's house, and she wasn't there. I was getting really scared, so I called the police. That must have been around eleven-thirty. The person who answered basically brushed me off, so I called Greg, and he got to my place about ten minutes later, so that would be eleven-forty or so."

I retraced that horrible night. It all sounded so routine, so clinical.

"Yeah, and just after I got there, Adam called to tell us he had Dawn," Greg added. "I'd guess it took us maybe fifteen minutes to get from Katy's apartment in Centretown to the treatment plant, so that would put us there at around midnight."

Benjamin nodded, taking notes. Then, ponderously, he scratched his large, shaggy head and looked directly at me. I could not read his expression.

"So you'd estimate that Mr. Cosgrove sat in your vehicle, uh, chatting with you, for how long?"

I blinked, trying to recall. It had felt simultaneously like six hours and like two minutes. I looked at Greg.

"I'd guess we talked for maybe half an hour," he said.

"And then what? He just jumped up and ran off into the woods?"

Benjamin sounded decidedly sceptical. My hands were sweating.

"That's right," Greg said. "We think he might have been scared off by the headlights of the police car that came by."

"Well now, see, that's the funny thing," Benjamin said. "We have absolutely no record of any police vehicle being in that area in that time frame. Yet Ms. Klein told me a police officer stopped to speak with you?"

"That's right," Greg said, apparently unfazed. "A man in a police uniform, carrying a flashlight, got out of his car, walked toward us and suggested we move along. He was just about to leave when Katy called him back and told him what had happened with Adam and Dawn. He wrote it all down, told her she didn't need to bother coming in to make a statement. Then he radioed headquarters for a K-9 unit or something, to search the woods for Adam. That's when we left."

Benjamin looked impassive. "There's no report of a request for the K-9 unit that night," he said. "And no reports were filed about any kidnapping."

"Is it possible he was with the RCMP?" I asked. "I thought the Rockcliffe Parkway was patrolled by the Mounties?" That must be it. I felt very pleased at my own cleverness, but Benjamin's expression did not change.

"Afraid not. We cross-checked with the RCMP, and they were unable to place any officer in that location at that time. Was the car marked with anything identifying it as a police vehicle?"

Greg and I shook our heads in unison.

"I'm sorry, but we really weren't paying close attention," Greg said. "We did have a few other things on our minds."

"You can't provide anything that'll convince me the person you saw was a police officer?" Benjamin ignored Greg's sarcasm.

"We're trying to tell you what happened," I said peevishly. "Adam ran off, the cop or whoever he was told us to leave, I told him what had happened, he radioed for the dogs and we left. That's all there is to it."

"Well, I'm going to have to assume you believe what you're telling me," Benjamin said. "But I have to tell you, this inconsistency doesn't make either of you look good."

"So — what are you saying?" I tried to sound confident. "Are you accusing us of something? Besides lying, that is?"

"I told you, Ms. Klein, we're not yet ready to lay charges in this case. I'll let you know the minute we are, how's that?"

My stomach lurched and cold sweat broke out on my back, but I said nothing.

Benjamin gave me a sharp glance, then changed the subject.

"What can you tell me about Mr. Cosgrove's state of health, Dr. Chisholm?"

Greg looked puzzled. "Not much, I'm afraid. I hadn't seen Adam as a patient in about twenty years, so I really couldn't say anything about that. Why?"

"Well, the results of the autopsy came in yesterday and it seems that the cause of death was a massive coronary." Benjamin read from a typed sheet he had pulled from a stack on his desk. "Ventricular fibrillation, leading to cardiac arrest, it says here. I was wondering if you knew about any pre-existing conditions."

"I was his psychiatrist, not his personal physician," Greg said. "And I was involved with his case a long time ago. But no, at that time I wasn't aware of anything."

"But if he had a heart attack," I said, "how did he wind up floating in the Canal?"

"That's exactly what we're trying to determine, Ms. Klein." Benjamin looked at me over his reading glasses, as though I were a backward child. "Unless he happened to have been walking along the edge of the Canal at the time of his heart attack, there really isn't any way he could have placed himself in the water, now is there?"

I gave him a dirty look, but he'd turned back to Greg.

"What about Mr. Cosgrove's … um, sexual life?"

"What about it?"

"Well, do you know if he had any … unusual preferences?"

"I told you, I knew him twenty years ago. At the time, it didn't seem likely to me that he'd ever had any sexual experience, so I really can't answer for his present-day activities."

"Why?" I asked.

Benjamin looked down and flipped back in his notes. Then he read: "Subject's back and shoulders show evidence of massive scarring … scar tissue both recent and distant … lacerations consistent with intentional infliction by subject or persons unknown."

"What does that mean?" I asked, puzzled.

"Looks like he was into S and M stuff. You know — whips and so on. You being a psychiatrist, Dr. Chisholm, I figure this kind of thing is familiar territory, right? I just wondered if you knew anything about it."

Greg just shrugged. "Nope. Sorry."

Benjamin sighed and closed his notebook, and we got up to leave.

21

Detective Benjamin wasn't about to arrest us for the murder of Adam Cosgrove, but I had the distinct impression he was having trouble believing our version of events. Well, join the club, I thought. He did suggest that if we could think of any further details, we should let him know at once, and his tone seemed to imply that we knew more than we were letting on. I wish.

Outside the police station, Greg hailed a taxi. His Audi was not ready yet, as even Marcel the Miraculous could not conjure up entire panels out of thin air. But there was a loaner awaiting him at the garage and Greg wanted to pick it up.

The taxi driver who took us from the cop shop to Marcel's place in the east end seemed to be having a bad day. Or perhaps he had just never been told that correct driving procedure does not include planting one foot on the gas and one on the brake, and alternating them at random intervals. We lurched and squealed across town, windows wide open, air conditioner and radio blasting.

Even the normally imperturbable Greg looked alarmed. He held his injured shoulder with his free hand to protect it from the worst of the jolts as we tried to discuss our meeting with Benjamin.

"So he died of natural causes?" I asked.

"Looks like it," he said. "Although it's possible to be provoked into a coronary, you know."

"What do you mean, provoked? Like someone could force you to have a heart attack?"

"Not exactly. But there are plenty of recorded instances of people just dropping dead of shock, fear, that kind of thing. Basically, the massive release of adrenaline just overloads the heart, and the person collapses."

"Do you think Adam was scared to death? Does that mean someone deliberately frightened him, or do you think he was just so petrified after we talked to him that he blew a gasket?"

"I don't think anything. I'm just saying it's a possibility. We didn't see anything, so how can we possibly know?"

We sat in silence for the rest of the ride. Well, perhaps not silence — the roar of the air conditioner and squeal of brakes competed with Led Zeppelin for dominance over our eardrums. I tried to focus on not throwing up until the Cab Driver from Hell stopped the car and demanded to be paid for causing us irreparable orthopaedic and middle ear damage. Greg withheld the tip and the driver actually managed to conjure up a look of injured surprise. However, our glares sent him hastily on his way.

Marcel galloped out of his garage to greet us. He wore a forest-green coverall over a clean shirt and tie, and his hair had that little-dab'll-do-ya look of a man who had not yet discovered the Dry Look. He wore thick horn-rimmed glasses, the better to compute your bill, my dear.

"*Dr. Chisholm!*" he boomed, approaching Greg and grasping his free hand in his own. "*So good to see you, Dr. Chisholm! Your car, such a beautiful car, we fix her up so you can never tell she even had a scratch!*"

I resisted the impulse to cover my ears.

"*I show you something, Dr. Chisholm,*" Marcel bellowed. "*You come with me, I want you to see something. We find it in the back seat while we're taking your car apart. We save it for you. Maybe you lose it awhile ago?*"

He dragged Greg into the office and I followed at a safe distance. From a locked cabinet, Marcel produced a small packet, wrapped in wrinkled, stained brown paper. It was tied together with a length of grimy string.

"Thanks, Marcel, I guess I must have lost that."

Greg took the package from him, turning it over in his hands.

"Can you hang onto this for me, Katy? I need to go over a few things with Marcel. Thanks."

I took the package and tucked it into my purse. A few minutes later, Greg emerged from Marcel's office, holding the keys to his loaner. We drove to his apartment, a short distance from Marcel's garage. This was convenient, considering the intimate ongoing relationship between Marcel and Greg's Audi.

I offered to drive, but Greg was chafing to get behind the wheel again. Despite his sling, he managed fairly well and I didn't press the issue. Instead, I took control of the stereo, ditching the classical music station in favour of Wilson Pickett.

Greg's two red-point Siamese cats, Gemini and Ezekiel, greeted us at the door, rubbing up against his legs affectionately, half-purring and half-meowing, urging him into the kitchen to feed them, feed them, feed them. While the kitties happily chowed down, Greg and I retired to his leather-upholstered sofa, the former cloth-upholstered one having succumbed to the Evil Shredders of Doom some time ago.

"Do you have the package?" he asked.

I dug it out of my purse.

"Thanks. I wonder what it is?"

"You mean you don't know? I assumed it was something you'd lost."

"No, no. Never seen it before," he muttered, fumbling with the string that held it closed. He untied it, spread open the paper and revealed a neat little stack of printed documents. On top of the lot was Adam Cosgrove's birth certificate.

"Oh my God," I breathed.

Greg started flipping through the rest of the papers. There was the birth certificate, and another for a child known as Arianna Cosgrove, born on the same day, forty-five minutes later. The twin sister. Adam hadn't been making it up.

There were also papers, in French, that seemed to indicate that both Adam and Arianna had been adopted at the age of one week, by a Mr. Julian Cosgrove and his wife, Micheline, residing in the Town of Mount Royal, Province of Quebec.

"Look, it says on the birth certificate that the mother was a woman named Debby Landreth," Greg said. "Father unknown. She gave up her parental rights when the kids were born."

"She was young." Seventeen when she gave birth to Adam and his sister, which would make her somewhere in her late sixties by now. I wondered what had become of her. "So this must be the twin sister in the pictures Adam gave me."

Greg gave me a hard look. "You never did turn those in, did you?"

"Well, Benjamin made me forget about them. He kept insinuating we were lying, and I was so busy defending myself that I forgot. He can just wait a little longer."

Greg shook his head, but let the subject drop. "Look. Here are a couple of news articles about Julian and Micheline Cosgrove. In this one, he's reported for slapping her around in a restaurant."

"Right. Of course!" I exclaimed. "I knew that! Peter told me, but in all the confusion, I forgot to tell you. He said Julian was involved in a whole whack of financial deals, and that he'd been arrested two or three times for assaulting the missus. Got off because she wouldn't testify."

Greg frowned. "Katy, do you think it's possible that old Julian killed that little girl? Is that what Adam remembered?"

He spoke very quietly, not wanting to jump to any conclusions.

"Not only possible, but likely," I said. "Adam kept going on about 'the father', didn't he? And Peter told me Julian died in the spring. When an abusive parent dies, the kids often start having flashbacks, right?"

Greg nodded. "Sure. Kids dissociate all the time — maybe it was too scary for Adam to acknowledge that the person he was supposed to trust to love and care for him had actually killed his own sister."

"Right! So he forgets all about it, pushes it into the back of his mind. It's out of conscious awareness, but it never really goes away. Until Dad is gone. Adam is safe, and the memories he's held back so long start to poke their way up to the surface of his mind. Only they don't make sense to him, because he's cut himself off from them so completely."

"Exactly. And if the father knew that Adam had witnessed the murder, maybe he threatened him — controlled and terrorized him. Convinced him that if he ever told, he'd be found out and punished."

"If Adam carried that around with him all his life, it's no wonder that talking about it made him feel he was about to die. Do you think that's it, Greg? He basically just scared himself to death? He'd broken silence after all these years, and maybe he thought his father would find out about it and punish him."

"Maybe. But it doesn't explain one crucial factor: how did he end up in the Canal?"

"Aaargh." I held my head, groaning in frustration. "Greg, what have we got ourselves into? I feel like I know just enough to scare me, but not enough to figure out what the hell is going on!"

But Greg wasn't paying attention. He had reached the bottom of the packet of papers. He stared incredulously at a scrap of paper with a key taped to it. An address was printed on the paper, in crabbed block letters. It was an apartment on Durocher Street, in the middle of Montreal's student ghetto.

"He wanted us to go to his apartment," Greg said, more to himself than to me. "He wants us to find his answers for him. Katy, we need to go back to Montreal."

"Hey, hold on a second," I protested. "You don't know that. He might have just dropped the package in your car when he was panicking, trying to get away. And even if he did leave it on purpose, what are we supposed to be looking for?"

Greg shot me an exasperated look. "You're the one

who keeps saying we owe it to him to get to the bottom of things, aren't you?"

"Yeah, well this is different. We're not private eyes, Greg. And I don't like the idea of rushing off to Montreal to dig around in a dead person's apartment." Especially not Adam's apartment, I thought. "Besides, shouldn't we be handing this stuff over to the police?"

"Aw, come on. It's just a daytrip to Montreal. We check out the apartment, satisfy ourselves there's nothing there, and get back here by bedtime. I promise: after that we'll pass everything over to Benjamin and go back to being good little law-abiding citizens, okay?"

"I can't just run off to Montreal, you know. I've got a business to run, and I can't leave Dawn here by herself."

"You're really scared, aren't you?" Greg sounded surprised. "We're not doing anything illegal, Katy. Adam left us the key, and the address, and a bunch of stuff that tells me he wanted us to find out what happened, even if he couldn't. I can't turn my back on that kind of request, and I didn't think you'd be able to, either."

I looked away, unexpected tears filling my eyes. He was right. I was scared. And in the past, I'd let my fear rule me; I'd let it push me out of a profession I'd loved. I'd let it silence me. I couldn't do that, not again.

"Fine, we're on our way." I met Greg's challenging eye. "Let me call Dawn. I'll take her over to my parents for the day — she'll be okay there."

It took eleven rings for Dawn to answer the phone. She sounded distracted.

"It's happening again, Mom," she complained. "When I check the logs, I get this phone number that makes no sense. The person has logged off, but never logged on. When I call the number, the receiver gets picked up, then put down again. So it's not a dedicated modem line, it's someone's voice line. All I can think is that I've got someone breaking into the computer through my server!"

"Let's talk about this in a few minutes, okay? Greg and I are going to drop you off at your grandparents' house, and you can tell me all your stories of cyber-espionage while we drive there. Ten minutes, okay?"

I hung up.

"What cyber-espionage?" Greg looked curious, and I repeated what Dawn had said.

"What program is she using?"

"I forget. Recluse, Remnant, something with an 'R'. No, it's Rebel. She says it's a hacked version of something or another, I didn't get all of it."

"That can be dangerous, you know. Hacked programs can be hacked. That means anyone can get into your computer and poke around. In fact, what I'd say is that someone went in, then erased the master log on their way out. The only thing they couldn't get rid of would be the record of themselves hanging up. Have any of your files been tampered with?"

"I haven't noticed. But that's where I keep my client records, and I'm not keen on having anyone hacking around with them." Client records. Adam's client records. An electric current went through me. "Mission Control, we have a problem," I said. "Greg, I have all my notes about Adam on that computer. Do you think … ?"

We bolted for the car and this time I drove, negotiating the streets back to my place in record time. I braked with a screech and we vaulted out of the car, slamming the doors behind us, to the chagrin of an elderly neighbour out walking her Shi Tzu.

In the apartment, Dawn was still in front of the computer, scowling at the screen.

"Dawn, Greg says you could be right: it is possible someone could be breaking into our computer. Do you mind if he has a look, just to check that out?"

Sighing, Dawn rose from her chair. With a sweeping bow, she gestured to Greg to sit down.

"Please, be my guest," she said. "I've been trying for the past hour to figure it out, and Billy the Nerd isn't home to help."

Greg sat down and his long fingers flew across the keyboard. He grunted a couple of times, then turned, looking grave.

"Are Adam's files stored in 'astrol.rec'?" he asked.

I nodded. "That's the directory where I keep current records. When I'm done with them, they get stored to a floppy disk, but while they're current, it's a lot easier to keep them on the hard drive."

"When did you last enter Adam's file?"

I thought. "This morning, while you were making your phone calls. I was doing some work on transits and progressions for the night he died."

"Not, say, at about one this afternoon?"

"Of course not. You know we've been running around all morning, and it's three-thirty now."

"Dawn? Would you have any reason to go into your mother's stuff?"

Dawn shook her head, tears forming in her eyes. "Mom is a bear about client confidentiality. I never touch her files. And now I've let someone else get into them. This is awful."

I put a comforting hand on her shoulder. "Don't worry, I know this isn't your fault. But I think we should disconnect your system for now, okay?"

Dawn nodded miserably.

"But Mom, why would anyone want to look at Adam's chart? I mean, no offense, but you're an astrologer. Anything in there is just going to be based on his chart — not on real life. You know what I mean, right? Most people would just say it was crap. Why would someone go to all this trouble?"

"I don't know," I said. "But Adam did tell me a few things about himself, and they're all in that file. Plus, I keep a record of my impressions — that might be of interest, I guess."

Greg switched off the computer, and he and Dawn went out to the car, leaving me to lock up. On impulse, I ran back to the computer, booted up, re-entered my directory, saved all the data from Adam's file onto a floppy and put it in my purse. I wasn't about to take any chances.

22

Dawn protested vehemently at the idea of being dropped off at her grandparents' house while we gallivanted off to Montreal without her.

"This just isn't fair," she raged. "I'm in this, just as much as the two of you are. You think just because I'm young, I'm going to get in the way, or something. Well, I'm not. And I have just as much right to know what happened to Adam as you do, you know!"

"Dawn, listen. I don't know for sure that we're even going to find anything. We could be going all that way for nothing. And you've already been placed in enough danger as it is — I'd feel a lot happier knowing you were at Zayde and Sabte's place."

"Well, what about you? How do you think I'll feel if the guy who killed Adam gets you, too? I'd practically be an orphan!" Her eyes filled with tears.

"Dawn ..." I tried to marshall an effective counterargument, but no words of motherly wisdom came to mind. "Oh, for God's sake, fine. It's not like we're doing anything really dangerous — right, Greg?"

"Of course not. If it were dangerous, we'd let the cops handle it. But Dawn, it's more likely to be kind of a boring trip. Are you sure you don't want to just do what your mother suggested?"

Dawn shook her head emphatically. "No way. I care about what happened to Adam, too. I'm going with you." And so it was settled.

The sky was beginning to cloud over by the time we crossed the Quebec border, wispy high clouds giving way to thicker grey ones that threatened rain by nightfall. We passed the town of Rigaud, then sped into the beginnings of urban sprawl that stretch out from Montreal's downtown core like the tentacles of a large, ugly octopus. Flattened futuristic glass and concrete monstrosities blighted the otherwise pleasant landscape. They might have been randomly dropped there as some sort of hideous joke by a cackling industrialist, now off enjoying his tax-free booty in more temperate climes.

Presently we could see the mountain that rises up in the centre of the city, an extinct volcano for which the place was named — Mount Royal. As we got closer, St. Joseph's Oratory became visible, clinging to the side of the mountain, a testament to the city's large Catholic population.

We merged into afternoon traffic on the Decarie Expressway, heading for the part of the city that lies between the mountain and the St. Lawrence River. Though it is a thousand miles inland of the Atlantic, Montreal is actually a port city, a dropping-off point for ocean-going freighters and tankers that wend their way into the heart of the continent via the navigable river. Here, they exchange cargo with the long, flat lakers, ships designed to ply the inland waters of the Great Lakes.

Durocher Street, where Adam had lived, runs south

from the Royal Victoria Hospital, just east of the McGill University campus. The address in Adam's packet led us to a nondescript three-storey brick building, built in typical Montreal style: black wrought-iron staircases leading directly from the sidewalk to the apartment in question.

No shared hallways reeking of cooked cabbage here. Rather, people regularly slipped on the icy outdoor staircases during the long, bitter winters. You pays yer money and takes yer chances, I thought. Adam's apartment was in the basement, as I might have guessed. For a person so paranoid and nervous, living sandwiched between two apartments would have been intolerable: too many dangerous opportunities for people to watch, listen, hear his thoughts, monitor his every move.

We trooped down the narrow stairway into a dank concrete hole. Greg fumbled in his pocket for the key and let us into the apartment.

"Are you sure this is the right place?" Dawn whispered. "It looks empty."

"No, no," I said. "It's not completely empty. Look."

Bleached white sheets covered all the windows, tacked neatly into place with heavy duty staples. The late afternoon light filtered into the place timidly, providing only enough illumination to allow us to enter without tripping over the doorsill. There wasn't much furniture. There was a narrow slab of plywood, supported on all four corners by green plastic milk crates. A single sheet and a thin grey blanket were neatly folded at the foot of the bed. No pillow was in evidence. No chairs, no carpets, no tables. Adam must have lived the life of an ascetic.

On every wall, crucifixes had been hung — solid

brass, each perhaps a foot and a half long by a foot wide. On each cross, there hung a despondent-looking Jesus, his face angled toward the floor, eyes rolled up toward heaven. His hands and feet were pierced realistically with brass nails, and dribbles of brass blood trickled from them. Each crucifix was decorated with a small piece of plaited palm frond.

The only other decoration was a small white marble altar, placed in a corner. The altar had been lovingly tended, and although Adam had been gone some time, surprisingly little dust had accumulated on its surface. A narrow band of crimson cloth had been laid across the top. A small brass bowl, a rosary and a tiny crucifix were laid out neatly, along with a bible, bound in matching red velvet. A glass vase contained a spray of flowers, now wilted beyond recognition.

"What's that thing, Mom?" Dawn pointed to a nasty-looking whip, its handle covered in braided leather, a cluster of knotted leather strips forming the business end. The knots were crusted in black, sticky tar. I fingered one gingerly, then dropped it as though it had burned me.

"It's blood!" I yelped. "Greg, take a look at this."

He stood next to me, staring in silence at the blood-encrusted lash.

"Yikes. This must be what Benjamin was talking about."

"What? What do you mean?" Dawn looked from Greg to me, her eyes wide.

"Well, it looks as though Adam was in the habit of punishing himself," I said carefully. "Detective Benjamin asked us about some scars he had. That's all."

"Why would he do that? That doesn't make sense," Dawn persisted.

"I don't know. I've read about religious people — not now, but a long time ago — who did this. They thought it would purge them of evil. Make God love them more. Something like that. Maybe that's what Adam thought, too."

"It's not uncommon for people who've been abused as kids to hurt themselves," Greg added. "It's like the emotional pain builds up inside, and the physical pain seems to let it out. If the person was a bit of a religious nut —"

"This is sickening." My stomach heaved, and tears burned my eyes. "Let's get out of here."

"No, wait," Dawn said. "We haven't checked out the kitchen and bathroom yet."

"Do it fast," I said. "I can't take much more of this."

Dawn wandered off to the kitchen, and I heard her rummaging around briefly. Then, "Mom? Greg? You should take a look at this."

The kitchen conformed to the apartment's minimalist decorating scheme: a single plate, a fork, a knife and spoon were arranged neatly on the counter. A small pot and frying pan had been washed and left to dry on a meagre square of cloth on the counter. There was no sign of any food.

From the drawer under the stove, Dawn had pulled out a shoe box filled with paper. She handed it to me and we carried it into the other room. Carefully, Greg pulled back a makeshift curtain to allow a little more light in. Clouds covered the sky completely now and the sun was low on the horizon, so the only illumination was a dull, smouldering grey light, filtered through dust-caked windows.

We knelt on the polished hardwood floor, forming a silent semi-circle around the shoe box. No one wanted to be the first to disturb its contents.

"It feels like he could be coming home any time, doesn't it?" Greg said.

I nodded. "I have this sense that I shouldn't be touching anything. It's like this holy shrine that he left, and it would be sacrilegious or something."

"Well, he wanted us to dig around. He practically said so, didn't he?" Dawn pulled some papers out of the box. "Here's his lease. Looks like he paid a year in advance, to Mme Pauline Dufour. She lives upstairs, it looks like."

There was also a will, made out in the name of Julian Reynolds Cosgrove, businessman, of the City of Montreal, Province of Quebec. I riffled through it quickly.

"Look," I pointed out. "It says Adam, as the only living heir of Mr. Cosgrove, has been receiving a stipend of ten thousand dollars per year, paid to him during Mr. Cosgrove's lifetime. Then, when his father died, he was to receive the balance Peter told us about. Except he gets it in chunks. Looks like his father was worried about him handling all that cash at once."

"Ten thousand a year? That's not a lot," Greg said.

"Well, it doesn't look like he was a big spender," I said, eyeing the nearly-bare room.

"Mom, Greg — what's Modecate?" Dawn asked.

"It's the brand name of a long-acting injectable antipsychotic drug," I said. "Fluphenazine decanoate. Why?"

"It says here that a condition of Adam's continuing to receive his allowance and collect the inheritance from his dad is that he continue in the Modecate program at the Allan Memorial Institute. I just wondered what that meant?"

Greg sucked in his breath and leaned an elbow on the marble altar.

"Basically, it means that Adam was going to the Allan once every two or three weeks to receive a needle containing a long-acting drug to keep his delusions and paranoia under control. If that's true, it means he was a current patient up there, at least until this past spring, when his father died."

"And if *that's* true," I added, "it means his file at the Allan should be current, not archived at all. Something stinks here, Greg."

He nodded. "It should be there, all right. It's like no one wanted any trace of Adam to exist there. Weird."

Dawn had pulled another piece of paper out of the shoe box. It was a letter, scrawled in pencil on a worn piece of paper that seemed to have been torn out of a child's lined notebook. The paper looked as though it had been opened and refolded many times. I read aloud:

Mon cher Adam:

I write to give you my best love and to hope for you to be living the best life you can live. I have not always seen what I should have been seeing, and I have not done things as they should have been done, but you know that I am always with you and you are in my heart. I know you will take care of these. Guard them with all your care. We will meet again in heaven. Pray always.

Avec mes meilleurs sentiments, Maman.

It was dated about eighteen years ago.

"Wow — his mother sounds so sad," Dawn said. "I wonder what she wanted him to look after so carefully? There's not much around here, that's for sure."

"What about all these crosses? They don't look cheap," I guessed. "That must be it. But there's something odd about the tone of this letter. Why would his mother 'hope for him to be living the best life he could live'? It sounds as if they were separated, or not speaking to one another."

"Right," Dawn said. "Saying they'll meet in heaven — like they won't meet again on earth? Maybe she was dying."

"I know what she wanted him to look after." Greg's voice was shaky. "She was talking about this."

Dawn and I turned to see where he was pointing. He had been leaning back against the altar, and his weight had shifted the top slab slightly. Pushing the slab aside, we found that the little marble shrine was actually a carved box, its insides hollowed into smooth whiteness.

It was hard to see in the gloomy half-light, but what I did see sent a jolt of dread through me. Bones: tiny, bleached white and fragile-looking.

"What're these from?" Dawn asked. "A dog, maybe?"

"No," I said. "Look there. A skull. It's human. This is — this was a child." Hauling myself to my feet, I stumbled from the room, retching. Dawn was not far behind me.

23

"Okay, this is the part where we bow out and let the cops take over," Greg said. "I don't know how these bones got here, and I don't know whose they are, but we're way over our heads here."

"No shit, Sherlock." I'd finished throwing up, but I still didn't want to sit too close to the cache of bones. I perched on the edge of Adam's bed, and Dawn sat glued to my side, pale and still. I kept a protective arm around her shoulders.

"I say we call Detective Benjamin from here and let his guys come in and pick up the whole thing. And then we leave and don't look back," I said.

"There's no phone here. And anyway, I was thinking of taking these back with us," Greg began, but the look on my face stopped him.

"Are you nuts?" I screeched. "Number one, I am not moving that box in any way, shape or form. We've disturbed it quite enough as it is. And number two, there is no way in hell I'm riding back to Ottawa with some poor kid's remains in the car. We are going home now, and we are going straight to the cops to let them know what we've found, and then we are washing our hands of this whole stinking business."

Greg conceded, reluctantly. We replaced the lid on the altar, smoothed the crimson runner back into place, lowered the sheet on the window and left, carrying only the shoe box with its hoard of documents. As we trooped up the stairs, though, I had an idea.

"You guys go ahead. I'll meet you at the car." I knocked on the door of the ground floor apartment. There was no answer immediately, but just as I turned to leave, the door opened a crack and an elderly woman peered out, blue eyes glinting sharply.

"*Oui*?" she said in a high voice.

Shit. I understand a smattering of French, but my feeble attempts to communicate have been known to provoke laughter in some circles. Like people who actually do speak French, for instance. But I'd knocked on the door; I had to follow through.

"*Bonjour, est-ce que vous êtes Madame Dufour*?"

"Oh, yes, dear." Mercifully, she switched to unaccented English. "What can I do for you? Are you collecting for the food bank?"

"You speak English! I thought — I mean, your name ..."

She smiled and bobbed her head like a sparrow. "Oh, I'm definitely *une anglaise*," she laughed. "But when I married Monsieur Dufour, God bless him, I learned to speak French. One needs it, living in this city, don't you find?"

I smiled agreement. "I'm a friend of Adam Cosgrove's. I haven't seen him for some time, and I was wondering if you might know where he is?" The lie flowed easily off my lips. Too easily, perhaps.

Mme Dufour closed the door for a moment, pulled the chain back and opened it again, inviting me into her apartment. Its layout was identical to the one downstairs, but the resemblance ended there.

This apartment was crammed with overstuffed furniture, doilies, cross-stitched samplers, photos in perfect brass frames and about a ton of that cranberry-coloured glass much beloved of ladies of a certain age. The smell was familiar — a kind of faint, dusty perfume that goes with sachets, underwear washed carefully by hand and pinned up over the bathtub to drip dry. The effect was cosy, bordering on claustrophobic.

"Please, dear, do sit down," Pauline Dufour said. "I've been worried sick about that poor boy. He almost never leaves his apartment, except once a week to get food, and then of course his visits to the doctor, but I haven't seen him, goodness, almost since the middle of June. He usually picks up my papers for me at the supermarket. I like to keep up, you know."

I nodded. "Adam said you were his landlady, and I was just wondering if he ever spoke to you about where he was going? I mean, when he left in June."

"Oh, no, dear. He kept to himself. But when he didn't come back, I began to worry, you know, because he's always been as regular as clockwork. Monday evenings, as soon as the sun sets, he goes out for his food and my papers. Then, every other Friday morning, the car comes to take him to his doctor. He told me once that the doctor helps him control his temper, you know. Not that I would ever think of him as having any kind of a temper at all — he was always so sweet-natured and quiet, just a lovely boy. A little lonely, perhaps, but then aren't we all?"

She peered at me for affirmation. I nodded again.

"The car?" I prompted. "You said a car would come to get him?"

"Oh yes. That poor boy's father takes such special

care of him. Every two weeks, just like clockwork, the car comes, picks him up, he goes to the doctor and comes back in exactly one hour. You could set your watch by it …" Mme Dufour's eyebrows puckered. "But you know, it's funny. I think the car stopped coming for him a few weeks before he left."

"That *is* funny," I agreed. "So he's been gone a few weeks? What about his rent?"

If Mme Dufour thought I was being nosy, she didn't show it. "Oh, my dear, his rent is always paid in full, once a year, you know. First of January, I get a cheque for the whole amount, from his father. Mr. Julian Cosgrove. It's nice, you know, because I just put it right into my term deposit account and it makes money for me all year. You can't be too careful, at my age, dear."

"Did … that is, does Adam have any friends around here?"

"Mmmmm …" she thought, tilting her head to one side. "No, I'd have to say no, he doesn't seem to have. In fact, it's almost as if he goes out of his way to avoid people, most of the time. Except for me, of course. He and I get along just fine. He's sweet, and he's very shy, of course. Not the talkative sort. But I do enough for both of us," she chuckled. "At first when he stopped coming by on Monday nights, I worried he'd hurt himself down there, you know, so I let myself in. But there was no sign of him."

"You've been inside his apartment?" I tried to imagine her reaction to Adam's monastic existence.

"Oh, yes, dear. It's not really my taste," she smiled, "but Adam is very religious, you know. I used to ask him to come to church with me. I've always been Church of England, though my husband was a dyed-in-the-wool Catholic — but Adam always says he prays and reads the bible every day, and he wouldn't like to have someone else tell him how to do it. He's a good, God-fearing young man, you know. That's not so usual, these days."

Mme Dufour wandered off into an editorial about the terrible moral and spiritual deterioration of today's youth. As soon as I could, I thanked her for her help and excused myself. She smiled sweetly, clearly happy to have had an audience, no matter how briefly.

"Please, if you see Adam, tell him to come home soon," she said as she saw me out the door.

I promised I would, and felt a pang of guilt. I just couldn't bring myself to tell the old dear the truth.

Greg and Dawn were waiting patiently in the car, and as we drove back toward the expressway, I told them about my conversation with Adam's landlady.

"So if Adam stopped going for his Modecate shots when his father died, the drug would have worn off within a few weeks," I said. "D'you think that's when the flashbacks started?"

"Sure," said Greg. "The meds probably kept things down to a dull roar for the poor guy. As long as they kept carting him off to the Allan for his shots, he would have been pretty quiet and inoffensive. When the meds wore off, though, all hell must have broken loose inside his head."

I rolled down the window. The blast of cool damp evening air felt good on my cheeks.

"Katy," Greg said suddenly. "I just thought of a phone call I have to make. I won't be a minute."

Without waiting for an answer, he swerved across two lanes of traffic and pulled the car into a no-parking zone. Jumping out, he ran to a phone booth, where we could see him thumping the top of the phone impatiently, then speaking rapidly to someone, waiting again, then talking.

He hung up and dashed back to the car.

"Would you mind sharing with the group just what the hell that was all about?" I asked, eyeing one of Montreal's dreaded Green Onions, a parking cop who was making his way purposefully toward our car. Oblivious, Greg pulled back out into traffic, then grinned like a kid who'd had a particularly good haul from the tooth fairy.

"I just remembered that I happen to know the nurse who runs the Modecate groups at the Allan," he said. "So I called her at home, and she was ever so delighted to hear from me. We're going to pay a little social call, my dears."

"Well, does anyone mind if we eat sometime soon?" whined Dawn from the back seat. "I don't know about you guys, but playing secret agent is really taking it out of me."

"Gawd, some mother I am," I laughed. "My kid's starving to death and I'm dragging her all over hell's half acre. I just hate myself!"

We found a fast-food joint featuring poutine, the good kind with dark gravy and real cheese curds, not the kind with watered-down gravy from a tin and shredded processed cheese I have sometimes found in Ottawa. We sat in the car to eat, and no one said much for some time, being too preoccupied with keeping gravy from dripping on our clothing.

Rain had begun to spatter on the windshield as we pulled up in front of Sherry Greene's house in a modest suburb west of the city. Her front lawn was immaculately groomed, trimmed all over to an even two inches and fertilized to within an inch of its life. It would take a tough dandelion to dare show its pesky little head in that soft carpet of grass, and I bet all and sundry pests had been eradicated from the perfect arrangement of flowers and shrubs surrounding the salmon-coloured stucco bungalow.

Greg shepherded us out of the car and up the walkway to the front door, which opened just as he lifted the knocker.

"Greg? Greg! It's so wonderful to see you!"

Sherry was an older woman, in her late fifties, stout and brisk, with a faintly English accent. Her hair was pulled back into a no-nonsense ponytail, and she had clearly been gardening when the rain started, for her nails were still caked with dirt. She smiled broadly at us while Greg made the introductions, but declined to shake hands until she'd washed up a bit.

"Come in, come in, make yourselves at home," she gestured, marching off to the washroom.

Looking around idly, I noted the collection of Elvis memorabilia: hand-painted plates of the King in his early, swivel-hipped career; others commemorating his later, white jewelled bell-bottom polyester jumpsuit era. A number of tiny Elvises were displayed in a backlit glass hutch.

"Ooh, I'm impressed," Dawn whispered, and I shushed her, trying not to giggle myself.

Sherry's taste in furniture tended toward Duncan Phyfe, dark, heavy wood with lots of carving and surfaces that probably ate up lemon oil furniture polish like candy.

Sherry returned, and this time she extended a plump dry hand to Dawn and me. Greg she hugged affectionately.

"I nearly fell over when I heard you on the phone," she laughed. "What are you doing in this neck of the woods?"

"We've just been on a daytrip to Montreal," he said, "and while we were here, I thought I'd call and see how you were doing. How's life at the Allan these days?"

She gave him a sharp look.

"Greg, don't play footsie with me. You don't just drop in on a person you haven't seen in — how many years? — anyway, you don't just drop in for no reason."

He laughed. "Okay, Sherry, you've got me. I'll tell you what's happening. You remember Adam Cosgrove? I treated him, ages ago."

Sherry jumped at the name. "What about him?" Her sunburned face got even redder.

"Well, he dropped in on me a couple of weeks ago, quite distraught, and I got him to sign a Form 14 for the release of his records from the Allan." Greg was becoming almost as good a liar as I was.

Sherry twisted a tassel on one of the many maroon pillows decorating her overstuffed couch. "I've been wondering where Adam got to." She studied the carpet. "Is he still in Ottawa?"

"Well, yeah." Greg watched the nurse carefully. "He's there, but when I tried to get the file released from the Allan, the records department claimed they'd never heard of him. And you and I both know he's been a patient for years, right?"

"Sure. He's been in the Modecate group for, oh, at least fifteen years now. Before that, his compliance stunk. But then, mid-May or so, he just stopped coming. No one could find him. He doesn't have a phone, and the only address we had was his father's house in Westmount. When I called, they said his father had passed away."

"Yeah, he died in early May," Greg said.

"Well, I'd heard something like it. In the papers. But I thought …" She stopped herself.

"Thought what, Sherry?" Greg's voice was soft, probing.

"I thought the father had made some kind of arrangement with Shapiro." Her hearty voice lost some of its edge.

Shapiro. Wasn't he the guy I'd met at my parents' place? What did he have to do with this? Mental note: ask parents about Dr. George Shapiro.

"What kind of arrangement?"

"Ummmm … I think it was kind of an under-the-table thing. You know, Shapiro doesn't do patient care any more, he's retired from that. He does research now. But he was the one who took over Adam's case when you left, and I guess he and Adam's father went way back. The deal was that if Cosgrove Senior could get Adam to come in, Shapiro would personally supervise the meds, make sure he got enough …"

"Enough for what?" I interrupted. "Aren't the doses pretty standard? And Shapiro is some kind of big *macher* in the psychiatric community, isn't he? Why would he consent to personally supervise Adam's meds?"

Sherry looked startled, and Greg gave me a warning look. "Sherry, why would Adam need especially high doses of Modecate? I never thought he was floridly psychotic."

Sherry blinked, and her face hardened as she realized she'd gone too far.

"Greg, you could charm the hind end off a mule, but this isn't any of your business. If you've got Adam at your hospital, you need to send him back. He was getting the treatment he needed, and he could be a danger to himself without it. In fact, I'm going to call Dr.

Shapiro right now. You can speak to him."

She marched across the room and picked up the phone.

Greg looked mildly at her. "That might not be such a bad idea, Sherry. Maybe he can explain why he was overdosing a patient with neuroleptics, just to satisfy Adam's father. What was it? Were they afraid if they stopped doping Adam up, some unsavoury family secrets would come out?"

"Get out of my house," Sherry said quietly. "I am not talking any more about this. Just get out."

"We were just on our way," I said. I didn't even stop to wave goodbye to the life-size bronze bust of Elvis, complete with realistic gold lamé scarf. We piled into the car and Greg turned it toward home.

24

Once, when I was a little girl, I owned a cat. I loved that cat, a big velvet grey beast named Doorknob, and it was my job to feed and groom him, to change the litter box and make sure he was healthy. I never minded the work; Doorknob was worth it. One summer morning, I got up and went to fill his dish with food. I was just about to scrape the old food out of the bowl when I screamed and dropped it on my mother's spotless linoleum, provoking a rare outburst from her.

"No, no, look, Mama!" I cried.

When she looked, she could see why I'd dropped it: the whole dish had been infested with maggots, and the white translucent worms were squirming blindly through what was left of the food, some falling over the edge and onto the floor.

I felt that same feeling of pained revulsion now as I contemplated each new revelation about Adam's life. The closer to the picture we got, the more the wriggling maggots came into focus.

"I can't believe they were just drugging him to shut him up," I said to Greg. "It must have scared the living shit out of him when the drugs wore off and all that stuff started to resurface."

"No kidding. And if Shapiro was giving him extra-high doses, that might explain why the records of his care were nowhere to be found. There's no way anyone would put something like that in a hospital file, where any clerk or nurse or technician could read it. That's the stuff of lawsuits — it could ruin Shapiro, not to mention looking bad for the Allan."

Dawn leaned forward in the back seat, listening intently.

"Do you think Adam knew he was being doped to the gills?" she asked. "I mean, if he knew it, he'd be even more paranoid than he already was, wouldn't he?"

"That's right. And as one of my patients once said to me, 'Sometimes being paranoid just means having all the facts!'" Greg chuckled. "No, seriously. That's one thing that can make patients stop taking their meds — they feel so sick and spacey that they decide the stuff they're taking must be poison, and the people giving it to them are part of the evil plot. And when they stop the meds, the paranoia just gets stronger, more vivid. It's a vicious circle."

"Poor Adam," I said. "Thinking the stuff that was supposed to make him better was really poisoning him. Where could he go? Who could he turn to? That must have been what made him decide to come to you, Greg."

"That's what I was thinking," Greg agreed. "And when I passed him off to another shrink, he decided to come to an astrologer — someone who could see things he couldn't. Poor guy."

"Listen, not to change the subject, but I think I might know Shapiro," I said. "I met him Friday at my parents' house. He was there for *shabbos* dinner."

"Pardon?" Dawn yelled. "You know this asshole? Why didn't you say something?"

"Hey, you just about deafened me," I complained, rubbing my ear. "And watch your language, kid. Yes, I know him, but don't worry — I don't like him. He tore a strip off me for daring to practise astrology without his permission. I don't know what your grandparents see in him, but I'm planning to ask."

"Well, I know George Shapiro, too," Greg said. "He's worked at the Allan for years, long before I ever got there. In fact, he's the one who referred Adam to me. I didn't know he'd taken him back when I left."

"Was he as obnoxious then as he is now?" I asked.

"It's just his nature. He's opinionated, that's for sure. A very vocal proponent of the biochemical theories of mental illness," Greg said. "Never had much patience with the talking therapies. I think he studied under Cameron, back in the fifties."

"Cameron? The one who did the CIA experiments? Well, that figures, doesn't it?"

"Huh? What experiments?" Dawn demanded. "What're you guys talking about?"

I explained. "Dr. Ewen Cameron was a psychiatrist at the Allan, who co-operated with the American CIA about forty years ago, subjecting his patients to various forms of brainwashing and experimental psychiatric techniques, without their knowledge or consent. He did a lot of damage, but none of this came to light until just a few years ago when there was a huge scandal. Somehow, Shapiro's affiliation with Cameron just doesn't surprise me."

"I wonder if your parents would be able to shed any light on this?" Greg asked. "They know Shapiro — is it possible they might have known old Mr. Cosgrove?"

"If they do, I've never heard about it. And I really

don't want to mix my parents up in this. Having Dawn involved is bad enough."

"Hey! I already told you, I want to be here," Dawn objected.

"Yeah, and I already told you, I don't really care for it. It makes me nervous," I retorted.

We lapsed into silence, and for the remainder of the trip, I dozed with my head wedged uncomfortably between the headrest and the window. Rain spattered intermittently on the windshield, not enough to warrant using the wipers, but threatening a downpour later.

I woke to the sound of the wipers flapping rhythmically, and rubbed the back of my neck to ease the stiffness. We were on the Queensway, city lights all around us.

"Greg, I think we should go straight to the police," I said through the cotton wool in my mouth. "Tell them about Adam's apartment."

"It's getting late. We can go first thing in the morning."

"Yeah, okay," I sighed. It was completely dark, and though I couldn't see my watch in the shadows of the car's interior, I guessed it was close to ten o'clock. My mind was staggering around in circles with the weight of all that had happened today, and I could probably use some time to sort things out before we were interrogated by the good Detective Benjamin. And I had no doubt we would be interrogated.

"You're probably right," I said. "It's going to be hellish enough talking to Benjamin as it is. If we go in tonight, we'll be there for sure till morning. He's probably not even working tonight, anyway."

"Benjamin's going to be pissed with us," Greg agreed. "We've been busy little felons today — entering

Adam's apartment, fiddling around with his stuff and leaving our fingerprints all over the place. And we removed evidence in the shoe-box, too."

I groaned. "Maybe we should just forget about telling him altogether — he'll have a conniption when he hears what we've been up to."

"Never mind. We'll deal with it tomorrow."

"All I want right now is to get to bed." Somehow, thinking of bed made me think of Brent. "Damn!" I exclaimed loudly, startling Greg and waking Dawn. At their alarmed looks, I realized just how tightly strung all our nerves had become. "Never mind, it's nothing crucial. It's just that Brent was supposed to call me after work today, and I wasn't there. He's not going to be impressed."

Greg and Dawn snickered in unison.

"Mom's got a boyfriend, Mom's got a boyfriend," Dawn chanted.

"Knock it off, you two. And he's not my boyfriend. I just don't want him to think I'm rude, okay?"

"Sure, Mom. But you know, I think it'll take more than you missing one of his calls to put him off your scent. He's got it bad for you, you know."

I pursed my lips silently and looked out the window. The road was shiny black, and the car hissed along, sending up a fine spray. It was raining hard, the windshield wipers slapping ineffectually at the sheets of water that poured down. Never mind, Brent and I could connect tomorrow, I thought. It's not the end of the world.

But when we pulled up in front of the apartment building, a familiar figure was once again lounging in one of the wooden Muskoka chairs on the front verandah.

Dawn and I said goodnight to Greg, and he drove off, promising to call me first thing in the morning. As the car's tail lights disappeared into the rain, Brent unfolded himself and ambled over to greet me with a hug and a peck on the cheek.

"Sorry we're late," I mumbled.

"Greg get run off the road again?" He smiled, but his voice had an edge to it.

"No, Mr. Smarty-pants, we had to check out a few things about that guy I told you about — the one who died over the weekend."

"So what? You're starting a new career as a private investigator? Last I heard, when people die under suspicious circumstances, the police take care of it, don't they?"

"Maybe so, but this is my business, not yours, Brent," I snapped. "Adam left Greg and me some of his personal effects, and it was pretty clear he wanted us to follow up, okay?"

"Hey, take a Valium, kid. I was just asking." His voice was mild. "Who was this Adam, anyway, that you need to go gallivanting all over the place for him?"

"He was a client. He wanted something from me, and I couldn't give it to him. Then he died, and I feel like this is the least I can do for him. And now, if you don't mind, I'd like to change the subject."

"Sure thing, honey. Say, have you two had anything to eat? I haven't had a chance to grab anything yet. How about it?"

Dawn went up and got Peter's enormous golfing umbrella, and we walked through the rain-soaked streets to a café that had just opened on Elgin Street, Ottawa's attempt at a cosmopolitan, hip and happening kind of neighbourhood. Restaurants and latte bars and clubs open and close regularly in this part of town, bowing to the food fashions as dictated in places like Toronto and New York.

The only difference is, there is a lag time of about two years before the Ottawa version opens. We don't like to jump into anything. Better to be certain that something really is trendy before adopting it as our own.

Brent chose a Tex-Mex place, and though the food was not spectacular, it was hearty and plentiful. We ate slowly, mainly because both Dawn and I had pretty much run out of rocket fuel. Brent, too, seemed quiet. Walking back home, he put an arm around my shoulders. Dawn trailed behind us, but not before winking ostentatiously at me to let me know she was deliberately giving us some privacy.

"Hey, honey, you seem pretty wiped out," Brent said. "Why don't I call you tomorrow and we can get together when we're both feeling more rested?"

"Or I could call you," I said. "I still don't have your number."

"Yeah, well, I'm hard to get hold of, most of the time," he smiled. "I've been working some crazy hours, trying to get this system up and running. It's probably best if I call you."

I shrugged. "As long as you don't mind leaving messages. My life has been a little hectic lately." Understatement of the century, Katy.

"Sure thing, babe."

I gritted my teeth. After five years together, surely a man as intelligent and sensitive as Brent could have grasped my hatred of that appellation. But I was trying to be nice, so I kept my mouth shut. Besides, maybe he'd forgotten.

We kissed goodbye, long and sweet, outside my

apartment building, as Dawn discreetly turned away and pretended to busy herself with the keys. Inside, Dawn and I barely spoke. Our brains had long since ceased sending coherent messages to our lips. By the time I slid under the covers, I was already asleep.

25

Wednesday was catch-up day. I'd lost Monday and Tuesday to Adam-related crises, and my regular clients were clamouring for some attention — the tape on my answering machine was full to overflowing. It would probably take me all day just to return the calls, let alone do any actual work. I set to work transcribing messages, then starting the long process of calling people back.

I did put in a call to Detective Benjamin, but he wasn't at his desk, which did not exactly break my heart. Greg had Adam's shoebox, and I figured it was more his job than mine to contact Benjamin. Besides, Greg had a secretary.

About halfway through the morning I was on the phone, arguing with a lady who wanted to know if I was a follower of Elizabeth Clare Prophet and the Ascended Masters, and if so, did I know which spaceship she should get on when they came to do the Big Airlift of Fate. This was not one of my areas of specialization, but I was having trouble convincing the woman. Fortunately, just at that moment, someone knocked on my door.

"Listen, I've got someone at the door," I said. "Can I put you on hold?" Without waiting for an answer, I hit the hold button and got up to answer the door. It took me a second to recognize the woman who stood in the gloom of my hallway, looking nervous and fiddling with the strap of her expensive handbag. Her smile was tremulous.

"Katy? Do you remember me? I'm Linda Marois."

Of course. Jean Marois' mammarily-enhanced wife. "Sure — we met at my parents' place. Great to see you!" I sounded more enthusiastic than I felt.

Linda looked older in the sunlight streaming through my dusty windows. Her makeup made her skin look cakey, tired.

"I hope I'm not disturbing you," she said.

"Not at all! Come on in, won't you? Just let me excuse myself from this phone call."

I picked up the phone again. "Ma'am, thanks so much for calling. Sorry I can't help you out. Bye!"

I gently laid the receiver in its cradle and turned to Linda, who had opened her purse and pulled out a quilted leather cosmetics bag. She was touching up the already thick makeup under her eyes, but stopped guiltily when I looked at her. Her eyes were huge and unblinking, and for a moment I was reminded uncomfortably of Adam. I brushed the thought away.

"So! Linda. It's nice to see you again. Is this a social call?"

She fidgeted some more with her purse strap,

stopped herself, bit at a perfectly filed and polished nail, and stared out the window at the brilliant sky.

"I just wondered … I mean, that is, I wondered if you could — you know, do my chart for me?"

"Sure." I hoped I sounded soothing. She looked as though a stiff breeze could knock her over. "Is there anything in particular you want to look for?"

"No, no! I mean, I just want … you know … some general information."

"Okay. Do you have your birth data? I need the date, time and place."

She gave me the essentials, and I had the screen up on the chart in seconds. I printed out a rough draft, and handed it to her, then settled in beside her on the couch.

"Okay. Here are the basics. You have the Sun in Cancer in the eleventh house, so you're an emotional person, with quite a tendency to worry. You might find yourself fretting over things that turn out to be less important than you thought, but worrying is just your way of keeping a handle on your world. You probably feel best when you're part of a group — either a social group, or a charitable organization. That kind of thing."

Linda nodded, biting at another nail. Some manicurist's hard work was about to go down the tubes.

I continued. "Now, here's your Moon, in Aries in the eighth house. That means you react really quickly to new situations, without really thinking things through. Your feelings run very high, so that you feel everything really intensely. When you combine this with your Cancer Sun, you can see that you probably get pretty carried away with your feelings.

"People might accuse you of being too reactive, but emotional sensitivity can be a good thing, depending on how you use it. Having the Moon in the eighth house can be a very sexy, sensual placement, so when you're in a romantic situation, you go completely on instinct. That feels good, right?"

Linda nodded.

"But there might be times when someone says something to you without thinking, and you take it too much to heart. Of course, if someone says something mean deliberately, it's like their words just pierce right through you. Does that sound right?"

Linda looked away, nodding quietly. When she turned back, tears had formed in the corners of her eyes. I put my hand on her arm.

"Linda, if this is too much, we can do it another time."

"No, I want you to go on," she said, though the tears threatened to penetrate the thick mascara barrier ringing her eyes. She took a tissue from the box on the arm of the couch and dabbed expertly at the tears. The makeup stayed intact.

"If you're sure. You stop me if you need a break, okay?"

"It's fine," she said.

"Okay. Let's look at your ascendant," I said. "That's your rising sign. You just barely have Virgo rising, and Pluto was coming up on the eastern horizon when you were born." I stopped, feeling a small stab of recognition. Pluto rising — just like Adam.

I cleared my throat. "Virgo rising means you like to look at each new situation in great detail, check out all the angles. You worry if things aren't exactly perfect. And wherever we find Pluto in the chart, there's going to be a lot of emotional power — so perfection and order in your life feel crucially important to you. If something is not quite right, you can get into a real state. You might not say anything — you're more likely to stew about it inside for a long time, then erupt."

Linda smiled. "You got that right, for sure."

"Good. Now, you've got this cluster of planets in the twelfth house — Venus, Mars and Uranus …"

Before I could continue, Linda interjected, "What about children?"

I studied the chart. "Kids are usually a fifth house matter. In your chart, that house is ruled by Capricorn. And Saturn is right at the door of the house, see?" I pointed. "Do you have any children?"

She shook her head.

"Do you want them?"

Her face clouded. "Yes. Yes, I do. But I don't know if I can have them."

"Well. Your chart doesn't say you will or you won't, but with this Saturn influence, having children must feel like really serious business to you. It's a place where you invest a lot of worry and concern," I said. "Oh, and Saturn here can also mean that you get romantically involved with older men."

"That's true," she said. "I mean, both things. I do think a lot about children, but Jean is older than I am, and he says he's already done the kid thing. He had some in his first marriage, you know. He doesn't want any more, and he wants me to get fixed — you know, get my tubes tied?"

She looked ready to dissolve, and I chose my words delicately. "Linda, did you and Jean ever … discuss having children before you got married?"

"Yes, and he said he never wanted any, but I thought he'd change his mind once we were married, you know — he'd see what a good mother I'd be, and understand how much it means to me. I thought I might be able to change him." Her lower lip trembled. "But he hasn't changed his mind, and now, you know, I'm running out of time. I'm almost forty. And he's past seventy — if we don't have them soon, it'll be too late!"

I handed her another tissue, and she blew her nose softly.

"That's hard," I sympathized. "What about Jean's kids, the ones from before? Have you been involved in raising them?"

"I've never even seen them. There was some kind of terrible fight, and anyway, they don't live around here."

She made a dismissive motion with her hand, and I caught the flash of a very large and brilliant diamond ring.

"But that's not what I want, anyway. They're grown-ups, older than I am. I want my own baby …"

She collapsed into racking sobs, shielding her face from me. I put a hand on her back, trying to comfort her. The longing for a baby is not a rational one, and you either have it or you don't. If you do, it can consume your life, make you feel that nothing else you do is important or worthwhile. And Linda definitely had it. I ached for her.

Finally, raising her head, she reached for a handful of tissues to repair her ravaged face. Where the makeup had been washed away, the skin over her left cheekbone was a spectacular rainbow: mottled purple fading to maroon, to deep mustard yellow and finally grey around the edges. I must have looked as startled as I felt, for she turned away from me a moment.

"Linda, what happened?" I asked, knowing the answer before I spoke.

"I walked into a doorframe," she lied, not even bothering to try.

"Look, we both know you never walked into any doorframe. Did your husband do this?"

She looked out the window. Damn. Double damn. I had actually liked Jean — his quiet, unassuming persona, his elegant bearing. And face it, I'd liked it that he came to my defense against Shapiro. So much for favourable first impressions.

"Linda, you can get help. I know some organizations where —"

She looked at me dully. "It was my own fault. He told me he didn't want to discuss it further, and I was irrational. I pushed him. I do push him, you know. I really get on his nerves, and then ..." she tried to smile, to wave it all away. "Who can blame him? I don't make much sense when I yell like that."

She looked at me earnestly, imploring me to believe that her husband, the soft-spoken, educated man I'd met at *shabbos* dinner, was really a nice guy, pushed beyond endurance by his carping and unreasonable wife.

"I don't buy that, Linda. I don't care if you pushed him or not. No one has the right to hit you, ever. I'm not saying you have to leave him, if that's not what you want, but both of you definitely have to get help. Him, especially. You understand, Linda?"

"He doesn't hit me that often. Most of the time, he just talks nasty, y'know?"

"Talks nasty?" I frowned, bracing myself for what would come next.

"Yeah. Like, he says I'm a bitch, and I'm fat and ugly, and everyone can tell I got my boobs fixed, even though he was the one who ..."

Oh, God, now I felt guilty for noticing the obvious enlargement.

She continued. "… and he says he can see right through me, that I'm so stupid that everything I think shows up on my face and he can predict what I'm thinking just by looking at me. He says I'm boring and not very bright, and completely predictable. But Katy, I try so hard …"

Another bout of sobs, with no attempt to stem the tears this time. I clenched my fists. It was a good thing Jean Marois was nowhere around.

"I've taken lots of university courses, you know, political science, history, things he's interested in, so we'd have something to talk about. But he says my profs are stupid, too, and I'm going to this nineteenth-rate university, not like McGill, where he went. And you know, ever since he got this new job, it's been worse. He's tired and cranky, really grouchy at the end of the day. Almost anything I say can set him off, so I don't say much."

"Did he get a promotion or something?" Not that I cared.

"Sort of. He used to work for External, years ago, but then they set up this communications security thing and he went over there a few years ago, and now he's in charge of the whole thing. It's supposed to be some big deal, but I don't really know what he does there."

I wasn't especially interested in Jean Marois' career as a public service czar, but Linda seemed genuinely proud of the man who had blackened her eye and abused her soul.

"Linda, look. He needs help just as much as you do, okay? More. Men who batter do it because they think it's their right, and they know they can get away with it if no one says anything. It has nothing to do with you, with who you are or what courses you've taken. It's in his own mind. You need to get to a marriage counselor, and maybe there's a chance he'll learn to stop and you can live a normal life again. I have some names, right over here."

I rummaged through my box of referral cards, pulling out a handful of names, therapists I knew who would take Linda's abuse seriously.

"He'd never go. He says I'm the one who's sick. And anyway, with this job, he'd never take the chance of anyone finding out he's seeing a counselor."

"Okay, I understand. But look," I scribbled my address on a piece of paper and handed it to her. "Take my address. If it looks like he's getting ready to hit you again, get the hell out. You can stay with us as long as you need to, make decisions, whatever. Okay?"

Linda had patched up her makeup, using a little brush and some thick flesh-toned stuff in a tiny white pot. This was obviously not a new skill for her. She tucked her equipment back into her purse and rose to leave. I saw her to the door, embracing her awkwardly. Those breasts really did get in the way, on a frame as small as hers.

"Remember — come right over if you need to," I called after her. She gave a small shrug as she left. Shutting the door, I sat heavily on the couch and closed my eyes. I focused on unclenching my fists, forcing myself to breathe deeply to relax my anger. Marois and Shapiro — man, my parents had picked a couple of real winners that night.

26

Greg caught me in the middle of wolfing down a couple of Jamaican patties for my lunch. He was calling from his office.

"Katy, Benjamin wants to see us." He, too, was munching on something.

"When? Is it important? I'm kind of swamped today." While I didn't regret having spent so much time with Linda, her visit had set my already over-burdened schedule on its ear.

"Yeah, yeah, me too. I told him we could meet him at the station about five, if that's okay with you."

"Not really, but what the hell. How did he sound?"

"Unimpressed with our Nancy Drew shtick, if that's what you mean. I told him about the box with the documents, and the skeleton and so forth, and he sounded like he was really working to keep a lid on it. You know, the tight voice right before the big lecture? I felt like I was in the mother superior's office at Holy Cross."

"Yeah, well, better you than me. That guy just rubs me the wrong way. I probably would have got us in even more trouble."

Greg laughed. "Probably. So I'll meet you there at

five, okay? Oh — and Katy? Maybe you'd better let me do the talking."

By the time we met outside the police station, the sky had clouded over again and the air felt thick and turgid. We were in for another spell of hot, damp weather. That's how it goes here: just when you think the heat has lifted, and your body is reviving from the putrid soaking air, it smacks you on your ass again. Bam. Ottawa's summer is just one of Nature's cruel jokes. And winter is even worse.

Benjamin was at his desk and didn't bother coming to meet us this time. I think we were beginning to get on his nerves. He wore glasses today — a big, shaggy reddish bear, wearing big, square black-framed glasses. His eyes looked smaller, buried behind lenses that made his face look bigger. He peered up as we slipped into our chairs in his cubicle.

"I hear you've taken it upon yourselves to do some police work," he launched right in. "You do realize that interfering with evidence in a criminal proceeding is a federal offence?"

"But I thought this was just a suspicious death, not a murder," I said, perhaps unwisely. "At least, that's what you told us last time."

He fixed me with his grizzly glare, which no longer seemed quite so comical, and pointed his pencil at me warningly.

"The point I'm making, Ms. Klein, is that if you find anything out about this death, you bring it straight to me. Me, you understand? Not Dr. Chisholm here, not anyone else. Evidence is police territory, and you have no business getting yourselves involved. You —"

"I bet you have a lot of Sagittarius in your chart," I interrupted, and he stopped, pencil in mid-air. "You've got the build for it, and the hair. And I'd bet on a fair bit of Capricorn, too. You really get bent out of shape when people ignore the rules."

Sensing impending disaster, Greg jumped in. "Look, Detective Benjamin, we just wanted to let you know what we found, okay? We didn't mean to cause you any problems. If there's anything we can do …"

Benjamin was still staring at me, but we'd stopped him in mid-charge. That was something, at least.

"Okay," he sighed. "What did you find, exactly?"

Greg described the parcel Marcel had found in the car, and how we'd concluded Adam must have put it there the night he died. He told Benjamin about the trip to Montreal, the monastic cell Adam had created, the self-flagellation, the marble casket that Adam had turned into the focal point of his shame and self-degradation.

Despite himself, Benjamin looked startled. "What, you mean this guy was beating himself with a whip in front of a box of bones? What's that all about? That's just sick."

"Well," Greg said, adjusting his glasses, "when kids are severely abused, they don't usually blame the abuser. They tend to take the shame onto themselves. It looks like Adam's mother sent him the altar, told him to look after it. Somehow, he had the idea that the other child's death was his own fault. So, especially if he was raised in a really religious household, he might think he needed to purge himself of the guilt, to punish himself for what happened. We can't exactly ask him, but the evidence seems to point that way."

Greg paused, wiped his glasses on a pocket hand-kerchief, then continued. "After we found the altar with the bones, and the shoe box with the papers, we put things back the way we'd found them, and we left."

Benjamin sat back, tapping his pencil on his knee. "Ms. Klein? Do you have anything to add?"

I told him about my visit with Mme Dufour, her story of the car that came to collect Adam every couple of weeks, her description of his quiet, reclusive behaviour. I told of the yearly rent cheques, paid by a father who wanted to ensure Adam didn't spill any inconvenient family secrets.

"Wait a second," Benjamin interjected. "This guy's getting ten grand a year? On top of having his rent paid? It's not a lot, but he wasn't exactly throwing it around, right? So where'd the rest of the money go?"

Greg and I shrugged in tandem. We must have looked like Tweedledum and Tweedledee.

"We don't know," Greg said. "We wondered that, too. Maybe he was giving it away? It'd fit the profile, if he was giving it to some church or local charity. But we didn't find anything in the apartment."

"Or maybe he brought it with him to Ottawa," I said. "In fact, maybe when he died, someone took it from him. That would make sense, wouldn't it? If someone rolled him for his money, I mean."

The more I considered it, the more the theory made sense to me. Adam packs his savings and photos, sets off for Ottawa to find the one person who's ever listened to him. He doesn't know how long he'll need to stay here, and security is a big issue for him. The money comes in handy, too, when he needs to rent a cell phone … or buy a knife. I shivered.

Greg was telling Benjamin about our visit to Sherry Greene, the Elvis Queen, and her revelation that Dr. Shapiro had been routinely overdrugging Adam, probably at the request of Adam's father. "And that's about it, Detective," he concluded.

At Benjamin's request, Greg wrote down Sherry's name and address, and the address of Adam's apartment building on Durocher. He handed over the shoe box and its contents, and we were excused. Greg offered to walk me home.

"I think we might actually have done Benjamin a favour," he remarked as we strode along Elgin Street.

"How so? He sure didn't act like it."

"Well, Adam died in Ottawa, right? So that makes it technically Benjamin's case. But a lot of the material evidence is in Montreal, under the jurisdiction of the Montreal police, so Benjamin would have to go through a mountain of red tape to get access to it. So he had to play tough guy about it, but really, I think he's happy we got him a bunch of information he couldn't have got any other way. As I understand it, police forces can get kind of territorial."

"Greg, get hold of yourself." I poked him in the ribs. "Now you're starting to sound like a cop. As of now, we have turned this investigation over to Detective Benjamin. Much as I may feel a personal repugnance toward his authoritarian attitude, I really do believe he is better equipped to handle this thing than we are."

Greg scowled. "Fine, if that's the way you want it. But I still say we can find out a few things about the case if we keep our ears to the ground."

"Greg, we've done our part. Adam lived a tragic life, and his death may just have put him out of his misery. I feel badly about that, but I don't think we should meddle any more than we already have."

"Fine, Ms. Smarty-pants. So what about the pictures? If you're so keen to turn everything over to the exalted Benjamin, why didn't you tell him about the pictures? Perhaps, unconsciously, you're trying to retain some connection to Adam, too?"

"Fuck you, Chisholm. I'm not one of your gullible patients, you know." I gave him another jab in the ribs. "I just happened to forget, okay? I'll drop them off tomorrow, first thing."

"Yeah, right." Was that a smirk I detected?

"Okay, fine. I admit, I'm not keen to give up the pictures. I feel like I'm holding them in trust for Adam. I don't want to see Benjamin stick them in little plastic bags as evidence, and file them away forever. It just doesn't seem right."

"Yeah, they're kind of a testament to the only happy times Adam ever had, aren't they?" Greg understood me perfectly.

Just then, I noticed the car parked in front of my building.

"Hey! It's the Flaming Deathtrap!"

"I thought Peter wasn't due back until tomorrow," Greg said. Just then, Peter himself came out onto the verandah, talking into my portable phone. He waved at us, said goodbye to his editor, pushed the antenna back into its receptacle and galloped down the front steps to plant a kiss on my cheek and shake Greg's hand vigorously.

Dawn followed her dad down the steps, clearly happy to have him home again.

"Let's go inside," I said. "For one thing, I'm starved, and for another, Peter, you're not going to believe what's been going on this past week." Had it only been a week?

Dawn produced a platter of hummus and triangles of pita bread, recipe courtesy of my mother. For a while, we were too busy stuffing our faces to say much of anything. Eventually, though, I related the tale of Adam's first visits and Dawn's kidnapping. Peter was outraged.

"How could you, Katy?" he kept saying. "She's my daughter, too, you know! You have no right to withhold information like that — you should have called me right away!"

"Peter, look, calm down, okay? I know she's your daughter, but by the time I was able to talk to you, she was safe and sound, and it seemed like a better idea to tell you when you got home. Why worry you when there was nothing you could do about it anyway?" I tried to sound like I actually felt on top of things.

"Dad, I was mad at her too, at first," Dawn said. "But I think Mom might have a point. I'm fine now. I'm still having dreams about it, but basically I'm okay."

"Honey, I didn't know you were still having dreams." I leaned forward to clutch her hand.

She gave me a wry smile. "Aren't you the big post-traumatic stress specialist? What did you expect? Anyway, you never asked."

Tears sprang to my eyes. "Oh, honey, I feel so guilty. How could I be so stupid? I'm so sorry."

"Katy, don't beat yourself up too much," Greg said. "Dawn's your daughter, not your patient. No parent wants to think their kid is suffering, they want to believe everything is just fine. So you missed it — now you know. Lighten up on yourself."

I looked at him through a film of tears. "That's not the point, but thanks anyway. The point is, Dawn is suffering because I was stupid and didn't just try to tell Adam what he wanted to hear. I could have done it, but I thought I would be violating some kind of code, telling him outright that his father might have killed his sister. So instead, I put Dawn's life at risk. And she's still paying for it."

Peter gave me a squeeze. "You can't predict the outcome of every move you make, Katy. You should know that by now. I don't care how good you are at astrology, you can't control what other people do."

"Don't I know it. But that doesn't help." I blew my nose with the tissue Greg handed me. "Okay guys, angst session is now officially over. Greg, why don't you tell Peter the rest of it?"

So Greg told the whole damned story one more time, from the kidnapping to Adam floating in the Canal; the photographs he'd left for me; Greg's mishap on the road from Montreal; the missing files at the Allan; the computer break-in, and so on down the line. Hearing it all related like that, I could see the places where we might have done some more thorough checking.

When he'd finished, I said, "Greg, you know what occurs to me?"

"What's that?"

"We know the name of Adam's birth mother. I wonder if she's still around, and if she is, could she add anything to the picture? I mean, she must have given those kids up for a reason. And her name was right there on the adoption papers. Adam must have known who she was. Did he ever contact her? I know a lot of adopted kids do try to contact their birth mothers, but did he do it?"

I was rambling, thinking aloud. Greg's eyes narrowed as he pondered. "You could be right. What was her name again? Debby — Debby something or another."

"Debby Landreth," Dawn said quietly.

"How did you remember that?" I asked. "I could barely remember the first name!"

"When we found the papers, I was thinking about

her, wondering how old she was when she had those twins. I was wondering what it was like for her, living in the forties and having kids she knew she'd have to give up. I guess I just noticed the name."

"Peter, our daughter is one amazing kid," I chuckled. He didn't disagree.

Greg said, "Well, I don't see how we can trace her, though. What're we going to do, go through every phone book in the country, checking for D. Landreths? Plus, what if she's married?"

There was a discouraged silence.

"Wait a sec," Dawn said suddenly. "I know where we can check a cross-country phone listing on the Internet." She jumped up and ran to the computer. She clattered away at the keys and in a couple of minutes she sat back in obvious satisfaction.

"Here's the list. Now I just have to input the last name ... there. It'll take a few seconds."

We gathered around the computer and, miraculously, three "Landreth, D." entries appeared on the screen. One was in Fort St. John, British Columbia, one was in Toronto and one was in Aylmer, Quebec, not much more than a stone's throw from Ottawa.

"Peter? I believe hunting down sources is your area of expertise?" Greg tried to hand him the phone. Peter looked hesitant. "I don't know," he said. "It's a little dicey, you know."

"What is, Dad? I see you calling people you don't know all the time." Dawn cocked her head to one side, like a quizzical sparrow.

"It's not that simple. I'm not calling her as a journalist, and I do have some ethics, you know, even if I work for the *Telegraph*."

"Well, can't you write a story about her? You know,

something about women who give up their kids for adoption or something?" Dawn wasn't about to give up, and Peter snorted.

"Katy, she gets this from your side of the family, you know. Okay, listen. I'll try to find this Debby Landreth person, but I'm not using my real name, and I'm not going over there to interview her. I don't have an assignment to do it, and if it ever got out that I'd tracked her down just to satisfy the curiosity of my nosy ex-wife and daughter, I'd be toast."

Dawn beamed. "Thanks, Dad! You're the best."

"Yeah, right," he muttered. "All right, here goes nothing. May as well start with the local one." He started dialling. "Hello, could I please speak to Debby Landreth? Oh, thanks." Putting a hand over the mouthpiece, he whispered, "I'm on hold. You might have lucked out."

Then, "Oh, hello, Ms. Landreth. It's Peter Klein calling, from the *Ottawa Telegraph*. Yes, well, actually, we're doing a story on adoption, and you were recommended to me as a source. No, no, of course, it's all confidential, no names would be used. I understand. Well, I was wondering if one of our reporters could come and talk with you. At your convenience, of course."

Peter could talk a very smooth line, especially when he was propelled by the fear that his source might hang up on him. And let's face it — if I'd given my kids up for adoption more than forty years ago, would I want to be reminded of it? Somehow, though, Peter was guiding Debby Landreth to the outcome we desired: an interview with "one of our reporters" — likely Greg, the second half of our one-two punch. Peter would prime the pump, and Greg would walk in, the caring, gentle therapist, and clean up. Quite the team.

27

Debby Landreth agreed to meet Greg that very evening. She said she wanted a chance to tell her side of the story, maybe get a few things off her chest. Peter says it often works that way.

Greg, of course, was our primary interviewer, and I would tag along in the background. This was decided on the basis that I refused to be excluded, and when it was suggested I stay home, I threw a major hissy fit and made everyone so miserable that the group consensus was that I should just go, for God's sake. That worked for me.

Debby Landreth was working that night, but she said the place would be quiet, so we might as well meet her there. "There" turned out to be a bar in Aylmer, a dark, damp, beer-smelling establishment with perhaps ten serious drinkers in evidence at eight o'clock in the evening. Some joker had plugged the jukebox with quarters, and "Wasted Days and Wasted Nights" blared over and over again into the dim, smoky air.

The bar was illuminated by a large electric clock surrounded by orange neon lights that flickered ominously, constantly threatening to give up the ghost, but never quite expiring. Clearly, the owners were having septic tank problems, for every now and then a pungent, fart-like gas would waft upward through the floorboards.

Debby, the bartender, was polishing glasses, looking thoroughly bored. The years had not been kind to Adam's mother. Her sparse dyed blonde hair was frizzed into an unlikely perm, which she fluffed up with her fingers in an unconscious gesture while she talked. The grey roots were visible, even in this light.

Her bony shoulders poked through the polyester scoop-neck T-shirt, but too much beer over the years had obscured whatever waist she might have had. She was thin everywhere else, but her stomach bulged above a pink vinyl belt. It was clear where Adam had got his pale, permanently startled eyes, except that Debby's were ringed with dark circles. Not bruises, I didn't think, but just fatigue and the vagaries of life.

I perched gingerly on a creaky bar stool and let Greg do the talking, as we'd agreed on the way here.

"Debby?" he asked, and when she nodded slowly, in a gesture that seemed to consume all the energy in her scrawny body, he moved closer and sat down, elbows on the bar.

"Hi, I'm Greg Chisholm. You spoke to my colleague, Peter Klein, earlier this evening."

Again the slow nod, but the pale eyes remained expressionless. That trait seemed to run in the family. A chill of recognition hit the back of my neck.

"Debby, do you mind if my intern, Katy, sits in with us? She's just learning how to be a reporter, and she won't get in our way."

At last Debby spoke, her voice a hoarse throaty whisper, almost inaudible in competition with the jukebox.

"I don't care, she can listen all she wants. Mebbe she'll learn something. Whattaya want to know from me?" Debby sounded at the same time belligerent and resigned, a woman who'd endured enough for one life and now just tried to roll with it, not letting anything get to her. This interview was appealing to me less and less.

"Well." Greg cleared his throat and smiled his most engaging smile. "As Peter told you, we're doing a story on adoption, from the point of view of the birth mother. I understand you've been in that kind of situation?"

She pulled a cigarette from a box behind the bar and stuck it in the corner of her mouth, talking out the other side as she fumbled for a lighter.

"Yeah, I done that. A long time ago, though. I figured it was for the best, eh?" She inhaled, then let the smoke drift out through her nostrils. "Anyways, who told you to talk to me?"

Greg smiled again. "Well, I can't really say, you know? If I told you who my sources were, you'd never be able to trust me to keep your identity secret, right?"

Debby Landreth gave him a hard stare. Then she seemed to come to a decision. "Sure, I get that. Well, like I said, I figured giving up my kids was the best thing. For them, not me. That's all there is to it."

Greg leaned across the sticky bar. "Sure. You wanted to do what was best for the children. Every mom wants the best for her kids, right?"

"Right. And this is back forty-odd years ago, eh? No such thing as 'single parent families' then," she snorted. "No daycare, no one'd even look at a girl been through that kind of thing. Not the age I was then, anyhow. Damaged goods, like."

"How old were you?" Greg kept it low-key, letting her take him wherever she wanted to go.

"Only sixteen. Fuck. Can you imagine? Sixteen years old, up in the fancy resorts there, workin' for them fuckin' rich people, and one of the boys sticks it where it don't belong, and bingo! Guess who's fired all of a sudden? They just let me go, no word of why, nothin'. Out ya go, like a load of trash they don't want around no more. Only I'm pregnant, and I'm broke. What'm I supposed to do, go home?"

She laughed, a sudden snort. At first I thought she was choking, but she took another drag on the cigarette and continued. "Home. That's a good one. So I'm outta there, right? They don't give a shit what happens to me, they just wanna make sure I don't corrupt the morals of all them rich kids, the ones who'll never have to wait a table or empty a trash can in their life. Like them kids aren't already fucking anything that'll move — me, other waitresses, each other …"

She drifted off for a moment, and Greg waited patiently.

"What a crock, eh? Like they're all so fuckin' pure. Ha. Anyways, only one lady was nice to me, gave me a bit of a hand, y'know? Old Mrs. Cosgrove, she figures she owes me some help, so she says, hows about I give her the kid when it's born, she'll raise it up proper, no waiting table or cleaning up other people's shit for my kid. What can I say? It was the best thing for the kid."

"So Mrs. Cosgrove, she helped you when the baby was born?"

Debby stubbed her cigarette out on the edge of the bar, then used a small brush to sweep the ashes into a large tin can that had once contained ketchup, according to the label.

"Sure, she helped me. Well, she felt like she had to,

didn't she?" She looked at Greg, challenging him to disagree. He nodded.

"Anyways," Debby laughed, "it wasn't just a baby
— it was two kids, twins. She let me name 'em, said I
should choose them and she'd go by what I said. She
was real nice, old Mrs. C. Her old man was a shit, a real
piece of shit, just like my dad, but she said that didn't
matter, she promised she'd keep my kids away from
him. He was never around the house, anyways. Out in
Montreal making money, humping his secretary, so I
heard."

"You didn't like Mr. Cosgrove, huh?"

"Fuck, no. He use to hit her, smack her around. I
think that's why her kid was so fucked up, too, y'know?
You hit a girl, she'll just take it, she might run away like
I did, but she's not gonna turn on you, hit you back. But
you hit a boy like old Mrs. C.'s kid, he's gonna get nasty
sometime or another. He might turn on you, take a strip
offa ya, or he might do it to someone else. And that's
how it all comes out, right?"

"So the Cosgroves had another child?"

"Huh. He wasn't *their* kid, he was hers. From before. His dad died, I guess. Maybe in the war or something. And he wasn't just older — he was old enough to
get himself in a whack of trouble. Him and his rich buddies, always gettin' in trouble, y'know? Mean stuff, too
— hurtin' people who couldn't fight back. But back then,
you didn't call the cops on rich kids. The parents just
kind of clean up the mess, no one mentions it, it's gone.
Never happened. You just get momma to take care of
things. Simple."

"Mmm. You knew Mrs. Cosgrove's son pretty well?"

"Like I'm trying to tell you, he was old enough to
get himself in trouble. And that's all I'm saying about

him. I seen him now and then a few times, and he's no better than he oughtta be."

So Mrs. Cosgrove's son was still alive. I wondered why he'd been omitted from his stepfather's will. Then again, if old Cosgrove had been smacking the kid around, and he'd fought back, maybe he'd been disowned or something.

"Anyways, I give the kids to old Mrs. C, Adam and Arianna, that's what I called them." Debby's eyes glazed over, the way a cat's do when that film comes down and they're not exactly closed, but you know they can't see you. "Cute. They were real cute. Blonde hair, big eyes — they looked a bit like me, not much like their dad. I didn't want to leave them, but it's not like I had a choice back then, right?"

"It must have hurt you a lot, giving them up."

Her eyes snapped back to the present, and for the first time her voice rose above a gritty whisper. "What the fuck d'you think? No kidding it was hard! But I'm not stupid, okay? I know those kids got a better chance with some rich family than they do with a sixteen-year-old kid who's gonna spend the rest of her fuckin' life with a wet rag in her hand, okay? It's better I don't see them again. It'd just hurt me, hurt them … Look, I changed my mind. I don't wanna talk about this shit any more. It's the past. It don't do no good draggin' it up now. I want you two outta here. Please?"

Her voice rose on the last word, high and plaintive. Tears gathered in the corners of her pale round eyes, and her thin lips quivered.

I felt like throwing up. We'd strolled into this woman's life and carelessly opened a wound that should have been allowed to rest undisturbed. I wanted to apologize to Debby, but more than that, I wanted to turn the clock back. I wanted to never have been here. I wanted Peter to never have made that phone call. I felt soiled.

As we slunk out of the bar, I glanced back at her. She pulled a bottle off a high shelf, poured herself a stiff shot, slugged it back. I tugged at Greg's arm and we quickened our pace. Outside, we gulped fresh evening air.

In the car, I rested my head against the headrest and let the shamed tears that had been burning behind my own eyes pour down my face. Greg started the car, and handed me a tissue. Driving back across the river, neither of us said a word.

28

Peter and Dawn were waiting for us. Dawn greeted us excitedly, practically bouncing up and down to hear how the interview had gone. Then she saw my face.

"What happened? Was it the wrong woman?"

"Sort of. It was Adam's mother, all right, but dragging information out of her like that made me feel sick to my stomach."

Greg agreed. "She's had a hard life, and it looks like giving up those kids was just one part of it. Us dredging it up didn't make it any easier. And we were there under false pretenses. It felt wrong."

Dawn looked subdued, and Peter stared into his glass of white wine.

"Well, at least we confirmed that old Mr. Cosgrove was an abusive bastard." Greg tried to salvage something from the ashes of the evening.

"We knew that already," I said. "The only thing we found out was that Mrs. Cosgrove had a son before she adopted Adam and his sister."

Greg's brow knitted, and he was quiet for a moment. Then he said, "I think Mrs. Cosgrove's son was the father."

"What the hell are you talking about? Debby never

said who the father was, Greg. And you accuse me of jumping to conclusions!"

"No, really. She kept hinting at it, didn't she? She said Cosgrove Junior was old enough to get into trouble, and talked about rich kids screwing around, their parents cleaning up after them. Well, isn't that exactly what Mrs. Cosgrove did?"

Despite myself, a growing excitement gnawed at the base of my spine. I sat forward eagerly. "Right! And she said Mrs. C. owed her the favour of adopting the baby and helping her out. Was that because it was Cosgrove Junior who'd fathered the children? Then Mrs. C. just adopted her own grandchildren!"

"Exactly. And it sounds to me like Cosgrove Junior inherited some of his stepfather's mean streak, too. Didn't Debby say something about the rich kids doing mean stuff?"

"Like what?" Dawn asked. "Did she tell you?"

"Not exactly. But she did mention something about boys who've been knocked around, how they're more likely than girls to turn on their abusers, or take it out on other people. She sounded like she knew whereof she spoke."

"D'you think Cosgrove's son beat up on Debby?" Dawn pressed.

"Possibly. It sure sounded like he beat up on someone. God, what a painful situation for Debby — she has to give her kids up to a family she knows are slapping each other around. All she can do is hope Mrs. Cosgrove can live up to her word and protect her kids."

"In the end," I said, "it's probably just as well she never knew what did happen, isn't it? Can you imagine knowing that the family you'd entrusted your kids to had actually killed one of them, and left the other an emotional wreck? She'd be in even worse shape than she is now."

Peter stopped us. "This is all very fascinating, people, but you are operating on an altered plane from me. Would you mind telling me exactly what Adam's mother did say?"

I described the whole interview, with Greg filling in the missing bits. It certainly did look like Adam's biological father was really his much older "brother."

"Well, it would explain the age problem, wouldn't it?" Dawn said. "I mean, you were saying that Adam's mother seemed really old to have kids that age, weren't you?"

"It also explains why I thought I remembered an older brother, but when we looked, we couldn't find a trace of him," Peter said. "I bet old Mr. Cosgrove wrote him out of the will."

"Well, Mom, don't you think we should try to find him?" Dawn asked. "I mean, Adam was his son, and now Adam's dead. Don't you think he should know about that? Even if he was mean to Debby back then, he might be different now."

"True," I said. "And we've been operating all along on the assumption that Adam had no living relatives. But I guess Cosgrove Junior does have some right to know. Besides, he and Debby would be the beneficiaries of Adam's estate, wouldn't they?"

Peter nodded. "That's right. When someone dies without a will, their estate usually goes to the next of kin. Of course, they'd have to prove they were related."

Greg started to laugh. "Every time I think this whole thing is safely dead and buried, something else pops up. Now it looks like we're going to have to find Cosgrove Junior before we can put Adam to rest for good."

"Hey, we're forgetting something obvious here, people," I said. "Maybe Cosgrove Junior really is somewhere around, and that's all very well, but if you look at those birth certificates, the space for 'father' is marked 'unknown'. Which means that anything in Adam's estate would go directly to Debby Landreth, right? I mean, presuming Adam had no children."

Everyone stared at me. "You're right!" Greg said. "You're absolutely right! This is something to tell Benjamin, Katy. Debby might be legally entitled to Adam's estate — he should go tell her. Can you imagine the difference something like this could make to her?"

"Well, there is the downside of telling her both her kids are dead," I cautioned. "That's not going to be easy for her to hear."

"Oh, that poor woman," Dawn said. "I'd hate to be her, wouldn't you?"

I hugged Dawn to me.

"It's not up to us, in any case," Peter said. "You two need to tell Benjamin tomorrow and let him figure it out."

That settled, my mind began wandering. I've never seen much in astrological lore about children who are adopted. It's not really something you can tell, just by looking at a chart. While the other three talked, I wandered over to the computer and called up Adam's chart onscreen. I stared at the circle on the screen, that mandala of life, sectioned into twelve houses, some empty, some containing planets, all linked and interaspected in a unique and beautiful pattern. To look at it, would anyone guess the horrors that had dogged its owner?

The father. Adam had feared the father. Had he meant his real father, the man who'd impregnated

Debby? Or had he meant his grandfather, the rich and overpowering investor, who'd arranged for his chemical imprisonment at the hands of Dr. Shapiro? I exited the file again, no further ahead. Then I looked at the directory, and something went *ping*! at the back of my brain.

"Dawn, you disconnected your server, right?"

"Yeah, of course. You watched me do it, remember?"

"There couldn't be any … I don't know, any copies of it left on the machine?"

"Mom, I turned the modem off. No one can get into our computer now."

"You haven't been in any of my client files, then, have you?"

"No, why?" She was on her feet, looking over my shoulder.

"Look at this, here. I wasn't using the computer at all yesterday, but it says the last time I saved was yesterday afternoon. We were in Montreal at that time."

"Mom, this is getting spooky." She sounded very young. "Someone's been in here, haven't they?"

"It sure looks like it," said Greg. "And whoever it is, they're very interested in Adam. This is too much!"

"Dawn," I said suddenly, "Sylvie doesn't have a key to our place, does she?"

"Mom!" Dawn yelped. "You know Sylvie would never do that! And anyway, no, she doesn't."

"I'm not trying to throw around accusations, honey. Don't be offended. But I want to know what's going on here. This is serious."

Peter had grabbed the phone, and I heard him say, "Yes, I'd like to report a burglary," then wait while the desk officer transferred the call.

"Peter, we have to talk about this first!" I whispered.

He shook his head, placing a finger to his lips, shushing me. It's one of Peter's more irritating characteristics: he doesn't consult, doesn't dawdle, just goes right ahead and acts, no questions allowed. Which is a fine quality, bound to get him ahead in the newsroom. But not in my apartment.

"Peter, get off the goddamn phone," I whispered, disconnecting him abruptly.

"Hey! Why'd you do that?"

"Because I want to think about what's happening here before the cops come traipsing through this apartment. Which, if you recall, belongs to me. Not you, me."

"Fine, have it your way."

"Stop sulking, Peter, it doesn't become you. Now listen. What just occurred to me was this — ever since Adam died, strange things have been happening, right?"

No one contradicted me.

"Okay. There's some kind of pattern here. Greg gets run off the road after mentioning that Adam's files are lost at the Allan. The computer starts getting broken into, and the only files that are touched belong to Adam. Sherry Greene goes ballistic when she realizes we know that Adam was being doped up by Shapiro. The log-off time on the computer yesterday is about half an hour after we get kicked out of Sherry's Shrine to the King. What does it all mean?"

"Yeah, I see what you mean," said Greg. "Someone wants to know how much you know, or how much you've guessed, and I'd bet the same person is trying to cover up Shapiro's tracks, too. What he was doing to Adam was highly illegal, and it would wreck his career if it came out. You can see why Shapiro might want to check you out, find out what you were doing. And why he'd want to shut me up, too, or at least scare me into silence."

Peter looked puzzled. "But why would he risk damaging his own career like this? Sure, what you're saying isn't impossible, but maybe that guy who ran you off the road really was just some punk taking it out on the first fancy car he saw. And sure, that nurse would be mad if she thought you'd tricked her into betraying her boss — she could get fired, right? Or maybe she just resented you pumping her like that. I run into that all the time."

"True enough," I argued, not yet ready to let go of my conspiracy theory. "But how do you explain the computer break-ins? It's happened more than once, and this last one was a physical break-in, not just over the modem."

We went around in circles for another hour until hunger and fatigue forced us out to the Party Palace, an Ottawa institution since the Second World War. The Palace is a greasy spoon in the greasiest tradition: cholesterol, saturated fat, white bread and overcooked vegetables form the dietary staples there. The coffee is always fresh, thick and strong. Food to put hair on your chest — big servings, and cheap.

We found a booth, and over plates of fried eggs, sausages and white toast slathered with butter, we tried to think about subjects other than Adam, his life and death. It was difficult, but we were all pretty burned out. The conversation turned to other crucial subjects, such as whether the video of Fergie cavorting with her former lover was real or fake. I voted for real, but I was outnumbered.

We left, satiated and buzzed on caffeine, since the Palace is not a place to succumb to passing fashion trends such as the recent decaf craze. Greg wandered back toward his car and Peter, Dawn and I went home.

"Oh, by the way." I linked arms companionably with Peter. "I saw Linda Marois today. Remember, from the *shabbos* dinner? She showed up in my office, right out of the blue."

Peter paused. "Oh, right, her. The one with the huge … no, never mind. I couldn't think who you meant at first. How's she doing?"

"Not great. Seems Jean is not the mild-mannered gentleman we met. He's been smacking her around." My voice tightened as I recalled that multicoloured cheekbone. "You'd never know it to look at him, would you?"

"Nope. Though I have to say he did look familiar to me. Couldn't place him, though. Did she happen to mention what he does for a living?"

"Mmm. Something about communications. I forget. Anyway, I gave her my address and told her to get the hell out of there if he starts in on her again."

"That's my girl. Save the world or die trying, huh?"

"Oh, shut up." Arm in arm, we walked home. Peter wanted to sleep at my place that night, and I might not have said no, but Brent's imprint in my bed was just a bit too fresh. I sent Peter upstairs.

But I didn't sleep well. Debby's lined, ravaged face and hoarse whisper kept drifting back into my dreams, and a couple of times I saw her and Adam together, staring at me with those identical pale blue-green eyes. Their combined pain was palpable, nudging at me over and over again, and I tossed around restlessly, waiting for morning to arrive. I wanted to shut both mother and son out of my mind.

29

THURSDAY, AUGUST 4
Moon square Uranus, square Neptune,
inconjunct Pluto ✦
Mercury square Pluto ✦
Mars opposition Jupiter, square Saturn ✦
Jupiter square Saturn ✦

I am not your basic morning person at the best of times. When I haven't slept, I resemble an irritated piranha, just waiting for someone to enter my space so I can take a chunk out of them. So I made a wide detour around Dawn, at least until I had some Grade A caffeine circulating through my veins. Even then, I was no June Cleaver.

The muggy heat was absolutely no help. No matter what I did, the slightest movement left me coated with a film of sweat. I hate sweat. In the shower, I turned the cool water up as high as possible. I stood in the old clawfoot bathtub for nearly fifteen minutes, letting needles of chilling water course down my body.

I got out and began to dry myself, and within a minute, the sweat had returned. I threw my towel to the floor in disgust, a habit I have long tried to eradicate in my daughter, and stalked off to my room, growling. I dug around for something to wear that wouldn't further debase my already foul humour. I found a sleeveless gauze Indian print dress that didn't stick to my skin in too many places, jammed my heat-swollen feet into sandals and said a quick goodbye to Dawn. She was too busy at the computer to pay much attention to my departure, which irritated me further, if such a thing were possible.

I had two clients to see today and a bunch of writing to do, so I trained the rickety fan's feeble stream of air on my face, stuck a disk in the laptop and pounded at the keys for a couple of hours, sucking back an Ethiopian Blend out of a politically incorrect styrofoam cup from Java De-Lux. By the time my first client arrived, I'd lost the fangs and most of the hair on the backs of my hands. I was ready to be the ever-understanding, wise and compassionate astrologer once more.

Gayle Fitzhenry was a small-business owner who liked to check in with me once per quarter about her financial prospects. Nice and simple, no horrifying family skeletons, no people driven bonkers by early childhood trauma. Or at least if there were, she didn't share them with me. I was profoundly grateful. We spent a pleasant hour going over the effects of a Jupiter ingress into her second house, and by the time she left, I was ready for some lunch.

That stupid white chip wagon was still parked on the corner, but once again it promised more than it delivered. So I wandered down Bank Street in search of cheap eats, preferably in an air-conditioned environment. I finally settled for one of my lunchtime regulars — an Italian trattoria featuring fresh pasta, rice rolls handmade by the proprietor's ancient grandmother and sandwiches on crusty Italian rolls. Even as I walked in, the woman behind the cash gestured to the cook to start making my regular: a smoked turkey sandwich, no butter, no mayo, lots of mustard, all the vegetables. She had the rice rolls heating by the time I sat down.

"How ya doing?" she called, and I waved back. Then I took out a paperback novel and settled in to await my lunch. This is one of the reasons I like this neighbourhood. Aside from the obligatory Birkenstock sandals that must be worn by all true denizens, and the occasional shop that sells useless but pricey stuff to people with cash to burn, the Glebe is basically a village. Everyone knows everyone, and most of us get along.

I'd managed to eat most of my sandwich without dripping too much mustard down my front when I looked up to see Brent, looming in front of my tiny table.

"Mind if I sit here, ma'am?" he asked, doffing that ridiculous Stetson. "Sure are lookin' pretty today."

Despite myself, I grinned. "Do you follow me around, or what, Wilkinson?"

He didn't answer, but eased himself into the chair opposite mine. He looked longingly at my rice rolls.

"Forget it, Brent, these are mine," I said churlishly. "Order your own."

"That's not very neighbourly of you, ma'am," he drawled, signalling to the waitress. He ordered a couple of rice rolls and leaned back, gazing at me appreciatively. "Hey, I'm sorry I didn't call you yesterday, but work has been kind of crazy. I figured you deserved more attention than I could give you."

"No problem, Brent. You don't owe me anything. It's not like we're officially going out or something, right?

One night of passion does not a relationship make, you know."

"You're a hard woman, Katy," he said through a mouthful of rice roll. "I thought it was a pretty damn good night of passion, myself."

"Maybe so, but all I'm saying is we don't have a basis for expecting a lot from one another. You know what I mean?"

"Is that the way it has to be?"

"Are you saying you want it to be different?"

"Are you?"

"Brent, we're talking in circles here. I'm just saying that we reconnected in a really nice way the other night, but I'm too old to put all my bets on one horse. Not that we can't ever get together, but I want to be very certain about what I'm doing." I looked down at the table. "I don't want to go through that kind of pain again."

"It hurt me, too," he said quietly. "You think it was easy? For years afterward, I kept asking myself what would have happened if I'd been more honest about how I really felt about you. If I'd been able to put aside my career for a minute to think about us. Then you got married and I got married, and it seemed like everything was more or less resolved. Only when my marriage ended and I started going out again, no one seemed right. No one made me laugh or feel things the way you did. One of the reasons I came to Ottawa was to see if there was any way to repair things. I figured you'd still be married to what's-his-name …"

"Peter," I reminded him.

"Yeah, him. Well, I figured you'd still be with him, and I didn't want to interfere with that, but I thought at least I could see you and apologize. I wanted to get — what's that word you use?"

"Closure?" I smiled.

"That's it. I wanted things to be right between us. It was important to me, Katy. I never even dreamed things would come out the way they did."

"And? Now that they have, where does that leave us?"

"It gives me hope, that's all."

"Me too. But hope makes me nervous. It makes me remember old feelings, and it makes me think about all the hurt we went through back then. I just don't know, Brent."

"That's okay," he said. "I don't either. But since we're both kind of clueless, can we at least keep talking? That would mean something to me."

I touched his cheek, running my finger over that familiar skin. My stomach lurched a little, not unpleasantly. "Brent, I'd be happy to talk to you. Whenever. You just have to give me the space to feel what I'm feeling, okay? And I'll try to do the same for you."

"That's all I want."

He took his paper napkin off his lap, arranged it alongside the plate that now held only the last crumbs of his rice rolls. He stretched out of the chair that was too small for his lanky frame. Then he insisted on paying the cheque, and we enjoyed a brief but very thorough kiss before he strode off down the street. I meandered off in the opposite direction, feeling much better.

I saw my second client, and finished up the chart for the newborn baby. By four o'clock I had a glow of virtue around me, the halo that comes from having applied one's self to the tasks at hand. It was only as I was packing up and getting ready to go home that I realized: I still didn't know how to reach Brent. I was going to have to wait for him to think of calling me.

Okay. I don't want to harp on power imbalances in relationships, but don't you think that if the man knows how to reach the woman, and can do so at his whim, whereas the woman doesn't even know where the man works or lives, there's a kind of inherent imbalance in the relationship? Well, I do.

On my way home I dropped in at the Post Office a few doors down from my office and found their Government of Canada telephone directory. Brent hadn't mentioned what department he was in, so I went straight for the alphabetical listing.

Nothing under Wilkinson. That was odd. Didn't he tell me he'd worked up north in a government job before he took this one? The directory is supposed to cover all employees, not just the ones in Ottawa. He should be in here somewhere.

I took the book over to the clerk behind the desk and asked if there was any other way to check the listing. She stood there, chewing her gum and looking at me, her head cocked to one side. Fine, there's no other way. I can take a hint, all right? I put the directory back on its shelf and headed home.

Maybe the directory was out of date. That's a possibility. Maybe I could get Peter to do some checking for me. He has all those on-line databases at his clever fingertips. The only problem was, I didn't feel like mentioning Brent to Peter. Not yet.

I couldn't exactly say why. I really didn't think Peter would be jealous of my new relationship, as he'd had his fair share of women friends since our marriage ended. I guess it was just the idea of Peter knowing I was getting involved with that particular man again. I'd spent years in our marriage telling Peter what an asshole

Brent had been — complaining about his inability to think about my needs, his grand assumption that I would just pick up and follow him wherever he went. No, I didn't want Peter to know about this yet.

The next option was to wait until I heard from Brent, then pry his phone number out of him. I'd tell him it was a question of principle, of fairness and decency. A mark of the trust we were trying to rebuild. Yeah, that would work.

Pleased with my resolution, I hummed to myself, crossing with the light at the corner of Somerset and O'Connor. There was a loud honk, and a screeching sound. I looked around wildly, jerked from my reverie. The car was headed straight for me, a beat-up old Chev or something like it, the driver intent on his task, eyes shielded by reflective shades. The car was light blue.

Flinging my briefcase and purse toward the windshield, I leaped desperately onto the sloping lawn past the sidewalk. The ground rushed up to meet my body, slamming into me hard. I lay there panting, my heart bursting out of my eardrums, as the car that had just tried to kill me squealed around the corner and sped off down O'Connor.

Another car, a black compact with fuzzy dice hanging from the rearview mirror, pulled over. A middle-aged woman with candyfloss blonde hair rushed to my side. Her eyes were as big as saucers.

"Are you all right, dear?" she asked. "I tried to honk, to warn you, but that maniac didn't even slow down! Do you need an ambulance?"

I shook my head, staring at her. In a daze, I gestured at my briefcase, its contents spilled out on the sidewalk. My purse lay in the middle of Somerset Street.

"Uh …" I struggled for the words. "Purse …"

"Oh, of course, dear, I'll just run and get it for you." She waited for a break in the traffic, then darted with surprising agility into the street to retrieve my handbag. "Here you are. Safe and sound. Now, you really must let me drive you home — you don't look at all well."

"No," I said. "I'm okay. Really. Thank you."

"Nonsense. Here, let me help you up." She grabbed my hand and helped me to my feet, steering me toward her car. My legs felt rubbery. As I climbed into the front seat, the shakes overcame me. My benefactress scooped up my papers and books and shoved them back into the briefcase, which she plopped into my lap, followed by my purse.

"Now. I'm taking you to the hospital." Here was a woman used to taking charge. "Let's see. The Civic's the closest to here."

"No." My teeth chattered uncontrollably. "Hate hospitals." My mouth was dry and I was shaking. I felt chilled, yet damp with sweat.

"Listen, my dear. I have been a nurse for thirty years, and I know a case of shock when I see one. We are going to get you to the closest hospital. Believe me, you need it."

My power to protest had diminished to nil. I allowed myself to be driven to the emergency room at the Civic, where the woman who had temporarily seized control of my life seemed to know a number of the staff.

I'm not really clear on what happened next, but when I woke up, I was lying on a gurney, my feet several inches higher than my head, my purse and briefcase on a table beside me. I was covered in heated flannelette sheets, and my right forearm ached. Something on my left arm felt unaccountably tight. A young woman in a peach-coloured polyester blouse leaned over me.

"Katy? Katy? Can you hear me?"

"What?" The word seemed to come from far away.

"Do you know where you are, Katy?"

"Hospital."

"You had an accident, and you went into shock, okay? Do you remember what happened?"

"Car. Tried to hit me." I tried to sit up, but the nurse put a hand on my shoulder and easily pressed me back down. I looked at my arm and realized that the ache was the result of an intravenous needle that had taken up residence there. Tubing led from my arm to a plastic bag that hung inverted from a stainless steel pole. Affixed to my left arm was a blood pressure cuff.

"Whassat?" I tried to point at the bag.

"We're just replacing some fluid in your body, making sure your blood vessels keep working, okay?" She flashed a bright smile and patted my shoulder.

"'Kay. Can I have a drink?"

"Well, you'll need to wait a few minutes until the doctor okays it, all right? Is there anyone you'd like us to phone for you? Your husband?"

"Um ... yeah. Greg." I gave her the number, and she used a phone on the wall.

"Hello, could I speak to Greg Chisholm, please? Yes, it's Emerg at the Civic here ... a lady named Katy Klein? That's right. She's had a bit of an accident and she came in in shock, but she's coming around now. No, but we're observing her. All right, I'll tell her that. Thank you." She hung up and returned to my bed.

"He'll be here in ten minutes, okay? Now, don't you try to move or anything. You just stay put and everything'll be just fine."

Not that I had much choice. I lay back and let the flannelette's warmth work its way into the deep chill I was feeling. And to think I'd complained of the heat this morning.

Greg sprinted through the swinging doors and galloped over to my side, his usually immaculate hair in disarray, his face red and anxious.

"What happened? Are you okay?" he panted.

"I'm fine now. A car took a swipe at me on the way home and some nice lady picked me up off the side of the road and brought me here."

"Someone tried to hit you?"

"Yep. Beat-up old car, light blue, I think. I threw my purse at it." Suddenly, the silliness of that gesture caught up with me and I started to laugh. Strangely, there were tears running down my cheeks.

Greg wiped my face and sat heavily next to me.

"Katy, that sounds like the car that tried to run me off the road. This is getting way out of hand. We have to tell Detective Benjamin about this. I'm sure it has something to do with Adam's death."

"Sure, I know. But I'm having trouble focusing just now."

So I just lay there, Greg warming my cold hand in his while we waited for my brain to catch up.

30

They kept me under observation for ages. According to Greg's watch, it was six hours before I got out of there. He'd called Peter and Dawn, so I was accompanied home by a committee. We were a very subdued group.

At home, Peter brought down some hamburgers and a salad. Dawn didn't say a word about the evils of meat.

"This kind of brings us back to the Shapiro conspiracy theory, doesn't it?" Greg said. Peter put up no arguments this time. "First thing in the morning, I'm getting Detective Benjamin on the phone and letting him know what the hell's been happening here. This is the end of the line."

"Greg, cut it out," I said. "You don't do tough guy. So fine, we call Benjamin, but I don't see how we can pin anything on Shapiro. There's no evidence that any of this even happened."

"What about the lady who rescued you, Mom?" Dawn asked. "Wouldn't she be able to recognize the car? Maybe she saw the licence number."

I shook my head. "I don't know who she was, honey. And I didn't question her too closely. All I remember are the fuzzy dice on her rearview mirror. They kept going in and out of focus."

Greg jumped to his feet. "I've got an idea. I'll talk to the admitting clerk at the Civic and see if she remembers who brought you in. Maybe we can track the woman down."

He dialled the number, and spoke briefly. Hanging up, he turned to us, downcast. "Shift changed," he said. "No one remembers who the woman was." Then he brightened a bit. "But that's okay. I know Laura, one of your nurses. She's looked after a couple of my people for me. I'll call her tomorrow, when she's back on. We'll get to the bottom of this, I promise you."

I swallowed the last bite of my hamburger, and put my plate on the coffee table. Pushing myself to my feet, I bade everyone a good night and staggered toward the bedroom. Immediately, three people leaped up and began guiding me, like tugboats steering an ocean liner. I shook them off.

"I'm not as decrepit as I look, you guys. I'm just a bit unsteady because my foot's asleep from sitting on it. Now everyone, as you were!"

They fell back as I closed the bedroom door on their faces, shedding my clothing as I approached the bed. I crashed on top of the duvet and fell into a deep sleep nearly as soon as my face touched the pillow.

When I awoke, it was bright outside. A bird was informing the world that it was just a wonderful place, and
why didn't everyone get up this very minute and join
him? I assumed it was a him. No woman I knew would
ever insist that just because she was up, everyone else
had to be. I groaned and rolled over, wanting to snatch
a few more minutes of delicious oblivion. It was not to
be; the phone was ringing.

"'llo?" My mouth felt like it was full of cotton batting.

"Katy? Is that you? It's me, Brent. Did I wake you?"

I lay back for a moment. "No, no," I lied. "No. I was
hoping you'd call."

"Oh, really? Why?" He had the nerve to sound smug.
Like I just couldn't wait to hear from him.

"I wanted to give you shit."

"Hey! What'd I do? I haven't done anything!"

"Well, it's like this." I struggled upright. "You've got
my phone number, right? Which is great, fine by me, no
complaints. But the problem is, I have absolutely no way
to get in touch with you, Brent. Like last night, I wound
up in the hospital, and it would have been nice to let
you know, but it's like you don't exist. No number in the
government directory, and your home number isn't
listed with the phone company, either. What's with the
secrecy?"

"Wait a second. You were in the hospital last night?"

"Yeah, but that's not the point …"

"What the hell do you mean, it's not the point? What happened? Were you sick?" His voice had geared up into hard, fast questioning mode.

"Relax, Brent," I sighed. "I'm fine now. I was in a bit of shock because a car sideswiped me, okay?"

Dead silence.

"Brent? Are you still there?"

"I'll be over in ten minutes. I'll be right there. Don't go anywhere." Click.

"Don't worry, boss, I won't move. I'll wait right here, just like you said." I stuck my tongue out at the dead phone receiver in my hand.

I got up and made some coffee. If I was going to be interrogated by an irate ex-boyfriend who might be about to become an irate current boyfriend, I might as well have my wits about me.

When the knock came at the door, I slowly replaced my mug on the kitchen table, where I was eating my morning bowl of cereal. I took my time on my way to the door.

He stood there looking down at me, his face all scrunched up like he was about to cry. Without a word, he gathered me to him and held me for a minute.

"Fine, I forgive you for being so bossy," I mumbled into his chest.

When he let me go, his cheeks were damp. "I'm sorry I was rude, before. I just thought … if something happened to you …" He cleared his throat. "What happened, Katy? If you don't mind telling, that is."

As I told of yesterday's misadventure, Brent listened, his eyes fixed on me intently. "Did you get a look at the driver?"

"Just a quick peek. He was wearing mirrored sunglasses and he looked … mean. Determined. I think if he'd really wanted to kill me, he'd have followed me up onto the embankment."

"So what do you think? He was just trying to scare you?"

"Yup. I think I've been treading a bit too close to something and he was the messenger, sent to tell me to back off."

"Katy, what the hell are you talking about? Back up and tell me the whole story, okay?"

I hesitated. For one thing, I didn't care for the idea of Brent just barging into my life and taking over. Not that I didn't want to share things with him, but I was damned if it would be a one-way street. Besides, he wouldn't even give me his stupid phone number. Why should I spill my guts?

"Later. Have some coffee?" Ignoring his look of outrage, I poured him a steaming mug. "You look so cute when you're mad, Brent."

"Katy, this is serious. If someone's trying to hurt you, I want to know about it."

"So you can do what? Git yerself a big ol' Colt .45 an' run 'em out of town? Get a grip, Brent. I'm telling the cops about what happened, and they'll take care of it."

"Look. I don't want anything to happen to you. I promise I won't interfere unless you ask me to, but won't you please at least let me know what's going on?"

"Yeah, okay. But first, I have a question for you."

"Shoot."

"Why aren't you listed in the government phone directory?"

He took a sip of coffee and put the mug down on the coaster I'd thoughtfully provided. "Okay, I'll tell you.

It's like this. The department I work for is kind of … well, it's confidential, okay?"

"What, you mean like CSIS?"

The Canadian Security Intelligence Service is Canada's secret service, a child of the former RCMP Intelligence Service, which got itself into major hot water a few years ago for spying on Canadian citizens, burglarizing offices and torching a barn in Quebec, all supposedly "in the national interest". There had been a huge public stink, with the result that CSIS was created and was supposed to report to a House of Commons standing committee. No doubt there was still stuff that didn't get reported, but by and large there was some public accountability now.

"Not quite like CSIS, no." Brent looked like his underwear had suddenly started to itch. "Actually, it's something called the Communications Security Establishment. CSE for short. And it doesn't have a listed number."

"I don't understand. How come I've never heard of this? And how come it doesn't have a listed number?"

"You've never heard of it because it operates on a very secret basis. And there's no number for the same reason."

"Brent, at the risk of sounding judgmental, what the hell are you doing mixed up in an organization like that?"

"They asked me. You know I've been into communications technology for a long time, right? Well, one day this guy meets me coming out of my office, asks if he can buy me a coffee, says he wants to talk to me. I wasn't sure. I thought he might be scamming me, but I went along. I figured in the worst case, I was bigger than him."

I didn't smile. "What then?"

"He recruited me. They were looking for people to integrate their computer system, bring it up to a world-class operation. I had the kind of skills and experience they were looking for. The pay looked good, and I'd have more or less free rein. So they sent me up north for a while, to check out some of the satellite receiving equipment up there, get a feel for the work and see how I could tolerate the isolation. Then they brought me here."

"So what you're telling me is, you're a spook."

"Katy, stop it. I don't wear a trench coat and run around with a gun blasting at KGB agents, okay? Not that there's a KGB any more, now that the Soviets no longer exist. I have a fairly interesting job that involves mucking around with computers and other stuff, and the only hitch is that I can't be reached at work."

"I need to give this some thought." I sat quietly for a few minutes. Brent looked at me like a puppy waiting for someone to rub its tummy. Then, something twigged. Communications security. Someone had been telling me about that, just recently.

"Brent, who's in charge of the CSE?"

"Guy named Marois. Jean Marois. Why?"

I sucked in my breath. This put a different spin on Linda Marois' story of abuse and humiliation. I wondered if my parents knew what their friend did for a living — they have strong feelings about secret government departments.

"It's okay. I know his wife, that's all."

"How? You're friends with her?"

"You don't want to know. Trust me."

"You means she comes to you about that astrology stuff?"

"You're getting better. You used to call it crap. But don't worry, she didn't give away any state secrets. Just the news that Jean beats the living daylights out of her from time to time."

"Wait a sec. How do you know this? Did she tell you?"

"No, actually she wasn't going to say anything. But something else came up and she started crying, and the makeup washed off. Your boss did quite a number on her. Technicolour."

"That's … unbelievable."

"You mean you don't believe it? Yeah, sure, Brent, I'm just making it all up. You know Katy, always going off the deep end about one thing or another …"

"Katy, that's not what I said, and you know it."

I subsided. "What did you mean, then?"

"I meant it took me a couple of seconds to digest, that's all. Listen, can you cut me some slack here? I want to do something about this, I really do. But if I go tearing into Marois' office and accuse him, it won't help anyone. I need to think, to plan out an approach. Can you sit on it for a few days? I promise, I'll try and figure out some way to help that poor lady."

"What the hell. She's been living with it a long time. Probably a little longer won't make much difference."

He looked grateful. Draining his coffee mug, he took it out to the kitchen and washed it carefully before putting it on the drying rack. If I'd been in shock yesterday, I nearly keeled over now.

"Brent? Is that really you? Voluntarily washing a dish?" Maybe he had grown up in some ways.

In fact, I was so blown away by this simple act of basic housekeeping that I didn't resist at all when he put a gentle hand on my back and started steering me toward the bedroom. It was nine in the morning. Time to get to work. On the other hand, my clients could survive without me a while longer. Dawn had already hightailed it over to Sylvie's, as they wanted to surf the net, or something.

All things considered, I opened the bedroom door and invited Brent in.

31

Somehow, sweat doesn't seem quite so objectionable when it is acquired through legitimate physical exertion. So I didn't really mind the salty film that evaporated slowly from my body as Brent and I lay panting, side by side on top of my crumpled duvet.

"Hey." I poked him gently in the ribs.

"Mmm."

"Don't you have to get back to being James Bond?"

"Mmm."

"What time is it, anyway?"

He rolled over and checked his watch on the bedside table. "Ten. Why, you in some kind of rush?"

"Not really. I'm my own boss, you know. Not a wage-slave like some people."

He bopped me with a pillow.

"You're a sneaky one," he said lazily.

"What? How come?"

"I told you mine, but you didn't tell me yours."

"Well, you distracted me. Your own fault."

"Okay, you've got the floor. Give, Klein."

I tried to give him the Reader's Digest Condensed version, but it didn't work. The past week had been full of nuance and detail, and they didn't abbreviate well.

He already knew about Greg's brush with the guy in the beat-up blue bazou, so I told him about Marcel's discovery of the package in the back seat of Greg's car, and our trip to Montreal, and our aborted discussion with Sherry Greene. Brent listened intently, propping himself up with an elbow on a pillow. His eyes, always sleepy looking, seemed even further away than usual; he must be doing some serious data processing.

Then I told him about what we'd uncovered about the blighted Cosgrove family history, our talk with Debby Landreth and our discovery that the apartment had been physically, not just electronically, burgled. His eyes snapped wide open.

"So why didn't you call the cops?"

"Because I wanted some time to think about things. And when I did, I realized that although Greg and Peter and I are pretty certain all this is connected somehow, it would be a hard sell to Detective Steve Benjamin. He wants hard evidence, not convoluted stories that make no sense. So Shapiro is probably into this up to his armpits, but when it comes down to it, whose word will the cops take? The eminent neuropsychiatrist from the world-renowned Allan Memorial Institute, or Katy Klein, failed psychologist and well-known loony astrologer?"

He conceded the point. "So what are you going to do now?"

"I'm not sure. I'll definitely keep you informed, though."

"Yeah, right, after the fact," he complained. "When you're lying in the morgue, or at the bottom of the Canal. Look, you're playing with fire here. I don't know what's going on, but the closer you get to whatever it is, the more you're going to keep having little incidents like yesterday's. You could have been killed, Katy."

"I'm being careful." My tone said, mind your own damn business.

"Katy, I'm saying this because I care about you. You know that, right?"

"I don't know anything just at the moment. When I do, I'll let you know. Anyway, I have to get to work, and so do you."

"Don't be that way. You don't want to hear about love, caring, whatever you want to call it, that's fine. But at least do me the favour of believing me."

I kissed his arm, draped damply across my ribs, and moved it to one side so I could get up and go to the shower. From safe within the confines of the curtained tub, cool jets of water streaming down my body, I shouted, "Okay, Brent, I believe you."

When I came out of the bathroom, he was gone, but on the kitchen table was a slip of paper with a phone number on it. He'd scrawled, "Here's my home number. Gimme a call sometime. B." There was a little heart drawn next to it. I hugged the paper to myself and practically danced out the door to work.

Greg had left a message on my machine, asking me to call him as soon as I got in. I dialled his number and sat tapping my foot impatiently as his secretary went down the hall to look for him.

"Katy? Thanks for calling back."

"What's up? Everything okay?"

"Oh, yeah. Fine. But I had a thought last night after I left you. I'd really love to confront Shapiro myself, you know. Let him know that we know what he's doing."

Oh, dear God — a chill went through me, and I tried to keep the bile down as Frank Curtis' purple face flashed briefly in front of my eyes.

"Greg, that might not be a great idea. That kind of thing can backfire. Badly." My voice shook.

"Oh, I know, I thought about that. But I was thinking I might have a better way to go about it. We could go see your parents, get some inside dope before we confront him. They know him, don't they?"

"Yeah, but what would be the point of that? I'm sure they wouldn't know he was keeping Adam so blitzed that the poor guy didn't know if he was punched, bored, drilled, or the seagulls pecked it out."

"Colourful turn of phrase," Greg chuckled. "No, they wouldn't know that, but they might know about his personal life. Know what I mean? It could give us some clues about how to deal with him. What buttons to push."

"I'm not so sure, Greg. I don't really want them involved in this, for one thing. We've already talked about that. Besides, what could they possibly tell us?"

Greg sighed. "That's the point. I don't know. We won't know until we get there."

"Just let me think about it, okay? I've already dragged Dawn into this, and the thought of bringing my parents in too — I don't know. They've been through a lot lately, with Dad's stroke and all. I'll give it some thought and let you know."

"Sure. Okay, well, talk to you later."

I did give it some thought. In fact, I argued fiercely with myself for most of the day. Argument A: They're old, they're tired. Dad has been sick. They won't be able to tell us anything useful, anyway. They'll want to know why we're asking, and they won't want to say anything mean about Dad's old friend. I don't want them to know what's been going on — at their age, the shock could kill them.

Argument B: What if they know things about Shapiro's wild youth that we could use to get a foothold? If he's one of Dad's old Montreal crowd, chances are they could tell us a thing or two. And I can't protect my parents forever. Sometime, they're going to have to find out. Besides, what about my obligation to Adam?

On the face of it, Argument A had it all over Argument B, but gradually the lure of more information tempted me greatly. I needed better weaponry in this battle against — what? Well, that was part of the problem. I had no idea what I was up against, and I wouldn't know until I had all the facts. And slowly but surely, the path to more facts was leading me to my parents' front door.

By mid-afternoon, I cracked. I called Greg, told him to meet me at my place by eight, and called Dawn at Sylvie's to advise her to eat at her dad's place tonight. If we had to spend any more time on this godforsaken quest, I was damn well going to work late. I needed to put in a few extra hours to catch up with all the work this week had cost me.

"Why, Mom? Is it something to do with the case?"

"I'm not exactly sure," I hedged.

"Forget it. Whatever it is, I'm coming with you."

"No, *you* forget it. You're already way more involved than I want you to be, Dawn. If anything comes to light, you'll be the first to know, all right?" I used my authoritative voice, but I should have known it wouldn't wash.

"That's bull, Mom. I'm coming along."

"Listen, kid, this isn't your call. I'm still your mother, and I'm legally responsible for your well-being. What I say still carries some weight around here, you know. You pulled this one on me last time, and look what happened."

"What? What happened?"

"Come on, Dawn, don't be silly. Adam's apartment wasn't something you should have seen."

"Mom, I'm okay with all that. Really. You remember I told you about the nightmares I've been having about him? Well, somehow, knowing the way he lived, the stuff he lived with, that makes it a bit easier for me." She sounded so earnest, I hated to burst her balloon.

"Well, that's good, but I still don't want you anywhere near this."

She was silent for a moment, then I heard a sniffle.

"Goddamn it, Dawn, don't do this." She didn't answer. "Dawn, please. We're just going to ask your grandparents a few questions about the old days, okay? It's not anything that would interest you. Let it go."

"Mom, you're not thinking about my feelings. I met Adam too, you know. I saw those tiny bones. I know what happened to you and Greg. And what can happen at Zayde and Sabte's? You can't protect me from this, and I don't want you to. I want to be with you. Besides, Dad has to go to an editorial board meeting tonight, and if I can't come with you, I'll have to stay here all alone. Since the thing last week, I've been kind of scared …"

"All right, Dawn," I sighed. "We can talk more about this when I get home. Meantime, you can do me a favour."

"Sure."

"Call over to your grandparents and ask them if tonight would be good, okay?"

It was all arranged. One of the valuable life skills I have struggled to impart to my daughter is the ability to negotiate, to get her point across, not to be pushed around. None of this namby-pamby passive acceptance of authority, just because the person happens to be older or wear a uniform. Still, it's a pain in the ass when she pulls it on me. While I wasn't thrilled she'd cornered me into letting her come, I pushed the whole issue aside. After all, as Dawn had said, we were only going to pay my parents a call. It's not like we were planning to beard Shapiro in his den.

Greg was waiting in his Audi outside my building at eight, and Dawn was just bounding down the walk as I arrived home. The evening air was no cooler than the day had been, even though the sun lay low, an iridescent orange-red disk floating above the western horizon.

Inside Greg's car the air conditioning purred happily, and within a few minutes I began to revive from the day's filthy heat. Dawn chattered away in the back seat, relating her day's adventures with Sylvie — shopping at the Market, surfing the Net. Strange how easy it was to forget that while my own life was drowning in the backwash of Adam's pathetic existence, other people's lives were carrying on around me, oblivious.

I felt like I was living inside a glass dome, segregated from the normal ebb and flow of mundane life, plunged into the phantasmagoria that had been Adam Cosgrove's life. I wanted this damn thing to be over.

32

Mama was outside, dragging the lawn sprinkler to a more advantageous location on the already lush lawn, fiddling with the controls to adjust the height of the spray. She looked up and waved a garden-gloved hand, bustling over to meet us. She hugged and exclaimed over Dawn, kissed my cheeks and greeted Greg warmly.

"*Gut shabbos*, everybody! Come, come in and see your father." She pulled us up the walk in the Rosie Death-Lock, hustling us inside before we could escape. *Oy vey*, and miss out on all the food she had waiting inside for us? What a disaster! This Friday evening, Mama was disappointed at not having had the opportunity to do the whole sabbath thing for us. However, she was down, but not out.

There was a predatory sparkle in her eye as she took this golden opportunity to break out a little snack for us. Nothing big, mind you: some hummus with wedges of pita bread; roasted eggplant relish with enough garlic to fend off all the vampires in Transylvania; "just a few" sugared almonds, heaped into an antique candy dish; cold gefilte fish from my parents' dinner earlier that evening; and a platter of toasted bagels that begged to be spread with cream cheese.

She sat us down at the kitchen table, where the sabbath candles still flickered, and called into the bedroom. Dad was taking his customary after-dinner nap.

"Bernard! Look who's here!" As if we'd just dropped in, unannounced. But to my mother, every new visitor is a gift. "Now, Katy, you look hungry. You should have just a little eggplant."

I hadn't eaten supper, so I heaped my plate with eggplant and took a generous slice of the fish. Mama tilted a critical head at my choice, went to the fridge, and came back with a jar of red horseradish.

"Dawn, *kinderleh*, I have some blintzes in the freezer, saving them for you. You want I should warm them up? It wouldn't take a second, and since you missed dinner last week …"

Dawn coloured, but said nothing about her absence. "Sure, Sabte, that'd be great. You know Mom never feeds me, right?"

My mother pinched her cheek and laughed. "You're humouring an old lady," she said. "I can tell."

Dad shuffled into the kitchen, looking a little better than he had last week.

"Dad," I said, standing to kiss him, "I know you're probably tired, so don't let us keep you up, okay?"

He nodded, smiling. I keep forgetting it's hard for him to talk. Every time I am reminded, a corner of my heart withers.

"Mama, Dad, you remember Dr. Shapiro? The one who was here for dinner last week?" I asked. "George, right?"

"Right." Dad enunciated carefully, so his dragging tongue wouldn't betray him. "I know him from Montreal. McGill. In engineering, transferred to medicine."

"I never liked that man." My mother was always

ready with an opinion. And people wonder where I get it.

"Why not, Mrs. Klein?" Greg asked.

"He's one of those *k'nackers* who puts up a big show about himself, but underneath it all, he's no better than anyone else." She looked to my father for confirmation. "Am I right, or am I right, Bernard?"

"Well ..." my father started, but Rosie took this as assent and carried on.

"You know he's some big *macher*." She translated, in deference to Greg. "You know, some ... hotshot in Montreal, head of this, that and the other, but you want to know how he got there?"

"Now, Rosie ..."

She shushed Dad, warming to her subject. "He let himself be bought, that's how! He's this little Jewish *nebbish*, a nothing, growing up on St. Henri, poor as dirt, but *oy*! Does he have ambition! So on the first chance, when this rich *goy* offers to put him through school, he takes it, and what happens? He's nothing but a *nafkeh*, a whore — whatever the *goy* says, little Georgie says, 'How high, sir?' And then! Then he has the *chutzpah* to tell my Katy she shouldn't be doing what she pleases with her own education, her education that she paid for herself, putting herself through school with her own hard work! Well, we did help her out a little, here and there, but not like the Great Doctor Shapiro, with his fancy-schmancy car and his big titles, who let the *g'vir* tell him how high to piss!"

"Now look what we started," I muttered to Greg. Usually, my mother's English was almost letter-perfect. Accented, maybe, but it was rare for her to pepper it with Yiddish as she was doing tonight. This she reserves for subjects on which she feels most strongly.

"Mrs. Klein ..." Greg said, and she waved her plump hand at him.

"Rosie! You should call me Rosie," she dimpled.

"Okay, then, Rosie — do you know who paid for Dr. Shapiro's education?"

"Oh, yes, we know," she said with grim relish. "It was that miserable old Mr. Cosgrove, him with the house on the Mountain, and his poor little wife, like a mouse she was, creeping around with her eyes always on the cat. She wouldn't say a word without that *alter kacker's* permission."

I was puzzled. "Mama, if you don't care for Shapiro, why did you invite him here?"

She snorted. "Ask your father! He's such an easy touch, his place in heaven is guaranteed!"

"George was one of the old crowd." Dad took advantage of Rosie's momentary pause. "We had some good times. Don't forget."

"*Feh*!" My mother mimicked spitting on the ground, which she would never do in a million years, especially since her hand-scrubbed and polished linoleum was the ground in question. "Good times! You were little boys playing at being big *pishers*, Bernard. If that old man let you little Jews come up to his villa, you thought it was such an honour —" She stopped, looking at our blank faces.

"In those days, there were signs on some places in Quebec," she explained. "'No Dogs, No Jews.' The only way to get into some of the fancy places in the Laurentians was to be a *goy* anglophone."

Greg and Dawn looked shocked. "You mean to say this went on in Canada?" Dawn asked. "Weren't there laws against that kind of thing?"

My father answered, his head shaking slowly from

side to side. "It was all over. Not just here. In those days, no one thought about it."

"So how come Mr. Cosgrove let you come up to his villa, then?" Dawn asked. "He doesn't sound like a very nice man, so why would he do that?"

"Mr. Cosgrove was not nice," Dad said. "His wife was a lovely lady. So sad …"

Mama took up the ball. "He let them in because his wife's son knew them. McGill had just started allowing Jews to attend, and the son could see that some of his classmates were smart, they had real promise — so his stepfather decided he might be able to make use of them."

"Dad, too?" I couldn't picture it. Shapiro I could see as a hired lackey, a *tuches lecher*, but not my father.

"Sure," Dad said, with a lopsided grin. "But just because he thought so, doesn't mean I had to go along with it, does it? And I paid my own way."

I chuckled. "Atta boy."

"Rosie," Dad said, "why don't you get out the picture box. Let the kids see."

Mama bounced up from the table and disappeared for a moment. She returned carrying a bulky brown velveteen-bound box, tied shut with a green ribbon. I'd seen it a million times as a kid. That's where they kept the pictures from the old days.

"Dawn, give me a hand to move some of this food out of the way," I said. "We don't want to get the pictures messy." Dawn and I started clearing, while my mother worked to untie the album. Her arthritis was getting worse, but I didn't offer to help; she would have shooed me away, hurt and offended.

Dad turned the pages labouriously, forcing his clumsy fingers to the task, and I had to restrain myself

from helping him, too. The doctors had assured my
mother and me at the time of his cerebrovascular accident that it would be better to allow him to do as much
as possible for himself. It would give him a sense of
pride, and help heal the wounded neural pathways
somewhat. Still, it pained me to watch him.

He handed me a bunch of photos. "These are from
the Cosgrove villa. Just after Mama and I came home
from Europe. Summer of forty-eight, maybe."

I recognized my parents, both wearing the full bat-
tle-dress swimsuits of the era, leaning against one another and grinning. My mother was still thin from her
ordeal, but starting to plump out. Behind them was a
stand of pine trees, and beyond that, only rocks and sky.

In another shot, three men stood shoulder to shoulder, posing with their heads inclined toward one another, grinning maniacally. One was my father.

"Who are these other two guys?" Dawn asked.

"There's Shapiro." Mama pointed a disdainful finger.

He looked nothing like the cold, patrician medical
elder statesman I'd met last week. Rather, he was ro-
bust, his naturally curly hair springing up in an unruly
mop, eyes glinting with the energy of youth. His smile
animated his face, and he looked full of mischief. How
had he become so withered and dry?

"He looks pretty happy," I commented.

"He didn't have advantages," Dad said. "He wanted
to be more than his own father."

Rosie butted in. "Who drove an old horse-drawn
cart and collected rags for paper. Old Mr. Shapiro was
poor as dirt, but at least he was honest. A hard worker."

"Rosie, George got a chance, and he took it. That
didn't make him a bad man."

I could see Dad's point. In those days, a poor Jew was damned if he didn't try to better himself, and condemned as a social climber if he did. Of course, none of this justified what he'd done to Adam.

Greg was on another track altogether. "Rosie, you said Shapiro had to answer to old Mr. Cosgrove. What did you mean?"

She made a sour face. "He was the family's personal bought and paid for doctor. If that man wanted the latest treatment for his son, the one who was a little *meshuggeh*, Shapiro made sure he got it. Or when his wife, poor thing, when she got so sick in the head and needed to be put away, Shapiro took care of it for him, made sure she got the best of everything …"

"Wait a second," Greg said. "She was put away? Put away where? What happened?"

"*Oy vey*," my mother said. "She was always so pious, praying always to her crosses and climbing up the thousand steps at St. Joseph's on her bare knees, and finally she could do nothing else but play with that little rosary and mumble prayers to her God. So they took her away to some place, some hospital, I think it was in one of the convents in Cartierville. Shapiro supervised her personally."

"Be fair, Rosie," Dad said. "George saw her more often than her own husband did."

"That's true," Mama conceded. "He really took good care, didn't he? Every two weeks, just like clockwork, he'd drive out there and have a little visit, keep her company."

I exchanged glances with Greg and Dawn. Every two weeks? Had he been drugging her, too?

"Is she still alive?" Dawn asked.

"No, no, she must have died … when was it, Bernard? At least ten years ago. I remember we saw the notice in the Gazette. It was a sad thing, very sad."

"What happened to her children?" Greg asked. "You said she had a son?"

"She did, and even with the way his stepfather treated him, like he was a *shmuts*, a piece of dirt, he never let it get to him," my mother said admiringly. "He was always polite, even to the old man, who deserved a kick in the *tuches* more. And he was a real ladies' man. Always the girls were flocking around him."

Yeah, like poor Debby Landreth, I thought, remembering her scrawny, work-worn frame.

"And there were other kids, too, right?" I prodded.

My parents exchanged quick glances. I remembered those brief flickering looks from my childhood: they meant, "Not in front of the child."

"Guys, I think I'm old enough to handle the truth," I said. Then I realized it was Dawn, not me, whom they were trying to shield.

"Zayde, Sabte, I can cope too," she laughed. "I'm a big girl now. I even know how babies are made."

My father laughed, then stopped to wipe the corner of his mouth. "Okay. What happened was this: Mrs. Cosgrove's son got someone pregnant while he was up at the villa that fall."

Mama grabbed the ball again and ran with it. "The girl was young, too young to support the babies, who turned out to be twins, a boy and a girl. And so Shapiro took her back to Montreal, put her in one of those Catholic homes, you know? For unwed mothers? And Mrs. Cosgrove started stuffing her dress with pillows, which your father knew because Shapiro told him, he thought it was so funny. And next summer, when the babies were born, Mrs. Cosgrove took them and raised them as her own. I don't think the old fellow, Mr.

Cosgrove, even knew the difference."

"So what happened then?" Dawn asked.

"Such sweet little things," Mama went on, as though she hadn't heard. "But then, when they were only young, not yet three, the little girl just disappeared, stolen from her crib. The little boy started to pine away for his sister. He was always a little *meshuggeh* after that, wouldn't speak. He looked like the devil himself was following him around. Those big eyes that just stared right through you …"

"And then Mrs. Cosgrove started to get a little crazy, too," Dad said. "Always praying, muttering to saints. She always prayed the kidnapper would feel sorry and bring Arianna back, but nothing ever came of it. Such a sad family."

Sad, indeed. I thumbed idly through the photos, mulling over the injustice of it all. Mrs. Cosgrove, Adam, even Debby Landreth — all scarred for life, while Mr. Cosgrove had lived in wealth to a ripe old age, and his son … A new question formed in my mind.

"Mama, Mrs. Cosgrove's son — you both knew him, right? Is he still around?"

"Of course, *mamaleh*! You had supper with him last Friday night!"

I felt like I'd been sucker-punched. It took several seconds to catch my breath. I stared at my mother, disbelieving. "Jean? Jean Marois? That's Mrs. Cosgrove's son? Why didn't you say so?" I was too shocked to raise my voice.

Mama shrugged. "You didn't ask, *mamaleh*. Why would it matter? We weren't talking about him, you wanted to know about Shapiro, and I told you."

"Who are you talking about?" Greg asked.

"What's going on? Who's Jean Mar — whatever you

just said, Mom? Come on, someone, tell me what's happening!" Dawn demanded.

"Dawn, just calm down, okay? I'll tell you later," I said. "Mama, Dad, I'll call you tomorrow, okay? You've helped us a lot. And thanks for the supper, it was delicious."

"But *mamaleh*, you hardly ate," she protested.

Dad put a hand on her arm. "Let the kids go, Rosie. Katy knows what she needs."

I rose to leave, and Greg and Dawn followed. My parents looked slightly mystified at our sudden departure, but over the years they've learned to take my idiosyncrasies in stride.

33

At the front door, we all exchanged hugs and kisses.
I thanked my parents again, and the three of us bolted
for Greg's car. Greg and Dawn peppered me with questions as we drove back toward the Queensway. I just
scowled and shook my head at them, trying to keep my
thoughts straight.

"Just a second, you guys. I need to think. Okay. We
already know that Adam's father wasn't really his father,
right?"

"Right. He and Arianna were adopted by their biological grandparents," Greg said. "So what?"

"So what is that Adam's real father is Jean Marois, a
charming and erudite gentleman I met at *shabbos* dinner a week ago, along with his wife Linda. Now, yesterday Linda shows up at my office wanting an astrology
reading. In the course of this, it comes out that her husband beats her."

Greg's eyebrows nearly met in the centre of his forehead. "So? He passes along the abuse he got from his
stepfather to his wife. That's too bad, but it's not unusual. I don't want to minimize the woman's pain, but
this isn't exactly a revelation."

"No, but what *is* unusual is that he's also the director of something called the Communications Security Establishment. Ever heard of them?"

Dawn looked blank, but Greg searched his memory banks. "Um, aren't they the ones who do all the satellite listening and so forth? I think I read a magazine article about that a while ago."

"Right. So think about this: Adam is terrified of people listening to his thoughts, tapping his phone, tracking his movements. Don't you think it's a bit of a coincidence that he fears all these things so terribly, when his own brother, who is actually his father, is in fact one of the few people in this country that actually has that capability?"

"Mom, I don't think even the Communications whatchamacallit can monitor people's thoughts," Dawn said. "Adam wasn't playing with a full deck, you know — he was a bit paranoid."

"Well, obviously!" I snapped. "But they could, at least in theory, monitor Adam's calls, keep track of him that way. And even if they didn't, even if they ignored him completely, what might it do to a man like Adam to know that his real father was capable of that kind of thing? It would fit right in with his delusions, wouldn't it?"

"You think that's why there was no phone in his apartment?" Greg was catching on.

"I'd say so."

"And Mom, I heard once that cell phones were the easiest things in the world to track. Do you think they were keeping up with him by the calls he made?"

"It's a definite possibility, honey. I think we need to have a conversation with Mr. Marois," I said. "Although, considering the state of his wife's face yesterday, I think it would be wise to go en masse. He's got a bit of a temper."

"So — do you know where he lives?"

I thought about that. If Brent was unreachable by phone, Marois was probably even more so.

"Greg, would you mind pulling over at the next phone booth? I want to call my parents back, find out if they know where Marois lives."

I hopped out at a corner convenience store and dialled my parents' number. No dice there, though. Mama put her hand over the mouthpiece to ask Dad for the number, but when she came back, she sounded disappointed. Apparently Marois had phoned them last Thursday, right out of the blue, and Dad, with customary gallantry, had invited them to dinner on the spot. Then he'd met Shapiro downtown near his doctor's office the next day and took the golden opportunity to invite him along as well. He'd never bothered to ask for phone numbers, let alone addresses.

I climbed back into the car. "Your grandparents are very trusting people," I told Dawn. "Dead end there. But Greg, I have an idea."

"Uh-oh." But his eyes were smiling.

"What about calling your good buddy Shapiro? Didn't you say you knew him at the Allan? He might know where to reach Marois."

"I don't think he'd give me the time of day. Katy, he's done everything in his power to put us off his trail! You don't send thugs to shut someone up, then just fold up when someone confronts you with the fact that you've been illegally drugging a bunch of people while working under the auspices of a respected mental health institution!"

"Okay, that's true, but now we know he not only doped Adam, but he parked poor old Mrs. Cosgrove in some mouldy sanatorium, then visited her every couple of weeks to make sure she didn't cause any trouble," I said. "I'd be willing to bet he gave *her* the royal treatment, too — that's information that the College of Physicians and Surgeons would find most interesting. He'd be up on charges, never mind losing his licence to practice. If we confronted him with that, don't you think he'd be a bit more ... flexible?"

"You are truly evil sometimes," Greg laughed. "But you might just be onto something. But what makes you think Shapiro will know where Marois is? And what's the big deal about finding Marois, anyway?"

"I just think we owe it to Adam to get this mess cleared up." For some reason, tears choked my voice. "I don't want to leave it hanging. Anyway, Shapiro was really deferential to Marois last week, like he was a bit afraid of him. It struck me odd at the time, but now it makes me wonder if they have an ongoing relationship of some kind. I'd be willing to bet Shapiro knows how to get hold of him. Just a hunch."

"Marois must know Adam's story," Dawn put in. "Maybe not how he died or who killed him, but what about those bones? I bet Marois knows something about that. After all, this happened to his family."

"Okay, okay," Greg said. "But how do you propose we get in touch with Shapiro? We don't know where he lives, and there must be fifty Shapiros in the Montreal phone book. And even if we do find him, he's not likely to invite us out to the McGill Club for gimlets, you know."

I rarely smirk, but this was an opportunity I could not pass up.

"Actually, I happen to know that Shapiro is in Ottawa at this very moment, attending an international conference on the neurochemical underpinnings of psychopathology. He said last week that he'd be attending, and I'm sure I read in the paper that it didn't end until tomorrow afternoon."

"Oh, right," Greg said. "I was invited to that one, but it wasn't exactly up my alley. Too much schmoozing and drug company propaganda, not enough patient care info. It's going on at the Congress Centre, isn't it?"

"I saw the sign when Sylvie and I were coming back from the Market this morning!" Dawn was bouncing up and down in the back seat like a six-year-old. "It's still going on, I'm sure of it!"

"All right, Robin! To the Congress Centre!" I yelled. I started humming the theme from the *Batman* TV show. Dawn and Greg joined in, and we zoomed down the Queensway toward Shapiro's last known whereabouts.

We took the Nicholas off-ramp and sped toward the centre of town. Old-fashioned streetlamps lined the Canal, shedding a picturesque light on its muddy waters. Pleasure craft bobbed quietly alongside the patio of the National Arts Centre, awaiting their turn to descend through the locks to the Ottawa River in the morning. If I'd been able to erase the thought of Adam's black-clad body floating in that still water, I would have thought it a pretty sight.

The Congress Centre is part of a shopping and hotel complex that replaced the funky, picturesque upper end of Rideau Street in the early eighties, tearing it all down to make way for this enormous, characterless white elephant known as the Rideau Centre. It's all glitz and polish, and could have been transplanted here from almost any major city in North America.

Ottawans had been deluded by the developers and their politician buddies that this monstrosity would make us a "world-class city"; but all it did was further gut the already deteriorating downtown core, creating a bus mall that screwed up traffic in ways too numerous to mention, and providing a warm dry place full of nooks and crannies where kids could shoot up in peace until the security guards found them and threw them out into the streets to freeze. Or boil, depending on the season. Now *that's* world-class.

The underground parking lot was full, so we circled back and found a spot near the Westin Hotel. I wasn't sure how we were actually going to find Shapiro, as the conference was a large one and we were not exactly dressed to impress. Greg wore jeans and a golf shirt, Dawn wore shorts and a tank top, and I had on a cotton sleeveless Indian print dress. We looked like a family coming back from a picnic.

But I should have given Greg more credit. Inside the Congress Centre, he strode purposefully toward the main conference area, gesturing to Dawn and me to remain inconspicuous. He made his way through milling groups of doctors and their wives, finally reaching the information table set up outside the main hall.

He spoke earnestly with the young woman who seemed to be in charge and she began to search through a printed list, then smiled broadly and handed Greg a white card. He held it aloft in a salute of victory, grinning at us from across the hall. Then he came back to where we stood.

"What's that?" Dawn asked.

"This, my dear, is my badge of entitlement. I told you I was invited to this thing, and my name hadn't been taken off the list because I never formally declined. So I told the woman at the desk that I wanted to attend the final plenary and she found my badge for me. Now we can go look for Shapiro."

"It doesn't look promising." I eyed the crowds of physicians and researchers milling about, slapping one another on the back and shaking hands. There was constant movement, some strange doctors' minuet. "This crowd is pretty dense."

"Yeah, we're never going to catch up with him in here," Dawn agreed. "Maybe we should split up and meet back here in fifteen minutes."

"Not necessary, I've thought of everything." Greg looked pleased with himself. "We're not even going to try to find him in here."

"Well now, imagine my relief. And would you care to share your grand plan with us, oh great and wonderful one?"

"Come along, my dears, and observe the master in action," he said.

We left the Congress Centre and found the main entrance of the Westin, only steps away. For some reason, the pimply teenaged doormen lounging in the breezeway sported scarlet Beefeater uniforms. Not exactly a perfect match with the overwhelmingly modern decor of the hotel itself. Were they supposed to impress the American tourists? I could just imagine the poor befuddled Yankees scratching their heads.

"But honey, I thought you said we were going to Canada?"

"Yeah, right — let me just check those tickets again …"

The hotel lobby was quiet, in pleasant contrast to the doctor-fest next door. Thick carpeting, comfortable-looking divans and the usual nondescript but tasteful art adorning the walls. There was an enormous chandelier dangling over the escalators, twinkling gaily.

Greg threw an arm around my shoulder, grabbed Dawn by the hand, and we approached the front desk looking, as I said, like a happy family returning from a day's activities in Canada's picturesque capital city. The desk clerk barely glanced at us. Greg leaned across the counter and aimed his most winning smile at her.

"Yes?" Her boredom was thawing already, under the warmth of the famous Chisholm smile. Dawn and I exchanged amused glances, but left the talking to Greg.

"Hi," Greg said. "We're just in for the conference next door, you know, and someone told us that a good friend of ours, George Shapiro, is staying here too. I know you can't give out his room number, but could you possibly call him for us? We haven't seen him in ages, and I know he'd be just furious if he thought we were here and didn't look him up."

"Sure," the clerk said, happy to oblige such an evidently nice family man. And a doctor, to boot.

She punched something into the computer in front of her, then picked up the desk phone. Dawn squeezed my arm in excitement.

"Gee, I'm really sorry," the clerk said, "but Dr. Shapiro isn't answering his phone. Do you want to leave him a message?"

We all looked downcast at this news, and Greg said, "Sure. Could I just have a slip of paper?"

She pushed some paper and a pen across the counter, and Greg scrawled, "Hi, George, just dropped in and thought we'd say hi, give us a call." He signed with an indecipherable squiggle, then folded the paper and put it into the envelope, which he gave back to the clerk. She put it into the appropriate room slot.

"Well, gang, we'd better go," Greg said. We sauntered toward the elevators, out of earshot of the desk.

"What the hell was all that about?" I hissed.

"Simple. She stuck the note in Shapiro's slot, which

just happens to have his room number on it. I saw this trick in a movie once," Greg said.

"Cool!" Dawn laughed. "Greg, I'm glad you're on our side!"

"Fine, so we know his room number," I admitted. "But if he's not in it, it's not much help, is it?"

"Not until we move into Phase Two of the operation," he said.

We took the elevator to the tenth floor, found Shapiro's room, and Greg rapped loudly at the door. There was no answer. "He's still over at the Congress Centre," Greg said, unnecessarily, I thought.

"So what do we do now, Sherlock?" I asked.

"We wait for him, I suppose. He can't be all that long — the closing plenary was starting when we were over there, and it was scheduled to last an hour or so. That was half an hour ago."

We took up a holding position around the ice dispenser. Every time someone emerged from the elevator, we pretended to be just kind of wandering nonchalantly toward our fictitious room. Greg even pulled a key from his pants pocket to add to the realism.

We had just returned to the ice dispenser when Dawn whispered, "Shh! I just heard something!"

"What was it?" I asked.

"I'm not sure. A popping noise. Down there." She pointed toward Shapiro's room, but there was nothing to be seen. Just then, a door slammed. I stuck my head out again from behind the ice dispenser, just in time to see a male figure striding quickly away from Shapiro's room toward the fire exit. He was through the door and galloping down the stairs before any of us could react.

"Was it him?" Dawn asked.

I shook my head. "I can't tell. It might have been. Tall and skinny, but not bald. Did Shapiro ever wear a rug, Greg?"

Greg shook his head. "Not that I know of. But that didn't look like Shapiro to me. What was some stranger doing in his room? This stinks, Katy."

"Come on, we don't even know for sure that the guy came out of Shapiro's room," I said. "We may as well go on home. I don't think we're going to find him tonight."

"Not so quick," Greg said. "I have an idea."

And that's how we reverted to Plan B. Since Greg had the appropriate hormonal complement — and a masculine voice — we sent him back to the lobby to order room service on behalf of the good doctor.

"And keep it simple," I said. "No champagne and roast duck, okay?"

Eventually we'd have to reimburse Shapiro, and whatever Greg ordered, it had to fit my budget. I had little use for Shapiro, but I wasn't going to stick him with a bill for our attempt to break into his hotel room. Greg reappeared, triumphant, a few minutes later.

"Did they give you any hassle?"

"Nah. They asked where I was calling from, and I said I was over at the Congress Centre and on my way back, and I'd expect the meal in my room by the time I got here. They were pretty cowed, I think. I got the impression they've already had a few run-ins with Shapiro."

"But Mom, if he's not in there, what are we going to do? They won't let us just come in and wait for him, will they?"

I hadn't thought that far ahead, but Greg just grinned. "Leave it to Uncle Greg, kiddo," he said. "Don't forget, I've got this badge — I'm Georgie-boy's best friend, don'tcha know. They'll let us in, all right."

I wasn't sure if the bellhop would buy this particular deception, but it was the closest thing we had to a plan. "Don't worry, Dawn," I said. "If they won't let us in, we'll go home and find him in the morning. No big deal." But somehow my words rang false in my own ears.

Now all we had to do was look inconspicuous while we waited for room service. Dawn suggested we hang out in the stairwell just down the hall from Shapiro's room and make our move when we heard the cart approaching. We huddled there, trying not to giggle with nerves, holding the door slightly ajar. In a couple of minutes, a uniformed waiter pushed a beautifully-appointed tray, complete with a cover to keep Greg's tuna sandwich at the correct temperature, down the hall toward our target.

34

We emerged from our hiding place, feigning breath-
lessness. After all, we were supposed to have just
climbed ten flights of stairs. We congregated noisily
behind the hapless young waiter, who appeared taken
aback by our sudden onslaught.

"Hi!" Greg greeted him. "Are you taking that food in
to Dr. Shapiro?"

"Yes …" the guy said, clearly wondering who we
were. Then he caught the conference badge on Greg's
chest and his expression lightened somewhat. A doctor — maybe we were more respectable than we looked.

Greg pressed his advantage. "We were just coming
to see him, too! How about that!"

"Uh, yeah, how about that." The waiter rapped
loudly on the door. "Room service!" he yelled.

Of course, there was no answer. I hid my smirk of
satisfaction at our cleverness. Now the problem was
going to be, how do we manage to stay in Shapiro's room
once the waiter left? He probably wouldn't just say,
"Sure, c'mon in! Dr. Shapiro won't mind if you just wait
for him here."

"Maybe he's in the washroom?" Dawn offered, trying to be helpful. "He's got a … a condition, you know."

Greg gave her a look, and I stifled a laugh. The waiter looked worried.

"I can't just leave the tray here," he said. "Hotel rules. He has to sign for it."

"Do you have a pass key?" Greg prompted. "I'm sure he'd like his food promptly — he's a bit of a stickler that way." Leaning conspiratorially toward the waiter, he stage-whispered, "George can be a little cranky sometimes, you know."

The waiter looked uncertain, hesitating between being chewed out again by a perennially dissatisfied guest, and getting in hot water for entering a room without authorization. We all tried to look trustworthy, not at all as if we were hustling this poor guy, who after all was only trying to do his job. He probably wasn't getting much more than minimum wage for all this aggravation.

He fumbled in his jacket pocket for the key and opened the door.

"Room service!" he called again, pushing the cart into the room. Then, just as rapidly as he'd entered, he backed out again, bumping into the three of us, who were crowding through the doorway. The waiter held a hand over his mouth and his eyes looked as though they were only attached to their sockets by a thread.

"What?" I demanded, shoving past him. Dawn was directly behind me, pushing to get past, but I blocked her, which turned out to be a good thing.

You know the old saying about fools rushing in? That pretty much sums it up, for me. The room had one of those beige-on-beige decorating schemes, designed to offend no one. While I can't say it was to my taste, I was less concerned with the pickled pine armoire and the champagne-coloured bedspread than I was with what was sprawled across the bed.

Shapiro had been in the room all along. He lay face down, half on and half off the expanse of king-size bed. He was immaculately dressed in a grey summer-weight suit, probably custom-tailored. His knees were on the floor, his arms spread-eagled, palms down. Under one hand was the television remote control. His head was turned away from us.

In the back of his head, facing me, almost hidden by his silvery hair and very close to where his skull joined his neck, was a small hole, surrounded by a tiny black halo. This innocuous perforation must have been the source of the crimson stain that blossomed out like a grotesque peony on the bedspread around him.

I had never seen a man who had been shot to death before. I hope I never do again. I only glanced at Shapiro for a second, but that was plenty for me. Backing rapidly up against Dawn and Greg, I bulldozed them unceremoniously out of the room, herding them backward.

"Go on, get out!" I shouted. Dawn loudly protested this cavalier behaviour, but I didn't care. To the waiter, I said, "Don't touch anything. Go down and call the police. Now!"

I didn't need to tell him twice. He stumbled toward the elevator, still cupping a hand over his mouth. He kept retching all the way down the hall.

Grabbing the arms of my two partners in intended crime, I hustled them back into the stairwell. On legs that wobbled only slightly, I led the way down all ten flights of stairs to the tunnel that led to the parking garage. It was only once we'd found Greg's car and I was safely ensconced in those soft leather seats that I caught my breath and steadied myself. I discovered that I was actually able to speak.

"What is it? What happened? Mom, what's the matter?" Dawn kept asking, looking like I'd taken away her all-day lollipop. "I thought we were going to talk to this Shapiro guy — what's going on here? Why'd you push me out of the room? I wanted to see, too!"

"Shapiro. Is. Dead." I took the minimalist approach. "Lying on the bed. I think someone shot him." By now, the chill in my hands and feet, the lightheaded feeling, the constant whoosh-whoosh of blood in my ears had almost become familiar to me. "Greg? Is it possible to go into shock more than twice in a week?"

He paid the parking attendant and we navigated the sparse nighttime traffic in silence. Dawn had quieted down, overwhelmed by this startling turn of events.

"Should we go to the police?" I asked.

Greg didn't reply immediately. Maybe it was a trick of the passing streetlights, but his skin had taken on a very peculiar greenish tint.

"They might think we did it," Dawn objected. Then she corrected herself. "But they couldn't possibly think that, could they? We'd have to be incredibly stupid to do that. And he was dead when we found him! Right, Mom?"

"Yeah, but we were trying to illegally enter his room, weren't we?" Greg said. "Plus, we left the scene of a crime. I think that's illegal, too. We're in big trouble."

"That's not the point," I said slowly. "Greg, you'd better take us directly to the police station." This business of living in crisis was really starting to get to me. Somehow my previous uneventful — not to say boringly decorous — life seemed really attractive at that moment.

"But Katy ..."

"Greg, Dawn is absolutely right. The cops have

every reason to suspect us. Every time a dead body has shown up recently, we've been connected to it in some way. If we don't go in and report this one immediately, Benjamin is going to be sure we killed him. Whereas if we go in now and tell him exactly what happened, there's a chance he might believe us. Or at least give us points for being honest."

Greg could see the logic in this. We'd been cruising down Colonel By Drive alongside the Canal. He turned right at the Pretoria Bridge, crossed over to Elgin Street and found a parking spot on a side street. We clung together as we walked, but we didn't look nearly as fresh-faced as we had in the hotel. My stomach was doing violent push-ups and despite the warm air, I felt chilled and clammy. Dawn squeezed my hand, but I barely felt it.

At the desk we asked for Detective Benjamin and within minutes he was in the lobby, looking not at all happy to see us. He resembled a basset hound on downers tonight — probably working the late shift. No Beau Brummel at the best of times, he'd discarded his worn suit jacket in favour of a green and white striped shirt, rolled up at the sleeves. Something suspiciously like the remains of a jelly doughnut adorned the placket.

"We'd, uh, like to report a murder," I said, not meeting his eyes.

Benjamin's eyes narrowed to slits and without a word he spun on his heel, beckoning to us to follow him. He needn't have bothered leading us; I already knew the way. I reflected that it is not an auspicious sign when the local police station begins to feel this familiar.

Benjamin sat on the edge of his desk, since we were using up all his allotted chair space. He pushed aside a couple of cardboard coffee cups and one sloshed its contents onto a file folder. He mopped at it ineffectually with a couple of tissues. Then he ran a hand through his hair and looked blearily at us.

"Now." He sounded grim. "Would you care to tell me what this is all about?"

"We found a body," I said. "He's — it's a doctor, a friend of my parents. Dr. George Shapiro, from the Allan Memorial Institute in Montreal. He's staying at the Westin, room 1006. We just wanted to ask him a few questions, and there was this guy from room service taking a tray in, so we just kind of followed him in, and Dr. Shapiro was lying on the bed with blood oozing from his head. I think someone must have shot him."

I decided not to mention that the room service waiter had only been there at our behest. It didn't seem relevant.

A muscle twitched in Benjamin's cheek. I wondered if he might benefit from some yogic breathing exercises. He scanned the tops of the room dividers surrounding his work area, then refocused on me.

"Would you like to explain to me exactly why you felt you had to question this doctor? No, don't tell me." His voice grew quieter with each word. "You decided to continue 'helping out' the police investigation into the death of Adam Cosgrove, and this was another of your little plans to gather more information, right?"

He was really quite red in the face. I wondered about his blood pressure; there were a few broken capillaries in his nose already.

Greg took over. "We'd been talking to Katy's parents earlier in the evening, and they told us some things that made us think Shapiro might know about Adam. Detective Benjamin, Adam was my patient. I feel we owe it to him to find out as much as possible about his life. And his death."

I nodded my approval, but Benjamin did not seem moved.

"Dr. Chisholm. Listen carefully. I have already informed you and Ms. Klein here that this is a police matter, have I not? And I believe I might have mentioned that if you should come across any more interesting information, you should inform the police, not act on it yourselves. Is that not correct?" He seemed upset.

"Detective Benjamin," I said, in my best, most calming therapist voice, "I know this looks very bad, but we didn't mean to cause problems for you. Really. We only wanted to talk to Dr. Shapiro, not get in the way of your investigation. We had no way of knowing he'd be dead. As soon as we realized the situation, we came directly to see you. Oh, and I also told the waiter to call 911."

Benjamin gave me a withering look, picked up his phone and barked something in police jargon. He listened, nodded, grunted a few times, then hung up. He didn't look at any of us, but seemed to study his brown loafers. This man could use a fashion makeover, I thought. I should introduce him to Carmen, my interior decorator friend. She'd do wonders for him. Carmen — God, I haven't called her in over a week. I hope she's still speaking to me.

"You're right, Ms. Klein," Benjamin said at last. "The body has already been called in. A waiter at the Westin. Fortunately for you, he told the 911 operator the same story you just told me. Now. I'm going over there, have a look around. When I come back, I'm going to want to talk to you some more. Is that clear?"

We nodded. Yes sir.

"So. For now, I want you to go home, stay there and

try to mind your own f-- … try to keep out of trouble for a couple of hours until I get to you. Okay?"

We nodded again. We will, sir.

"And keep your phone line clear. I'll call when I'm ready for you, probably in a couple of hours. Now get out of here. I've got work to do."

I was not pleased with this abrupt dismissal, but I was relieved we wouldn't have to spend the rest of the night in these uncomfortable moulded plastic chairs, drinking stale coffee and awaiting Benjamin's return.

35

We sat listlessly in my stuffy living room, waiting to hear from Benjamin. The vivid image of Adam lying in the morgue had been displaced from my consciousness by another, equally morbid one: Shapiro, collapsed across his hotel bed, neatly combed hair nearly obscuring the small black hole. And blood, blood spreading out around him like a ghastly overblown flower.

"Greg, if he was hit in the back of the head like that, would he have felt much?" I asked.

"He probably heard the killer behind him, but no, I doubt he would have felt anything," Greg said. "I've read about this kind of thing. It looks to me like a close range execution-style killing, not a spur of the moment thing — you know, where he and the murderer were struggling and the gun just kind of went off. It wasn't like that. It was very neat. And you saw he was holding the TV remote in his hand, so I think he was feeling at ease when it happened. Not expecting anything."

"You saw it, then?"

"Yeah, sure, until you frog-marched us out of there. God, you can be bossy sometimes."

"Yeah, well, you don't have kids. You don't know

what it's like — I wanted to get us out before Dawn saw. You didn't see it, did you, honey?"

Dawn shook her head. "I was just trying to get past you when you started pushing us. Anyway, how long do you think Shapiro was lying there?"

"I'm no pathologist," Greg said, "but it seems to me it would have taken ten minutes for the blood to spread like that. Plus, he had minimal lividity."

"What's that?" Dawn leaned forward.

"Well, when a corpse has been lying around for a while after death, blood starts to pool on the bottom side of the body."

"Can we please stop talking about this?" I asked. "I almost lost my supper back there, and this isn't making things better."

"Hey, you were the one who started it," Dawn protested. "Besides, we need to get our story straight for when that authoritarian asshole cop calls us back."

I was too tired to even attempt to correct her language. "Yeah, well, I don't need any help remembering what Shapiro looked like. That image is now permanently engraved on my retinas." Then something else occurred to me. "Oh shit, I just remembered something. I promised I'd call Brent if anything else happened."

"You also promised Detective Benjamin you'd stay off the phone," Dawn reminded me.

"This'll only take a minute." I was as good as my word — I left a terse message on Brent's machine, asking him to call me. Then we sat back and waited some more.

Dawn was falling asleep, her head lolling back against the chair, when the phone rang. Her head snapped upright. I jumped to snatch up the receiver, but it was Brent, not Benjamin.

"What's up? I got your message."

"I can't stay on the phone. The police want to be able to get through, and it's a long story. Can I tell you about it in the morning?"

"The police? What the hell have you been up to now?"

"Oh, sure, it's bound to be my fault," I snapped. "How come everything is always my fault, Brent? We just happen to have discovered a body. No one you'd even know — a Dr. Shapiro. So now we have to wait and speak to the police, who have asked me to keep a line clear. Which is why I have to hang up now, if that's all right with your royal majesty."

There was a silence. Then, "Fine, Katy. Have it your way. I'll speak to you in the morning." Click.

Damn. Unexpected tears sprang to my eyes. I hadn't meant to push him away quite so hard. This relationship thing was going to take more work. I went to the bathroom and grabbed a handful of tissues and blew my nose loudly.

When I came back, Dawn's eyes were at half-mast and she was yawning. Greg was trying to talk her into grabbing some sleep, but she didn't want to miss anything. Finally, though, the two of us managed to convince her we'd wake her as soon as anything happened. She went to her room.

"But I'm not getting undressed," she said defiantly.

"I don't care. Just go," I replied. "You need the sleep."

I fixed Greg and myself some herbal tea, turned the TV on to Leno and we settled in to wait for Benjamin's call. Half an hour later there was a tentative rap on the door. That would be Peter, back late from his meeting. Probably saw the light on. Editorial meetings often went on into the wee hours, winding up downtown in some of Ottawa's seedier drinking establishments, so Peter was actually a little early. Anxious to fill him in on the day's events, I struggled out of my comfortable chair and slipped the chain off the door.

"Hi," I said, but the man standing in front of me was not my ex-husband.

It was Jean Marois, smiling at me. He was holding a big, ugly gun, which he pointed directly at my stomach. As he pushed the door open with his foot, he nudged me with the barrel and I jumped backward.

Have you ever felt so frightened you were actually unable to breathe? That's how I felt. My chest heaved desperately, but no air came in; I just made a funny, high-pitched wheezing sound.

"You are not going to invite me in, Katy?" Marois asked. It surprised me that his voice sounded just as cultured, as gently refined, as it had at my parents' house.

I still couldn't talk, but I moved back from the door and Marois entered. Greg, thinking he was about to greet Peter, was approaching the vestibule with his hand extended, a friendly welcoming grin frozen on his face. He looked from the gun to me and back again. His eyes registered confusion, then fear.

"Katy?" he managed. His mouth kept opening and closing, like a fish surprised to find himself flopping around in the bottom of a rowboat.

Marois herded us back into the living room, motioning with the gun for us to sit. I sat. All I could think was, *Please, God, don't let Dawn wake up. Don't let him hurt her.*

I've been an agnostic with atheistic leanings for many years, but this was the second *shabbos* in a row in which I'd prayed for my daughter's safety.

I sat on the edge of the couch, numbly watching Marois. To be precise, I watched that very large gun, which seemed to grow in his hand. It was strange. I used to work every day with patients who'd suffered trauma, and one of their main symptoms was dissociation — the ability to exist in a terrifying situation while feeling as though they were elsewhere, perhaps watching it all on television or something. I'd always sympathized, I understood the concept, but I'd never really lived it. Now I could honestly say I had some idea of what they were talking about.

"What … do you want?" I managed finally. It took great effort to force the words past my frozen lips.

Marois looked relaxed, tranquil, on top of things. Well, no shit. He was the one holding the gun.

"I just felt it would be beneficial to have a word with you, Katy. But I had no idea you would have a guest. Would you care to introduce me?"

Bile backed up into my throat. I swallowed hard, willing myself into composure.

"This is Dr. Greg Chisholm," I said. "Greg, this is Jean Marois. Director of the Canadian Security Establishment," I added, feeling it was only polite.

"Ah, so this is Dr. Chisholm." If Marois had not been pointing a gun in our direction, I think he actually would have leaned forward to shake Greg's hand. "I believe you once treated my unfortunate half-brother, is that not so?"

"Was he your half-brother?" Greg replied. "I was under the impression he was your son."

I made a small noise in my throat. Please, Greg, don't antagonize him.

But Marois only raised an eyebrow. "You have been doing your homework, Dr. Chisholm." He seemed pleased at Greg's acuity.

"I have. And I wonder if you might perhaps explain a few things to me." Greg smiled conversationally. "For example, I realize you killed Adam, but I've really been at a loss as to exactly how you did it. It was all so neat. Very tidy."

What the fuck are you doing, Chisholm? I glared at Greg, but he ignored me.

Marois, though, had cocked his head to one side. "It was not difficult, really." He was all modesty. "You must understand, Adam was always a very ... predictable person. Predictable, yes. I merely followed you to the site he'd arranged with you, waited for him to bolt into the woods when the car approached, and had ... my assistant administer the lethal injection. Rather like putting down a rabid dog, you understand."

A chill passed through me. "But — they didn't find any poisons in his body. They said he'd had a heart attack. How could you make someone have a heart attack, for God's sake?"

"Katy, I don't think Monsieur Marois here would have been clumsy enough to use anything detectable. Am I right?" Greg asked.

I was beginning to catch on. Greg was flattering Marois, buying into his narcissism — the complete, single-minded self-absorption that fuelled the man. Greg understood Marois' need for admiration, and he was giving him what he wanted, subtly drawing him out.

Sure enough, Marois rewarded him with a smile. "Of course not, Dr. Chisholm. As you know, Adam was of a nervous, a rather anxious disposition. For some reason, he was always very distressed by my presence. It was an easy matter to augment that distress, raise him to an even greater degree of anxiety. Enough to simply cause his heart to stop beating. Nothing painful, you understand — just an exacerbation of his existing state."

"No, of course not. Very clever indeed." Greg sounded admiring. "May I guess that you used an injection of epinephrine?"

"Well done, Dr. Chisholm. I really don't consider that murder, do you?"

My mind worked furiously. In Adam's state of abject terror, his adrenal glands would have been working overtime, pumping out adrenaline, otherwise known as epinephrine, at a tremendous rate. Adrenaline is the natural hormone that prepares the body to fight off threats, or to flee them — it's sometimes known as the "fight or flight" hormone. It speeds up the heart rate, increases blood pressure. If Marois had administered enough epinephrine to a man already pumped as full of it as Adam had been, it certainly would have caused heart failure.

"You mentioned an assistant?" I asked, though I already knew the answer. It would have taken two people to give Adam the shot. The state he was in, he certainly wouldn't have held still long enough for someone to prepare the syringe, find a suitable injection site and administer the drug.

"You are intelligent enough to guess that, I think, are you not, Katy?" Why had I not noticed the flat vacancy of his eyes last week?

"Shapiro," I guessed. "Which of course is why you had to kill him tonight? You knew we were beginning to see his connection to Adam's death?"

Marois waved the gun dismissively. Despite myself, I flinched.

"He was my stepfather's tool," he said contemptuously. "I no longer had a use for him. Tiresome man."

"Yet you seemed to be friends when I met you at supper last week," I said.

"You may have noticed, my dear, that what I seem and what I am are two different things." Marois actually seemed to be enjoying this. Yeah, well, he'd probably been the sort of kid who'd liked burning bugs to death with magnifying glasses, too. "Shapiro was a sycophant, my stepfather's possession. So long as his interests coincided with my own, I saw no reason not to allow him to live. But when those interests diverged, well …" He shrugged eloquently.

"But …" I searched for words. "Even Shapiro … I mean, he was willing to keep Adam sedated all that time, and I suppose he did the same to your mother, but to actually kill someone …"

Marois sniffed. "It is clear that you misunderstand people like Dr. Shapiro, Katy," he explained. He sounded almost grandfatherly. "You must realize that a man who has allowed himself to be bought and paid for over a period of four decades is not likely to suddenly become a free agent. Shapiro had no mind of his own. I simply acquired my father's mortgage over him. He did what I asked, because he knew the consequences if he chose to do otherwise."

"While we're on the subject of the older Mr. Cosgrove," Greg said, "we've both been wondering whether it was you or your stepfather who, well, you know — the little girl?"

"She was a very noisy, unpleasant child," Marois said. "Much like her brother — a cringing, whining brat. I did tell my mother what might happen, I warned her of the outcome, should she choose to believe …" and here he spat the words, "… that servant-girl. That whore. She could provide us with no evidence of paternity. No proof whatsoever. My mother, the poor fool, agreed to take responsibility for that unfortunate young woman's spawn, and of course it was a catastrophe."

The mask of civility was cracking. Greg had eased his way into the heart of Marois' corrupted psyche, peeling back the layers of acquired gentility and education, the years of practised civility, to expose the raw sewage below. There was something satisfying in watching the façade degenerate: it was like watching the truth emerge from a forest of lies and subterfuge.

"She annoyed you?" Greg prompted.

Good, Greg — focus on his feelings, how she made him feel.

"She would not shut up!" Marois snapped. "She cried, and I warned her she was irritating me. She angered me to the breaking point, only it was really her own breaking point, you understand?"

Marois smiled and snapped his fingers in the air. My stomach lurched sickeningly as I took his meaning. In the back of my mind, I heard Adam, choking and sobbing as he described the stark horror of his sister's death: " … screaming, crying, until the end … and then, there's nothing."

I clamped my teeth together to keep my throat from opening in an hysterical wail of mourning. Pain eddied up through my body as I fought to stay in control. I wanted to throw myself across the room, smash this smiling, genteel monster who held us hostage with a gun he cradled as casually as a lit pipe.

"How …" I began, but the word remained a whisper, blocked by a lump the size of a tennis ball in my throat. I coughed slightly and tried again. "How did you keep it quiet? Didn't anyone wonder what had happened to her? Weren't you worried your mother would find out?"

Marois looked at me levelly. He seemed oblivious to the effect of his words, and it struck me forcibly: nowhere in his blandly toxic psyche had he any understanding of the horror of his actions. To him, the child had screamed, he'd wanted her to stop and he'd shut her up — just as Adam had made a nuisance of himself, coming off his medication, running around talking about the past. He had to be stopped, and Marois had done it. Uncomplicated and straightforward — there were no inconvenient moral ambiguities for Jean Marois.

"You are underestimating me." He shook his head at my lack of perception. "My mother was a weak, easily led woman. I told her the brat had died in her sleep, and my mother had no wish to contradict me. I told her to dispose of the remains and she did it — I believe she had some little sarcophagus made, and added it to her ridiculous collection of religious artifacts. She was a weak, spineless woman."

"But Adam saw," Greg said softly. "That must have proven awkward for you."

Marois glared at him and raised the gun slightly, a quiet reminder of exactly who was in control. Greg ignored the implied threat.

"Why didn't you just kill him too?" he pushed. "He got in your way, too, didn't he?"

"Adam," Marois spat. "Mewling little cretin. He was even more gutless than my dear sainted mother. Of course, he was just that much easier to control. Very susceptible to the power of suggestion, you know." Marois smiled to himself, and once again his sadism showed through, raw and unguarded. "Adam," he murmured. "I could silence him with a look, a whispered word, and the little dimwit would flee, cowering off to his room. You know, he actually stopped talking once, simply because I told him to shut up! He didn't utter a word for years. No, he was no trouble to control."

Staring at Marois, all I could think of was Pluto. Pluto rising in Adam's chart. Pluto the destroyer, the blindly destructive rapist and murderer, emerging from the bowels of the earth to control and shatter lives. Uncaring, unfeeling, acting out his own needs and desires with no concern other than this: my will be done.

This was the Pluto I'd seen in Adam's chart, the one I'd pointed out to Linda — the Pluto of raw, untrammelled power. The power to demolish without batting an eyelash. And always hidden, acting behind the scenes, invisible even to his victims, wreaking his damage and leaving them to blame themselves for his rampages of terror.

"I'm curious," Greg said, as though Marois had described nothing out of the ordinary. "How did you know about Katy's and my involvement in Adam's life?"

"Did Katy not explain to you the position I hold?" Marois asked, shaking his head in disbelief that anyone could possibly be so dense. "I have access to certain electronic devices, shall we say, that enable me to keep track of people in whom I have an interest. When Adam first telephoned Katy, I thought little of it; but her continuing interference piqued my interest. So I simply assigned one of my employees," and here he smiled benignly at me, "an old friend of hers, in fact, to report to me on her actions."

I sat up very straight, my mouth dry. Brent? Had he been assigned to monitor my calls, watch my activities, report them to his superiors at the CSE? I wanted to rage, to cry, but I did neither. I just stared at Jean Marois, who was clearly enjoying my distress.

He raised an eyebrow in mock concern. "You really ought to be more careful, my dear. What is it they say — 'when something seems too good to be true, it probably is'?"

Greg had another question, but I barely heard him speak. Brent. I couldn't let myself believe he'd had anything to do with this, but —

"What about the fellow who tried to run me off the road?" Greg asked. "Was he one of yours, too?"

Marois waved a dismissive hand. "Pah. No, he was an old patient of Shapiro's. Clumsy, an unfortunate waste of time and energy. But you see, Shapiro had not the same judgment, the same ability to plan that I have. He panicked, when it was not at all necessary. I had everything in hand."

"Was Shapiro's thug the same person who posed as a police officer the night Adam died?"

"Very good, Dr. Chisholm. You have a good eye for detail."

This was starting to sound like one of Peter's news conferences. Marois, bland and confident, the consummate government official, sat answering questions, putting just the correct spin on things. Revealing only what he wished.

I said nothing. I was less concerned with Brent's betrayal or Shapiro's hired hand than I was with my daughter. For directly behind Marois, perhaps three feet from the chair where he sat, the door to Dawn's room began to slowly open.

36

I couldn't look at that door. I could barely breathe, for fear of giving Dawn's presence away to Marois. I began to babble.

"Well, Monsieur Marois!" I raised my voice several notches, in hopes of alerting my daughter. "What do you propose to do with us? I take it you don't plan to sit there all night with that *gun*, right? I mean, you must have had some kind of plan in mind when you came in here. You've already killed Shapiro, so I guess we're next on your list."

I sounded moronic, like someone from a bad movie. My voice nearly squeaked with the effort to reach Dawn, to let her know what was happening. Stay in your room, Dawn, don't come out here, keep your door closed … I clenched my hands till they lost all sensation and every muscle in my body was on high alert. I concentrated all my will on keeping Dawn in the relative safety of her room.

Marois looked puzzled at my sudden loquacity, but the stupidity of mere mortals such as myself should have long since ceased to amaze him. I hoped.

"Is it not clear that I shall have to kill you?" he asked. "It will pain me to do so, of course. After all, the only daughter of an old friend …" He shook his head sadly, but then brightened. "However, one must look at these things philosophically, no? Once you and Dr. Chisholm are no longer meddling in the affairs of my family, I shall have many fewer concerns in my life. Less stress, as they say. And that is something for which to be thankful, I think."

Dawn had heard me. The door stopped moving. I can't say I relaxed, but something like relief flooded through me. I hoped she would have the presence of mind to escape through her bedroom window, maybe even go for help. Yes, now there was a plan. Keep Marois talking until Dawn had a chance to summon assistance.

But even as I opened my mouth to implement my clever scheme, I was thwarted. The telephone rang on the table next to me. I flinched. Then I remembered: Benjamin was supposed to call. Could I somehow let him know we were in trouble?

I looked at Marois, uncertain.

"Pick it up," he nodded. "But I suggest that you re-assure the caller that everything is fine. We would not wish to have any unpleasantness, no?"

I lifted the receiver, acutely conscious that Marois was watching my every move. In the brief moment before I could say hello, all hell broke loose in my very small living room.

Dawn burst from her room, screaming at the top of her lungs, an avenging warrior queen. She was wielding some kind of large rectangular package. Marois, momentarily distracted, turned his head to see what the hell was happening. As he moved, Dawn smashed him on the side of his head with a very large, very heavy hardcover copy of the *Larousse Encyclopedia of Animal Life*, a Channukah gift from my parents.

Marois cried out in pained surprise. He clutched at his ear, dropping the gun, which spun across the floor and landed under the couch. He grabbed blindly at his unseen attacker, who nimbly hopped back, then darted in again, cracking the book down on the crown of his head this time, eliciting a yowl of enraged pain.

Greg and I dove for the gun simultaneously. However, I still held the phone, which gave Greg the advantage in our brief struggle. Then I realized: I am fighting Greg for the gun. Greg is on my side. I backed off.

Greg stood facing Marois, holding the damn gun nervously with both hands. I could tell he'd never held a gun before — he kept giving it nervous glances, as though he'd accidentally picked up a rattlesnake. He kept it pointed at Marois, though, and that was all that was necessary.

Dawn, realizing that she'd merely winged Marois, not actually killed him or even rendered him unconscious, kept pounding him relentlessly about the head and ears with the book, as though he were an insect that refused to die. Finally he slumped forward in the chair, out cold or conceding to her superior weaponry. I couldn't tell which, and I wasn't eager to find out.

"Okay, Dawn, I think that's enough," I yelled finally, and she reluctantly dropped the book on the floor. If I hadn't told her to stop, I swear she'd have kept right on pulverizing Marois' skull all night. Now, though, red-faced and puffing with exertion, she pulled a silk scarf, another gift from her grandparents, from her shorts pocket. She handed it to me.

"What the hell am I supposed to do with this?"

"Tie the fucker up, Mom!" she snapped. I didn't even bother to correct her language.

I tied Marois' hands together behind his back, just

like in the movies. It was only as I was testing the strength of my knots, and blessing Mrs. Vangelis, my Girl Guides leader, that I realized I'd left the phone receiver lying on the floor. Someone on the other end of the line was shouting to me to pick the damn thing up.

"Hello?" It was Benjamin. "Yes, Detective, what can I do for you?" I was caught somewhere between crying and laughing with relief and joy.

"Ms. Klein? Katy? Is that you? What's going on there?" He sounded genuinely worried, as well he might.

"Um, nothing, now. That is, everything's all right. I think we're okay now. But could you get over here? Now? We've caught the guy who killed Adam and Dr. Shapiro, and I think he's unconscious at the moment, but I don't know how long he's going to stay that way. We've got him tied up, and Greg's pointing the gun at him and all, but I still don't like having him here."

Words tumbled out of my mouth in a torrent that I felt powerless to restrain. Still, it was a damn sight better than the abject terror I'd been experiencing only moments before. Given a choice, I now know that I'll pick babbling hysteria over numb fear by a margin of two to one. Live and learn, I guess.

"We'll be right there, Ms. Klein," Benjamin sighed. "Don't go anywhere, okay?" He didn't sound surprised that we'd apprehended the bad guy. Just kind of patient and resigned. And what did he think, that I was planning a night on the town, or something? Where could I possibly go? I wouldn't have minded a stiff drink, maybe even a coffee, but there was no time to act on the idea.

Police cars started to converge on the apartment building within minutes. What with the howling sirens and flashing lights, I was sure my gossiping neighbours would have a field day.

More than anything, I wanted someone to cart away the slumped over, trussed up Marois. I wanted him out of my life. Having him here, even unspeaking and immobile, felt like having something toxic and foul in my apartment. I wanted him gone.

Benjamin was the first officer to reach my front door, and sure enough, he came in kvetching. We'd gummed up the fingerprints on the suspected murder weapon, we'd practically killed the suspect himself — well, excuse us for living! There was no pleasing the surly detective, so I gave up trying.

They did remove Marois, though it was necessary to call an ambulance to do so, since he only began to come around shortly after the cops started to arrive. According to Greg, Dawn's attack had left Marois with a massive hematoma on his scalp. He'd probably have the headache of a lifetime when he woke up, but no real long term effects. My heart bled cold borscht, I can tell you. I'd been hoping for a more lasting kind of damage, but I was willing to settle.

37

SATURDAY, AUGUST 6
Mercury inconjunct Saturn ✦
Venus inconjunct Pluto ✦
Mars opposition Jupiter, square Saturn ✦
Jupiter square Saturn ✦

Eventually, with Marois and his gun removed from the premises, and most of the cops dismissed from the scene, Benjamin dropped into an armchair. He rubbed his temples with the tips of his fingers, looking weary and pained.

"I need to get this all straight," he said, and then the real questions began.

A female officer, whose name I didn't catch, sat on a kitchen chair taking notes. Greg, Dawn and I stayed up with them for several exhausting hours, recounting the saga of Adam, Arianna, Shapiro, Mr. and Mrs. Cosgrove and, finally, Jean Marois.

By the end, Benjamin seemed, if not exactly sympathetic, at least less hostile. And he actually seemed to enjoy the story of Dawn pounding away at Marois' skull while the adults scuffled over the firearm.

"You've got guts, little lady, I'll say that for you," he said. Dawn sat up very straight, looking him directly in the eye.

"Yes, and if you call me 'little lady' again, I will do the same thing to you," she exploded, her eyes blazing. I tried to shush her, but she shook me off angrily.

"Really, Mom, I hate that!" she cried. "Just because I'm young is no reason to patronize me. I don't put up with that kind of sh—"

I clapped my hand over her mouth. Mental note: have a discussion with Dawn about her colourful use of expletives.

"I can see your point," I assured her, "but there's no reason to be rude in return."

Fortunately, Benjamin was amused, and not inclined to cite my daughter for threatening bodily harm to a police officer, or some such thing. He flipped his notebook closed, said he'd contact us later if he needed anything from us, and reminded us to let him know if we thought of anything else to tell him, no matter how insignificant it might seem to us.

"Oh, one last thing," I said. "I was just wondering about something."

"Yes?" He sounded forbearing.

"Well, it's just … If they killed Adam out there in the woods, you know, injected him with epinephrine, induced a coronary, like Marois said — well, why would they have thrown him in the Canal? Why not just leave him out there, let him rot?"

Benjamin scratched his head. "I'm not really sure. Maybe because floating in the water for a while would make his skin puff up a bit and hide the injection mark? Needle marks are usually hard enough to detect, even if they're recent and the corpse is in good condition, so letting him float around a while would have made the mark pretty much invisible. But we haven't questioned the suspect yet, so I really can't say for certain."

"Thanks. Just wondering."

I saw Benjamin and his colleague out, settled Greg in Dawn's room for a few hours' shut-eye, and collapsed on my own bed, Dawn curled up against me. The sun had already begun to peek over the windowsill, but I barely noticed it. Suddenly, all the fatigue I'd held at bay over the last ten days or so came crashing down on me. I slept, a long, black, dreamless sleep.

When I awoke, a strange odour reached my nostrils. I had to shake my head vigorously to identify it: someone seemed to be in my kitchen, cooking bacon and eggs and coffee. Dawn still slumbered next to me, so it couldn't be her. Besides, the chances were remote that she'd voluntarily prepare such a fat, cholesterol and caffeine extravaganza. Or even voluntarily allow the ingredients into the apartment.

What time was it, anyway? Oh God, almost three. Was that morning or afternoon? It was light out. Okay, that meant it was daytime. I thought. I lay there for some time, alternately waking and dozing, until the bedroom door creaked open and a familiar pair of eyes peered round at me.

Oh, it was just Brent. Right, I forgot — his main culinary achievements centred around bacon and eggs. I nearly dozed off again, until the events of the previous night began to filter through the fog. Remembering, I struggled upright in bed, thrust my arms into my dressing gown and my feet into slippers, and shuffled out to the living room. I blinked at the sudden sunlight. To say that I felt like the living dead would be a gross understatement.

"Brent?" My voice came out somewhere between a caw and a croak.

"Right here, honey. Ready for some breakfast?" He emerged from the kitchen, all dolled up in one of my aprons, brandishing a spatula and a cup of coffee. Under other circumstances, I might have thought he was cute, and I was certainly grateful for the coffee.

"Sit down, Brent," I said ungraciously, though I did accept the steaming mug he handed me.

He looked anxious. "What's up? I came in a while ago, and it was like walking into that fairytale, you know — the one where the whole kingdom falls asleep …" He stopped when he saw my face.

"First, how the hell did you get in here?"

"Oh, that!" He looked relieved. "I talked to Peter, told him who I was, and he let me in. He's not a bad guy, Katy — we had a good chat. Anyway, I'm sorry. I thought you'd be glad to see me."

"Brent, you've been spying on me." Flat, unemotional. Just the facts.

The colour drained from his face, and he studied the coffee cup he was holding. "It's not how it looks, Katy," he mumbled.

"That's bullshit, Brent. Your esteemed boss, Jean Marois, was arrested last night for the murder of one Dr. Shapiro, and I imagine they'll eventually figure out a way to connect him to Adam's death, too. The little girl he killed all those years ago — well, I guess she'll have to go into the 'unsolved' pile, even though Marois admitted last night that he broke her neck. And while he was in the mood for confessing, he let slip that you had been providing him with all the information he needed to keep tabs on me."

Brent looked stunned. It was a long time before he

answered. The air hung still and heavy between us, and all I could hear was his breathing. I realized that under my rage at him, beneath all my pain and sense of betrayal, I still harboured a tiny spark of hope. I wanted him to deny it, to tell me Marois had been lying. I wanted him to say he loved me, and scoop me into his arms, and hug and kiss me. And then my pain would be all blotted out, and I wouldn't feel like someone was gouging my heart out with a pickaxe.

None of that happened, though.

"Let me tell you what happened," he said at last. "I told you I got recruited, and I accepted the job and came to Ottawa mainly because of you. That's the truth. But what I didn't know is that one of the jobs they'd assign me was tracking this guy, Adam Cosgrove. I was supposed to be developing computer systems, and here they had me out doing surveillance work. But in my business, people who ask too many questions don't last long. I figured they were testing me a bit."

He took a sip of coffee, sitting with his long legs drawn up and his shoulders stooped. "I didn't know anything about the poor guy, just what I was told. He was crazy, and he was a threat to someone high up in the government. You have to understand, at the Farm we operate on a need-to-know basis. Like, I only get told what I need to know to get the job done. Probably only two or three other people in the whole place are in on what any other operative is doing. Security stays tighter that way.

"Anyway, I'm tracking Adam, who we know came to Ottawa, because someone at the Allan tipped us off that he might try to find your friend, Greg. From there, someone at the Royal Ottawa confirmed that he'd come in, so I was tasked with picking up all Greg's phone calls.

That's when I heard your call come in to him, last week."

"You mean, when I called to give him shit for sending me Adam? That call was bugged?"

Brent nodded, but he wouldn't meet my eyes. "The way it works, I'm not in charge of what happens to the information. I just make the tapes, run them through a machine, a computer that can pick out key words. Like for instance, Adam, or Cosgrove, or whatever. Then the tapes go up the line. I don't even know how far they go, because like I said, it's all on a need-to-know basis. But the next thing I know, I get tasked with tapping into your conversations.

"Katy, I did it, but I didn't want to, you understand? And I took some stupid chances. I came to meet you that first day in the coffee shop not because I wanted to spy on you, but because I couldn't stand the thought of being so close and not seeing you again. And when we met that day, I knew I couldn't just leave things the way they were. I swear, I wasn't spying on you then."

He talked into his knees, but now he raised his head. Tears shone on his cheeks. They should have moved me more than they did.

"I have a question." I sounded like a student in a lecture on spying techniques. "That white truck, the chip wagon outside my office. Was that you?"

He nodded. "The trucks are kind of like portable labs, air-conditioned, full of electronic equipment. I used that to get a fix on your office phone, but your home phone was a lot easier. It's a portable — those things broadcast for a few blocks, you don't need much special equipment to pick them up. They're not very secure."

"And the computer break-ins?"

"Yeah, I'm afraid that was us. Not me, actually, my partner. By that time, I was getting pretty freaked out about spying on you, so he did most of the B and E by way of Dawn's server. Not the apartment break-in, though," he added hopefully. "In fact, when you told me yesterday about someone getting in here, I realized this was getting way out of hand. I applied to get myself off the case."

"That was very noble of you."

"Katy, I had no idea in the beginning, and when I realized what was happening, I had no way of knowing how Marois would use what I was giving him. You've got to understand: this was my job."

"I've heard that one before, Brent. The one about 'only following orders'. Or have you forgotten, my mother came out of Auschwitz? That particular argument has never gone over well in our family."

He winced, my words hitting him like poisoned darts.

"Brent, you spied on me. You passed on information that put not only my life, but Dawn and Greg's lives, in danger. Your information got Adam killed. In fact, it nearly killed all of us. Marois was here last night, and he was planning to murder us, just like he murdered Adam. He would have done it, too, if we hadn't been able to stop him. And that was just luck. I can't forgive you for this, and I can't ever forget it. I want you out of my life."

Saying it felt like I was ripping my heart out of my ribcage with my bare hands. I couldn't even cry. I'd passed that stage. I was one gigantic gaping wound, and I wasn't sure I'd be able to heal, but I was certain I needed Brent to get far away from me. Now.

"Katy, don't do this," he said. "Please."

But all I could do was shake my head.

"Go," I said. And he did.

EPILOGUE

I ate the breakfast Brent had prepared for me, chewing mechanically and swallowing because I knew that it was what one was supposed to do. And that's how I went through my days for the next several weeks — on auto-pilot.

Greg owns a small cottage on an island in one of the Rideau Lakes, just a short distance from Ottawa. It was at his insistence that I packed up Dawn and drove down there, hiding out until the end of August. I really couldn't afford to do that, but as Greg pointed out, I also couldn't afford not to. He is an exceptionally kind and understanding friend.

Benjamin was exasperated at my unavailability for those few weeks, but Greg assured him that we had not skipped the country. In our absence, Greg spent a lot of time going over and over the statements we'd given that Friday night, or Saturday morning, or whatever it was. In the end, Benjamin was more or less satisfied, I think. He didn't send anyone around to arrest us, anyway.

Nor did the police ever catch up with Shapiro's hired thug, the guy who'd run Greg off the road and tried to hit me with his car. Benjamin agreed with us that the same guy was likely the one who'd shown up in the parking lot dressed up in a police uniform the night Dawn had been kidnapped. So I guess he's still out there somewhere.

Meanwhile, Dawn and I spent a long time just sitting on the porch, watching the old blue heron that lives off Greg's front dock. It was a beautiful bird, sleek and grey-blue, standing patiently for hours in the shallow water, watchfully waiting for little carp and sunfish to swim past its feet, then swiftly dipping its beak into the lake, wriggling its neck back and forth as the fish slithered down its gullet. Lunch over, the bird would resume its original position, standing there like a statue.

We also picked berries, blueberries that grew in the springy, dried-out bog on the other side of the island, and some raspberries from old bushes Greg had planted here years ago. They stained our fingers red and purple, and we licked the juice off, uncaring. The sun was hot on our backs and legs, and we picked in silence, sharing glances from time to time, then retreating back into ourselves.

Once I tried to apologize to Dawn for not protecting her well enough, for allowing her to become involved in any of it, but she just hugged me, and that was enough to make both of us cry and cry. After that we spoke little of it, preferring to swim and read and lie on the dock in the sun.

When we got back to the city, I decided I'd had enough of my own cringing silence. One day I went to Greg's apartment and sat with him and told him the story of Frank Curtis. It was hard, very hard to speak of my shame and humiliation, and when I was done, we sat quietly on his couch, watching those bloody cats rip a brand new set of curtains into long, thready strips.

"I wish you'd told me, Katy."

"I couldn't. If I'd told you, that would have made it true."

And that is where we left it. But two months later, amid great media coverage, Dr. Frank Curtis resigned his position as Director of the Forensic Unit at the Royal Ottawa Hospital. His resignation had been prompted by a hospital investigation into his untoward sexual activities with certain patients, who were now being encouraged to come forward with their stories. A trickle turned into a flood, and soon there were more than twenty charges pending against Dr. Curtis.

Greg told me what had happened when the hospital board had called Curtis on the carpet:

"He was standing there, all defiant and blustery, demanding to know why they were wasting his valuable time. The secretary of the board read from a list of allegations, and Curtis just stood there, getting redder and redder in the face. Then the secretary told him the board was going to have to suspend him until the allegations had been investigated by the Royal College of Physicians and Surgeons, not to mention the police. Curtis looked around at them all, and said, 'Well, I was thinking of retiring, anyway.' And that was that."

So it was. He went to his office, packed his belongings and left the hospital. Just as simple as that.

Only one loose end remained after Marois' arrest, and it took a few months to resolve. Debby Landreth, Adam's biological mother, was in fact his only documented living relative. Now that the lawyers have finished wrangling over the question, I understand she will be inheriting the money old Mr. Cosgrove left Adam. It seems only fair.

It has been several months now since Adam exploded into my life. I have seen Brent only once, at a shopping mall. He was having lunch with some people I'd never met, and I turned around and walked quickly back in the opposite direction. He might have called after me; I don't know.